Disquiet

By Georgie Reed

I dedicate this story in memory of my Grandad,

George Edward Reed

Chapter 1

A mobile phone rang in the dead of night, abruptly rousing Alfie Sayers from his slumber. He awoke, drenched in sweat, gasping for air, and tormented by the same recurring nightmare that had haunted him since his past. With trembling hands, he wiped his eyes and took deep breaths to quell the fear that clung to him. Lying in bed, he stretched his arm towards the bedside table and retrieved his mobile phone, answering it without bothering to check the caller ID at this ungodly hour.

"Hello," he mumbled groggily, still half-asleep and yawning as he attempted to moisten his parched voice, making it sound more coherent. Beside Alfie, his fiancée, Charley, lay in bed, her golden-brown eyes partially open, blurrily looking up at him.

"They're dead!" a voice on the other end of the phone shrieked. The words resonated so loudly that Charley heard them clearly, stirring from her slumber, her eyes snapped open as she sat up, watching Alfie. The shock of those two words reverberated through Alfie, prompting him to sit up at the edge of the bed. Charley sat behind him, listening intently to the phone call.

"Teddy? What? Who's dead?" Alfie asked, his bewilderment evident in his voice. His heart raced, and his body tensed at Teddy's shocking revelation. He absorbed every word Teddy uttered, though the distressing news left him struggling to contain his emotions. Teddy was hysterical; Alfie tried his best to calm him down. Hearing voices in the background, a male voice came to the phone and introduced himself as "Officer Henby." Clearly, he described the scene to Alfie, sending shivers down his spine. Alfie's mind was overwhelmed by the image painted in his mind. Giving short replies, the police officer handed the phone back to Teddy, whose voice crumbled in despair. Hearing his friend's torment, Alfie pulled himself together.

"Okay, Ted, mate, I'll pick you up from the police station; you can stay with us," Alfie replied, swallowing his shock to sound strong for his friend. Hanging up the phone, Alfie dropped his device on the bed. Charley, filled with worry, placed her hand on Alfie's shoulder. She could tell from Alfie's tone of voice that he wasn't okay.

"What's going on?" she asked softly, hiding her anxiety for Alfie. Turning around, he looked at Charley to tell her the news.

"Teddy's mum and Eva have been murdered," Alfie revealed, his voice filled with anguish as tears began to trickle from his eyes. He inhaled deeply, attempting to contain the flood of grief. Standing up, Alfie fumbled around, unsure what to do first. Crawling to the edge of the bed, Charley knelt up, pulling Alfie close to her. She placed her left arm around him, her right hand gently cradling the back of his head, running her fingers through his light brown hair while squeezing his toned physique. Leaning her face into his shoulder, she reassured him that all would be okay. She knew Alfie inside and out; she could see him struggling to bury his emotions deep within. She was fearful; the last time a tragic event had unfolded, Alfie disappeared for a period of time, leaving her in the lurch. She could see the anxiety brewing inside of him.

Alfie sniffled, pulling himself away from Charley, and turned his head to wipe his hazel eyes dry, trying to halt the tears that threatened to fall. He moved into the adjacent bathroom, just steps away from their bedroom. Standing before the sink, he turned on the cold tap and splashed his oval face with water. As he gazed at his reflection in the small bathroom mirror, a man appeared, staring at him. Alfie squeezed his eyes shut, taking deep breaths and exhaling rapidly in an effort to regain his composure. When he looked back at the mirror, the man was gone. Leaving the bathroom, he returned to the bedroom. Charley watched him silently, noticing a change in him as he got himself dressed, her concern etched on her face.

Alfie opened a chest of drawers and retrieved a tracksuit, hastily pulling it on and grabbing his running trainers, sliding them onto his feet. Feeling Charley's gaze upon him, he avoided eye contact as he sorted himself. Edging out of the room, Charley called to him, and unable to ignore her, he turned to her.

"Let me come with you, Alf," Charley implored. Her voice carried a clear tone of concern, desperate to be by his side and not leave him to take on the burden of Teddy's pain.

"You can't. Who's gonna look after Oscar? We can't wake him up, and it's too late to find someone to watch for him for us," replied Alfie, his tone subtly reassuring her of his well-being. He continued in a calming tone, "I'll be fine," as he walked over to the bed, stroking her blonde hair from the side and giving her a tender kiss on the top of her head.

Leaving the bedroom, the dread of loss plagued him as he looked upon the closed bedroom door down the hallway. Slightly opening the door, he peered inside to take a quick glance at his son Oscar sleeping peacefully. Oscar's angelic face bore a striking resemblance to his father but more childlike and with a darker shade of brown hair. At the foot of Oscar's bed lay Bulldozer, the Doberman Alfie had acquired and trained to protect his family and home when he wasn't around. Bulldozer lifted his head, eyeing Alfie's entrance. Upon recognizing him, he settled his head back down and nuzzled the duvet for comfort. Alfie quietly shut the door.

Descending the stairs in his detached house, he entered the kitchen to pour himself a glass of water. His mouth remained parched from his earlier awakening. Gulping down the water, he exited the kitchen and paced through the hallway, picking up his keys from the table by the front door. Glancing at himself in the mirror above the table, he ran his hand over his angular jaw and pinched the top of his moderately soft nose, nibbling on the bottom of his full, red lips. With a loud exhale, preparing for what he was about to emotionally endure, he left the house.

The night air hung heavily, a blanket of oppressive humidity settling over the dimly lit street, casting an eerie pall. Alfie paused for a moment, his gaze tracing the shadowy contours of the silent thoroughfare. The unsettling stillness gripped him as he stood, a solitary figure under the weight of the sombre night.

His eyes were drawn towards his car, its presence now ominous against the backdrop of the obscure street. A spectre dressed entirely in black loomed across the road, their malevolent intentions palpable as they locked eyes with Alfie, a chill sweeping through him. Their ominous stare seemed to linger before they melted into the street's obscure recesses, swallowed by the night.

Inexplicably, Alfie's gaze remained fixed on the shrouded path leading to the alley, where he sensed the intruder lurking, an unseen presence that bore into his very soul. His unease festered, compelling him to turn and intently strain his ears for the faintest echo of approaching footsteps.

As he gingerly secured one of the three locks on his front door, he cast a wary glance around the desolate street, yet it remained devoid of any life. Anxiously, Alfie continued his cautious steps, his eyes glued to the menacing alleyway. He braced himself for an imminent, menacing figure to spring forth and launch an attack, clenching his house keys like a concealed weapon, poised for an aggressive defence.

Reaching his car, he swiftly activated the door mechanism, granting himself refuge inside. He locked the doors and, with trembling hands, ignited the engine, infusing the street with an eerie glow that illuminated the lurking shadows.

As he drove slowly away, he looked into his rear-view mirror, searching for movement in the alley. The night's events yearned for a face to put to the inscrutable malevolence. As he sped away, his eyes remained locked on the rear-view mirror, scouring the darkness for a figure to recognize.

The weight of paranoia gnawed at him as he drove. He reached for his phone, calling Charley in a fevered rush, imploring her to bring Bulldozer and Oscar to their bedroom. He felt the overwhelming dread of leaving them alone in the dead of night, all the while grappling with the haunting reality of Teddy's unsettling revelations earlier that evening.

As Alfie navigated the dusky roads, his car pierced the dimly lit streets with its piercing headlights. The evening was cast in a soft, ethereal glow as he ventured on. Eventually, he approached Teddy's home and made an abrupt stop to survey the area. The scene before him was a stark tableau of chaos and despair. Police car sirens danced and sang in unison, their vivid blue lights flickering and fracturing the obsidian darkness, casting an eerie aura over the entire street.

The small, detached house stood shrouded in the unforgiving embrace of yellow crime scene tape, a symbol of the grim incident that had transpired within. The solemn scene overwhelmed Alfie, prompting him to pause for a lingering moment, his gaze fixed on the scene that had so violently upended Teddy's life.

His mind, unable to escape the tendrils of the past, spiralled back to his teenage years, where he had once stood amid a strikingly similar scene, a traumatic memory now echoing in his troubled thoughts.

Flashback:

Amid the blinding glare of the police lights, Alfie's gaze fixated on the woman. She was drenched in blood, her face contorted in agony as she clung to the lifeless figure in her arms. The harsh, cold illumination rendered her a spectral figure, while the vivid red and blue flashing lights punctuated her suffering with an eerie rhythm. Her screams tore through the night, echoing a gut-wrenching howl of despair that seemed to pierce Alfie's very soul. Shivers ran down his spine as he stood there, paralyzed and trembling.

A tap on the window abruptly interrupted Alfie's thoughts. He turned his attention to the police officer who had knocked on his window, undoing it as he did.

"Excuse me, sir. What are you doing here lurking at this late hour?" the police officer asked bluntly, bending down to peer directly into Alfie's eyes.

"Sorry, officer. That house is… I'm... my friend lives there. I'm just on my way to pick him up," Alfie explained to the officer, struggling to find the right words. The officer looked at Alfie with suspicion.

"Hang on a minute, you're that guy... Alfie Sayers... aren't you?" the officer replied, recognizing Alfie's face as he inspected him closely.

"That's me," Alfie replied modestly. He had encountered this too many times in the last week, and after his recent TV appearance a few hours ago, he knew his celebrity profile would only grow, much to his dismay.

"I've been following your story since you were in the paper. Well done to you!" The officer said enthusiastically, a congratulatory smile on his face. Alfie gave an awkward smile back.

"Thank you... but I should really be picking my friend up from the police station," replied Alfie, making an excuse to escape the praise.

"Who's your friend?" asked the officer, sounding more interrogative.

"Teddy Brackman, he lived in the house you have taped off," replied Alfie, pointing to the house. The officer looked at Alfie, a torn look on his face as he debated what to say.

"Him, ahh well, between you and me, Alfie, and I shouldn't be saying this but, I'd keep my distance from him for a while..." the officer began, but Alfie cut him off, thanking him for the advice and excusing himself to drive away.

Alfie and Teddy had been lifelong friends. Both their mothers had been friends since their teenage years, sharing many life events together. They were inseparable, just like their sons, until an unthinkable event drove them apart.

Driving towards the police station, he couldn't help but contemplate the identity of the psychopath responsible for the deaths of Teddy's loved ones. He couldn't comprehend who would want to harm Teddy's mother, one of the most gracious women he had ever known, second only to his own mother. She had always made Alfie feel like a part of the family, looking out for him, particularly during what he considered the worst period of his life. The thought of the torment and pain she had endured at the hands of some malicious individual weighed heavily on his mind.

Parking his car outside the police station, Alfie remained seated, attempting to regain his composure. He knew he couldn't display visible distress in front of Teddy. Glancing at his phone for the time—1:49 am—he sent a text message to his mother to see if she was awake. He didn't expect a response, but he wanted to talk to her after hearing the devastating news about his best friend's mother.

Stepping out of the car, he took a deep breath, the empty streets around him providing a sense of isolation. The night breeze hit him in the face as he looked at the police station in front of him. He anticipated the pain Teddy was in as he strode across the road, his heart heavy with worry for his friend.

Walking through the front doors of the police station, Alfie headed toward the reception, where a young man sat with his head buried in his phone. The stark fluorescent lights hummed overhead, casting an uninviting glow throughout the lobby.

"Hi, I'm here to pick up Teddy Brackman," Alfie softly stated, placing his hands on the reception desk. The man at the front desk put his phone aside and looked up at Alfie, his eyes widening with recognition.

"Oh my God, you're Alfie Sayers. I watched you earlier on the Jane Moore show," the man replied, clearly taken aback. Alfie gave a slightly complex smile, feeling annoyed by the admiration he was getting from the people who were meant to be solving his friend's mother's murder.

"Yeah, that's me. Could you tell me how long Teddy Brackman will be, please?" Alfie inquired impatiently while trying to maintain politeness.

"He's just giving a statement, so he shouldn't be too long. You can wait over there for him," the man at the reception answered, pointing Alfie toward a cold-looking area filled with rows of plastic seats.

Thanking the man, he gave a half smile while walking over to the waiting area. Sitting in the cold blue plastic chair, he fidgeted, trying to get comfortable. The strong disinfectant smell from the shiny floor filled his nose. Glancing at the clock on the wall, he pulled out his phone to send Charley a text message, letting her know that he was waiting for Teddy, and it shouldn't be too long. The uncomfortable seat dug into his back, causing him to shift restlessly in an attempt to find a more comfortable position. Distracting himself from the wait, he began playing with his phone, flicking through photos until he came across a simple family photo from a picnic in the park. It captured Alfie's world.

His heart sank, and his stomach churned as he imagined himself in Teddy's shoes, pondering the loss of any of his loved ones, even the dog. Putting his phone down, he looked around the room; it was silent, and he was the only person waiting. A heavy burden he'd held for years jumped to the front of his thoughts. The current situation made Alfie question if he should finally tell Teddy after all these years, but a looming doubt of making things worse and revealing things he wanted to keep quiet silenced him.

Jittering his knee, Alfie stood up and began pacing around the room, his mind filled with too many thoughts stirring up an episode of anxiety. Leaning against the wall, he slid down, sitting on the floor and pulling out his phone to look at his social media. Several clips from his TV interview earlier were tagged, and he needed a distraction, so he sat and watched the interview.

Five hours ago... Jane Moore Interview:

Hiding behind a curtain, Alfie's palms grew clammy with sweat. For the first time in a long while, he was nervous about his image. He peeked from behind the stage curtain, catching sight of his family and friends sitting in the front row. Their faces radiated excitement and pride. Alfie had been anticipating this interview for a week, ever since the news broke that he was among the top 10 earners of the year. Typically, the list featured well-known entrepreneurs and celebrities, but Alfie had surpassed most of them in his last year, even though his company had been in operation for eight years, catapulting him into the public eye.

"And now, I'd like to welcome my next guest, the entrepreneur, multi-millionaire, who needs no introduction. If you don't know him, you must be living under a rock. He's been all over the news for the past ten days. Let's give a huge round of applause for... Alfie Sayers!" Jane Moore introduced with a gleaming white teeth smile.

Taking a deep breath, Alfie wiped the sweat from his forehead. With a broad smile, he walked onto the stage, and the audience erupted into cheers, leaping to their feet, giving him a round of applause. He warmly shook Jane's hand and gave her a friendly hug before waving to the enthusiastic crowd.

"Alfie, how are you today?" Jane inquired; she had a smitten look on her face.

"I'm well, thank you," he replied in his soft baritone voice looking her directly in the eye.

"So, you've been the talk of the media this week. As soon as I read your story, I told my team, 'I want him on my show! I want to hear his story personally,'" she complimented leaning closer toward him.

"Thank you. Yeah, well, you know, it's been unreal. This week has completely taken me by surprise. I never expected my small business to garner this much attention. To be completely honest, I never dreamt it would become what it is now. I didn't think a company could become this famous unless it's something like Disney. It's just unbelievable," Alfie humbly responded as he kept his focus on the interviewer trying to ignore the gushing from the audience.

"Well, I wouldn't call it a small business anymore, Mr. Sayers. You're now number four on most successful lists for this year," enthused Jane, glancing at the audience encouraging applause. Turning back to him she continued, "So, what's your story, everyone wants to know about the mysterious Alfie Sayers but so far it's just been business talk?" another white teeth flash as she pushed for information on Alfie's life.

"To make a long story short, I started a marketing and advertising company when I was 25. Seven years later, I'm now the go-to advertiser for more businesses than I ever dreamed of. It all began when a certain company approached me with a 6-month contract. I won't reveal their name, as I prefer to keep certain things confidential due to the nature of business. But they initiated a private bidding war with me, offering a life-changing amount of money, which was more than I earned in my first three years combined. Other companies joined the bidding, making it quite a peculiar situation. At the time, I had a small team and faced the dilemma of choosing a contract. I was concerned about my reputation and dividing my resources. They offered me a life-changing amount of money for 6 months of work. Once I worked with them, my reputation soared, and my price increased. I still have a small team, along with our trusted freelancers. It's a dream come true. However, I have my two right-hand men, Thomas Mellor and Stewart Dowler, to thank," Alfie modestly explained, gesturing to the two men seated in the audience. He didn't want to divulge his personal life publicly.

"Just for clarity, Alfie's company, Say Advertising, is responsible for many commercials you see online and on TV, including major brands, movies and musicians," Jane boasted as a show reel played behind Alfie.

"When did you realize how big Say Advertising was getting?" Jane inquired.

"I don't think I realized it until last week when the media picked up on us. My focus has always been to make a living for my family," Alfie truthfully said, taking a glance at his family and friends.

"So, what about growing up? Did you always know you wanted to get into the advertising industry?" Jane asked.

Alfie chuckled buying time to think of what to say. His heart raced as he dreaded speaking about his past. On the outside, he maintained his composure, concealing the tension within. He then lightened the mood with a joke, saying, "Not exactly. I just wanted to be a superhero as a kid, save people, and run up buildings." He laughed, catching his mother's gaze who gave him a nod letting him know that he'd handled that well.

Present:

Teddy walked into the reception area, his dark blonde hair dishevelled, his face notably paler than usual, and his piercing green eyes now carrying a sorrowful weight. Alfie couldn't help but notice the unmistakable anguish etched onto Teddy's face. He knew his friend well enough to discern when something was amiss simply by the look in his eyes.

Alfie swiftly stood up from the floor, watching as Teddy approached. Teddy turned to the police officer who accompanied him; they had a brief hushed chat that was too low for Alfie to hear. Slowly making his way to Alfie, Teddy collapsed into him, tears flooding from his face. Placing his arm around Teddy, Alfie reassured him, swallowing the lump stuck in his throat.

"Come on, let's get out of here," Alfie softly said as he tapped Teddy on the back. Walking out of the police station, both men walked silently to Alfie's car. Watching Teddy get in the passenger seat, he could see the torture on his face. Alfie sat in the driver's seat, turning on the engine as he watched Teddy from the corner of his eye.

With worry on his mind, Alfie drove back home fast, focusing solely on the road as the car filled with a mournful silence, Teddy's grief hanging heavily. Every passing moment felt agonizing, and Alfie struggled to contain the overwhelming empathy and sadness he felt for his friend and the woman he had known throughout his life.

Parking his car outside the house, undoing his seatbelt, Teddy sat still. Peeping at the side of Teddy's window, Alfie searched for movement from the mysterious shadowy figure he'd seen earlier in the dark alleyway.

"I don't know what to say, Teddy. What happened?" Alfie confessed softly, showing his support. Turning to Teddy, eyes welling up, Teddy turned to him as tears fell like a waterfall.

"I came home from work this afternoon, got changed, and then went back to work to cover for one of the guys... that's why I couldn't make it to your thing tonight. So, I went back to work," He spoke with deep breaths, holding back the pain that was trying to burst free. He paused, the weight of his regret and sorrow deep in his voice. "I came home... and... I opened the door... and... I saw my Mum at the bottom of the stairs. She was covered in blood, I tried... I tried to do CPR on her and then I heard a crack... I called for an ambulance, I told them I think I hurt her, I think I broke something.... But she's bleeding, I was shouting at her... Wake up... Please wake up! But she wouldn't move," His voice trembled with despair as he continued, "The operator told me the ambulance won't be long... so I repeated the address... so they knew the right house to come to. I sat on the floor holding her, asking her to wake up, then the ambulance came, and they told me to give them some space and then they said she was.... She was... Dead!" His voice broke as he acknowledged that his mother was gone. In heavy breaths he tried to continue but broke down in tears.

"I'm so sorry, Ted," Alfie said, placing his hand on his shoulder.

"But... Then... I walked into the living room... and... it was like a scene from a Horror Film... Like," Teddy's voice trembled as he continued. "There was blood... everywhere. It was on the walls, the floor, and... and Eva..." His voice caught in his throat, and his trembling hands covered his face, as if trying to shield himself from the horrifying images that would forever stick themselves into his mind. He couldn't find the words to convey the shock and devastation he had experienced.

"I yelled," Teddy panted, his voice barely audible, his body shaking with the memory. "And one of the paramedics came into the living room... and she took me out of the living room." Tears streamed down Teddy's face as he sobbed uncontrollably, unable to comprehend the tragic loss he had suffered. His voice was filled with a mixture of grief, anger, and disbelief, all intertwining into a heart-wrenching symphony of pain.

As Alfie looked at his friend, he felt helplessness, unsure of how to provide the comfort that Teddy needed. He couldn't begin to fathom the pain Teddy was in, the trauma, and repercussions this would have on him.

Hearing about Teddy's trauma and seeing the anguish etched onto his face, Alfie's mind flashed back to a young boy with his head soaked in blood, cradled by a woman screaming in distress. It was a memory that had haunted him for years. Alfie rubbed his eyes with his thumb and index finger.

"Let's get inside," Alfie murmured softly, opening the car door. Both of them walked to Alfie's front door, and after unlocking each lock, Alfie gestured for Teddy to go inside first. Alfie took another inspecting glance toward the dark alley to assure no one was lurking. After going inside, Alfie shut the door securely, turning around to head into the living room, where he noticed a brown envelope. Picking it up, he found his name written on it suspiciously. Footsteps came running from the living room into the hallway; Charley, unable to sleep, waited for them to return.

Upon seeing Teddy, she gave him an intense hug, and Teddy broke into tears as Charley reassured him that she and Alfie were there for him. Leading Teddy into the living room, she began asking him questions, encouraging him to let out his feelings.

"I'll go make us all a cup of tea," Alfie gestured, standing near the living room door frame. Going into the square kitchen, he placed the envelope on the side, grabbed the kettle, filled it with water, and put it on boil. Gazing out of the kitchen window, he looked at the empty dark street, wondering if the figure was just in his head. As the kettle boiled, he grabbed three mugs, placing them on the side. The brown envelope in his sight, he opened it and pulled out the contents. His fingernail had a speck of blood on top of it. Pulling out a sheet of paper, he read it silently.

"Do you remember what it feels like to kill?

Tonight was because of you, Alfie.

Who's next?"

Reading the note repeatedly, he turned pale as a shiver rattled down his spine. Reaching inside the envelope again, he pulled out two photos. The first was of Teddy's mother dead at the bottom of the stairs, smothered in blood. The second photo showed Eva's lifeless body lying on the sofa with blood smeared all over the living room, a knife stuck in her chest. Eva's dark grey eyes stared lifelessly at the camera, as though looking directly at Alfie. Inside the envelope, Alfie noticed a splatter of blood, which he could only assume was either Teddy's mother's or Eva's.

"Are you okay out there?" shouted Charley from the living room, startling Alfie, causing him to drop the note and photographs on the floor.

"Yeah, I'm fine," Alfie replied shortly as he bent down, picking up the note and photos off the floor. He put them back into the envelope and folded it up, placing it in his jogger's pocket. Noticing the blood, he quickly washed his hands, splashing water on his face to calm himself. After washing his hands, he quickly made the cups of tea, taking Charley and Teddy's into the living room.

Going back into the kitchen, leaning over the countertop, his mind raced. He knew he could only confide in one person: his mother.

Overwhelmed, he envisioned the silhouette in the shadows, now certain that someone was watching him and had left this message. But who? He went over the note's wording in his head, **"Do you remember what it feels like to kill?"** Only one person alive knew the full story of his past, and one who knew bits. The note's claim that tonight was because of him baffled him. He couldn't understand how it was his fault or why someone would target Teddy's mum and girlfriend if it was because of him. While he cared deeply about Teddy's mother, there were closer people to him who could have been targeted to hurt him even more. The line, "Who's next?" worried Alfie the most as everyone he cared about, from family to friends, raced through his mind.

Charley called out to Alfie again. Inhaling a deep breath, Alfie grabbed his tea, going into the living room to sit with Charley and Teddy.

"Have you told any of your family?" asked Alfie as he sat down, facing Teddy and Charley. Alfie pushed his worry aside, focusing his mind on Teddy.

"No, not yet. I don't think I can..." Teddy replied with fear in his voice.

"I'll help you make those calls while Alfie's at work tomorrow if you want me to," offered Charley as she rubbed Teddy's arm.

"Would you? I'd really appreciate it. I don't know how or what I am going to tell everyone," Teddy replied, sniffling. Alfie and Charley exchanged glances of sympathy for their friend as he stared at the floor.

"Do they have any idea who did it?" Charley asked. Alfie looked at her, then back at Teddy, hoping for an answer, but Teddy didn't have one or he would have said from the beginning.

"No, but I had to give the police a list of people that I know or knew after I gave my statement," explained Teddy, resuming talking normally. "Give it a few days; they'll get evidence from the house and put the scumbag away!" Alfie stated angrily, not wanting to find out who was next.

"They won't. Apparently, when they tried to get evidence from the house, there was nothing there. It's like they cleaned up after themselves," replied Teddy, his voice slightly changing before returning to his sorrow.

"Really? How would they have had the time to do that?" asked Charley, baffled.

"I don't know…they said they'd been, you know, long before I got there," replied Teddy, seemingly angry with himself for not being there to protect his loved ones.

"So, what happens next?" asked Alfie, hoping for an answer that would soothe his anxiety.

"I have no idea. I mean, I'm not going to be able to go back to that place, so I have no idea what I do next," replied Teddy.

"Don't worry about that, mate. You can stay with us as long as you want to," responded Alfie, trying to ease Teddy's concerns, knowing that Teddy would be worried about imposing himself on anyone.

"You guys have a child, and you're moving out in a few days. I can't put myself and all this on you both like that," said Teddy, sounding guilty. Alfie leaned over to Teddy, so he faced him.

"How long have we been friends? We're family; you are always welcome, and the new house has more than enough room for you," Teddy leaned forward, embracing Alfie gratefully, trying to smile but breaking into a flood of tears. Alfie hugged him again.

"It's okay, Ted, just let it out," Alfie reassured, patting Teddy on the back.

"You're always welcome with us, Teddy," Charley reaffirmed, placing her hand on Teddy's knee.

The three of them stayed up talking all through the night. Alfie's mind jumped between questions of who'd done this while listening to Teddy let all his pain free. He looked at both

Charley and Teddy, haunted by the line "Who's next?"

A bright light shined into the living room where the three of them sat. The summer sun was rising, brightening the sky. Alfie felt his phone vibrate in his pocket; he took it out, seeing a text message from his mother. Footsteps loudly thumped in the hallway, and a dog collar rattled upstairs; Oscar and Bulldozer came rushing downstairs, noticing Teddy sitting next to his mum. Oscar hurriedly jumped over the sofa and latched himself onto Teddy's back.

"Uncle Ted," he shouted gleefully. Bulldozer walked around the sofa, sniffing Teddy as Oscar greeted him. Bulldozer then paced over to Alfie, sitting at his feet, watching as Oscar jumped all over his uncle Ted.

"Are you here to help us pack?" asked Oscar with childlike innocence.

"No…" Alfie interrupted as Teddy spoke over him.

"I am," Teddy said, smiling at Alfie and gesturing warmth toward Oscar, giving Teddy something to focus on other than his grief.

Standing up, Alfie excused himself, walking out of the living room. Bulldozer watched Teddy and Oscar more intently as Alfie made his way to the kitchen to see Charley.

image of the postman lurking in the shadows opposite his house. However, a disturbing realization gripped him; the postman appeared taller than the mysterious figure he had observed before, or at least that was his impression.

As the postman approached Alfie's mother's house, Alfie's gaze remained unwavering, his eyes locked onto the man doing his morning route. The postman deftly inserted mail through the letterbox, a seemingly mundane act that sent shivers down Alfie's spine as his mind pictured something worse. His fixated stare lingered until the postman finished the delivery and moved on to the adjacent house. The intensity of Alfie's surveillance mirrored the escalating tension within him, a turbulent blend of fear, suspicion, and the unshakable sense that danger loomed ever closer.

Slapping himself on the head, Alfie muttered, "Get it together, Alfie!" The words, a desperate plea to quell the rising tide of anxiety, echoed repeatedly in the confines of his troubled mind. Frustration clung to him like a heavy cloak as he worked himself into a panic, the gnawing unease tightening his chest, rendering him weak and vulnerable. In the grip of this internal storm, Alfie fought to regain control, his efforts manifested in deliberate, laboured breaths that only offered fleeting relief.

Closing his eyes, he attempted to visualize the elusive figure that had vanished into the shadows, aggravating his sense of paranoia. Each attempt to summon a face, a motive, or even a semblance of reason proved futile. Mind drawing blanks, he felt the weight of his own powerlessness, grappling with the frustrating realization that he couldn't pinpoint a credible threat among those he had known. The futile mental exercise left him emotionally drained, his frustration reaching a crescendo as he slammed his hand against the top of the steering wheel, a raw expression of his internal turmoil.

"FUCK!" The exclamation, an outburst of pent-up tension, reverberated through the quiet surroundings. Grabbing his work bag in a desperate attempt to anchor himself in the tangible, Alfie stepped out of the car. Shutting the door behind him, he scanned his surroundings with a hyper-vigilant gaze, examining every inch of the space within his visual field. The fruitless search for any anomaly intensified the sense of vulnerability that clung to him.

Crossing the street rushing, he approached his mother's front door, the nagging apprehension persisting. Ringing the doorbell, he awaited the familiar face of his mother. As the door opened, revealing a petite woman with softer feminine features and brown eyes – a mirror image of

Alfie – his eyes met hers in search of solace. Yet, the remnants of anxiety lingered, compelling him to continue scanning the surroundings, looking for shadows or signs of the elusive threat that haunted him. The internal debate of what to disclose to his mother added another layer to his turmoil, leaving him caught between the desire to confide and the fear of sounding irrational.

"What do I owe this morning surprise visit by the local celebrity," she asked jokingly, her eyes assessing Alfie's expression. The humour in her tone faded into concern, fuelled by the instincts only a mother possesses. A sense of foreboding settled over her as she recognized the familiar look of dread etched on Alfie's face. "What's the matter?" she asked, her concern deepening.

Without responding, Alfie walked past her, entering the house, and making a beeline for the kitchen. He placed his bag on the large round table at the room's centre, the place where many burdens were bared. As he began unravelling the distressing events involving Teddy's Mother and Eva's murder, his mother's concerned demeanour quickly transformed into shock and horror. Tears welled up in her eyes, a sadness for the friend she once trusted and for Teddy whom she'd seen grow up.

"Do they know who did it?" she asked, her worry now encompassing both Alfie and herself. Alfie observed the turmoil reflected in his mother's eyes as tears started to fall. "I know we weren't as close after we found out about Teddy; she was wrong for what she did… but she didn't deserve this," she sobbed, reflecting on the complex history and unspoken tension between her and Teddy's mother.

As the smell of grief suffocated the room, Alfie recognized a regret in his mother, he consoled her reassuring her that she didn't need to feel any guilt for how their friendship ended.

"How's sweet Teddy coping," his mother asked with a motherly concern, intensely looking at Alfie she slowly sat in the chair next to him, she brushed Alfie's bag with her elbow as she leaned forward holding her son's arm.

"His struggling, we were up all night with him, and he was all over the place," Alfie confessed not looking his mother in the face, "His mum and girlfriend gone in one night, that's going to take a lot to heal from, we know how much damage that does," Alfie continued softly finally looking at him mother.

Allowing his mother to immerse herself in empathy for Teddy's loss, Alfie hesitated, grappling with the decision of whether to disclose the remaining details. Despite his selfish need to unburden himself, he acknowledged the weight he was placing on her shoulders. He knew she would be worried and scared, yet he also recognized her as the steadfast anchor in his turbulent life.

"They don't know who did it, but when I got home after picking Teddy up from the police station last night, there was an envelope on my floor, it was blank, and it had a note inside it… for me," Alfie spoke pacing his words until he finally revealed all to his mum. Unzipping his bag he took out the envelope. Holding it in his hand tightly he looked at his mother cautious to show.

"What did the note say?" She asked looking at the envelope in his hand. Snatching the envelope out of his hand, his mother reached inside, a splatter of blood stuck to the top of her hand as she pulled out the contents.

"Whose blood is this?" His mother asked as she looked disgusted dropping the note and photos on the table, she got up washing her hands in the sink. Alfie took them off the table as his mother sat back down. he handed the note to her, explaining,

"They sent this note with two photos inside." She read the note aloud, the chilling words echoing in the room. **"Do you remember what it feels like to kill? Tonight was because of**

you, Alfie. Who's next?" Her stunned eyes oscillated between her son and the ominous message in her hand. Re-reading and repeating the words, panic flickered in her face as she looked at Alfie in alarm.

"What do you think they are talking about?" she asked, her gaze penetrating Alfie's, a note of worry in her voice, her maternal instincts urging Alfie to uphold their silence.

"I don't know," stressed Alfie, his brow furrowing as he reflected on the people in and out of his life.

"Does anyone know what happened when you were younger?" she asked, scrutinizing him, her protective mother instincts kicking in.

"You, me, and Charley knows some of what happened, not everything, just minor details, to add depth to what everyone else knows," Alfie confessed, fidgeting under his mother's intense scrutiny.

"What about what me and you did?" she asked, examining him further, her eyes narrowing with concern.

"No one… there's no need for anyone to know!" Alfie replied adamantly, looking at his mother.

"It's impossible for anyone else to know then; it was covered up, it died with him," she reassured her son, a sense of relief crossing her face. Holding the photos in his hands he handed them facedown to his mother. Gasping in horror, a high-pitched squeal escaping her lips, she cried out with a mix of repulsion and sadness as she saw the photo of her deceased old friend.

"Was that blood from there? Asked his mother instantly as she threw the photos on the table. Witnessing the anxiety on her son's face, she momentarily buried her own feelings to assure him that she was there for him. Staring into the note once more, she rubbed her face, trying to comprehend the cruel reality unfolding before them.

"I don't understand. Why are they dead because of you?" she asked Alfie, looking back at him. "If they wanted to send a message to you, why not to me, or Charley, or heaven forbid, Oscar," she continued, attempting to rationalize the situation. She hesitated before adding, "Maybe you just have a psycho from the past jealous of you making stuff up," She knew that dismissing the matter wouldn't be so simple.

"But then this… Do you remember what it feels like to kill? It just doesn't make sense. Who would know?" She was confused, desperately attempting to provide Alfie with an answer to ease his chaotic mind. The situation had even freaked her out, she just needed to ease Alfie;

knowing how much he'd conquered in the past. She feared this would be send him spiralling back. She could already see that the entire thing was messing with his head.

"Maybe someone is just trying to scare you," she replied, hoping to alleviate his fear, but she knew better. This situation had unnerved her too. She managed to conceal her worry better than her son, a mother's trick she had mastered over the years.

"It's already worked," Alfie's soft nose twitched as he exhaled, releasing all the terror that was eating him up inside. He confessed what his mother already knew. Alfie sat down, burying his face in his hands. Closing his eyes, another flashback pierced his mind.

Flashback:

"Alfie!!!" A deep, penetrating voice roared aggressively, its resonance echoing through the corridors of Alfie's memories, a haunting spectre of his past and an unwelcome visitor in his present. Alfie locked eyes with the man, his small frame trembling under the weight of intense fear. In that moment, the very air seemed to thicken with an oppressive terror that clung to him.

His breaths became rapid, each inhale a struggle against the suffocating grip of panic.

The man's eyes bore into Alfie's, an abyss of menace that sent shivers down his spine. The terror held him captive, rendering him helpless in the face of impending doom.

A cold, fleshy fist, calloused and unyielding, collided with Alfie's tender cheek. The impact sent shockwaves through his young body, the pain radiating like tendrils of agony. In that brutal meeting of flesh, the world transformed into a nightmare for Alfie, his innocence shattered in the cruel hands of a menacing force. The echoes of the encounter reverberated in his soul, leaving an indelible mark of intense fear that would haunt him long after the physical pain subsided.

Present:

Jumping out of the chair, Alfie let out a deep, terrified screech. His entire body trembled uncontrollably as the echo of his own fear lingered in the room. His wide eyes frantically scanning the room, struggling to distinguish the present from the haunting memories that had invaded his mind. It took a moment for him to grasp his current reality, realizing he was stuck in a daydream where his mind relentlessly dragged him back to relive the painful past. The anxiety, like a malevolent force, warping his perception, blurring the lines between what was real and the haunting echoes of his own past.

His mother, burying the worry from her face, stared at him with her own mind racing as she could see the anxiety problems he'd faced crawling back into his life. Alfie, still visibly shaken, slowly lowered himself back into the kitchen chair, silently calming his erratic heart from the scars of his past.

"Are you okay?" she asked sympathetically, touching his shoulder as her fear revealed through her eyes, flickering through all his episodes from the past. The look of terror on his face slowly began to disappear, but the reassuring smile he attempted failed to convince her.

During his teenage years, an event ignited which created his anxiety. It took him three years to overcome, with a few hiccups here and there. Another occurrence had set him back to square one in his late teens. There was a period after Oscar was born where his mother stayed with him, witnessing his ongoing struggle with anxiety although it was mild because of Oscar. She was angry that her son was being dragged back into the severity of his panic.

"Stupid question, I know," she tried to soothe him with her light-hearted reply. With his head within his palms, he shook his head, attempting to rid his mind of the memories that flickered.

"I just need to make sure you, Charley, and Oscar are safe," Alfie expressed his concern, revealing the protective nature that his mother had observed in him since childhood. "Can you come and stay with us until this is over, please?" Insisting, he looked at his mother with a non-negotiable expression.

"I've seen enough horror films to know that's the smart thing to do in these kinds of situations," she responded trying to lighten the tension, and to ease Alfie's panic. Walking out of the kitchen and into her bedroom, she pulled out a suitcase and began packing her clothes. Sitting at the table, Alfie pulled the note into his eye view, re-reading it again and again, trying to find a clue in the writing from the mystery sender. He pondered on what his mother had said about it being someone jealous of him. He couldn't accept that it was a stranger; it wasn't just threatening, it was personally aimed at him, insinuating his dark secret.

Calling Alfie into the bedroom, she asked him to help her throw her clothes into another suitcase. Once everything was packed, Alfie walked back into the kitchen, placing the photos and note back inside the envelope and then into his bag. Walking back into the hallway, he grabbed her suitcases, and they made their way out of his mother's house.

Opening the front door, Alfie's eyes widened as he noticed a large, ominous brown envelope resting on the doorstep. The atmosphere seemed to grow heavier as he took the suitcases outside, a sense of foreboding settling over him. Bending down, he cautiously picked up the envelope, and his mother promptly locked the door behind them, heightening the tension.

Scanning the mysterious package in his hands, Alfie flipped it around, desperately searching for a name, an address, or even a stamp. The suspense mounted with each passing moment. However, this time the envelope remained blank, not even his name written. His mother observed the blankness in Alfie's hand, her mind jumping to the same as his.

"Is that my post?" she asked, attempting to take it from him.

"No… No, it's not," he replied, pulling it away, his stomach tying up in knots. A chilling realization dawned on him – the sender of the ominous note knew where his mother lived, he was right. Scrutinizing the street, Alfie looked for any signs of the mysterious sender, analysing everyone who passed by.

Holding the enigmatic envelope in his hand, he pulled the suitcases towards his car, his mother following behind looking around. In public, she maintained a worried silence, her apprehension intense. Swiftly putting his mother's suitcase in the back seat and slamming the door, Alfie rushed to the driver's side. As he sat in the car, he slammed the door shut, his mother joined him in the car. Both stared at the envelope, a heavy sense of dread settling in the air. The thought loomed – had someone else been harmed? Alfie's heart raced, each beat echoing loudly in his chest.

"Open it!" demanded his mother impatiently, her eyes fixed on him. Wearily, Alfie ripped the tip off, nervous about the contents. His mother watched with growing impatience, eager to uncover the secrets hidden within the envelope. As it finally opened, he pulled out another note and a photograph.

"Remember what you did?

You can't save anyone this time!

Not even them!"

The warning words deepened his worry, intensifying the chilling atmosphere that surrounded them. Alfie silently read the note to himself. Handing it to his mother, he stepped out of the car, scanning his surroundings with a fuelled anger that left him light-headed. His eyes darted to every person on the street as frustration built up within him. In a brief moment, he forgot about the media attention he was attracting and couldn't contain the urge to coerce his tormenter whom he felt was watching.

"COME AND GET ME THEN!" he bellowed, his voice echoing, foam forming at the corners of his mouth. His intense gaze locked onto every person who dared to look in his direction.

Sensing the escalating situation, his mother swiftly grabbed the bottom of his shirt, forcefully pulling him back into the car. Alfie bent down, slamming the door shut, frustration evident as his hand smacked with the top of the steering wheel.

"Stop!" demanded his mother with a stern look. "It's not going to help drawing attention to ourselves, especially with everything going on with your work." Alfie, realizing the truth in her words, tried to relax himself. He apologized to his mother, taking a deep breath.

"I know what the note is referring to," Alfie revealed, looking at her with a shared understanding. "No one was saved the last time," he confirmed, the weight of the past hanging heavily between them.

Pulling a photo out of the envelope, Alfie stared at it, and an immediate surge of dread gripped him. His heartbeat accelerated rapidly, the rhythmic pounding echoing in his ears. Pains began to pierce through his chest, intensifying with each passing second. Overwhelmed, he dropped the photo, clutching his chest in agony, convinced he was experiencing a heart attack.

Struggling to calm himself, he found it challenging to take breaths; the pain consumed his mind, rendering concentration impossible. He was caught in the clutches of a dangerous panic attack, a torment he hadn't experienced so violently in years. Closing his eyes in an effort to regain control, he felt suffocated by the overwhelming angst, his attempts to exhale met with strained grunts.

His mother, no stranger to Alfie's struggles, had witnessed numerous panic attacks before. Reacting swiftly, she grabbed his nose and held his mouth, a technique she had perfected over the years. Alfie resisted, struggling against the grip on his face, but his mother persisted until he finally managed to take a deep, shuddering breath. Panting heavily, it took some time before he could inhale normally, and the panic attack subsided. His mother understood that shocking him and redirecting his focus was crucial in breaking the vicious cycle of anxiety that had taken hold.

"Are you okay now?" his mother asked, checking on him. Bending down, Alfie picked up the photo to show his mother the reason for his panic. From a distance, the image displayed

Charley and Oscar outside his school. Judging by the jacket Charley wore, the photo was taken within the last two weeks. Frustration gripped him as he scanned through everyone he had ever met once more, unable to determine who might be behind this disturbing intrusion.

"They know where you live, they know where I live, they know where Teddy lives, they know where Oscar goes to school... Who the hell is this? What else do they know?" Alfie voiced his disquiets out loud, disturbed by the unsettling darkness of the situation.

"I don't know, darling. They've cornered us. Going to the police isn't an option – it'll open a can of worms you can never close. You're moving house tomorrow, far away from here... I'll stay with you until we find out who it is!" his mother replied, determined to protect her son. Taking the envelope from him, she felt the edge of paper dig into her fingertip. Opening it carefully, she found another photo stuck face down on one side. Carefully pulling it off to avoid damaging the actual photo, she looked inside with widened eyes.

"Alfie, I haven't seen this photo for years... Last time I saw it was in our old house!" Surprised, she leaned over to him, putting the photo in his face. It was an old picture from Alfie's thirteenth birthday, featuring smiles with Teddy, Lucy, and a couple of other friends and family. Her finger pointed at someone in the photo, glancing at Alfie, tears flowed down her eyes. A shiver stroked down his spine as he looked at the familiar face that erupted emotions hidden.

"Guess that confirms it further," Alfie replied cutting his focus away from the photo. His mother covered her mouth as she stared at the picture, wiping her eyes. Turning the ignition, Alfie began to drive back to his place, a heavy silence cloaking them.

Alfie's mind was erratic, while his mother stared out of the window, thinking about the photo. That envelope wasn't just for Alfie; they wanted to throw distress her way too. She knew that when push came to shove, Alfie was a survivor and he'd survive, but the mental torment would be his downfall. He wasn't equipped to deal with things emotionally or mentally; the burdens would destroy him. Stopping outside of his house Alfie parked the car.

Charley gazed out the window, watching Alfie pull up to the curb. She observed his mother exiting the car as they parked outside. Alfie, still inside, swiftly stashed the new note and the two latest photos back into the envelope, sliding it into his work bag. He emerged from the car, locking the door, Charley stepped outside to greet her mother-in-law.

"Diane, what are you doing here?" Charley asked pleasantly. They shared a good relationship, akin to that of a mother and daughter, a bond that had developed over the years.

"I thought I'd come and stay, help you all move to the new place," Alfie's mother replied, smiling as she exchanged a subtle glance with Alfie. Their unspoken communication always worked seamlessly, a testament to their close connection whenever something was amiss.

"I thought it would help if Mum came and helped us, and the new house is big enough, so we'll have room for her to stay with us while we settle in," Alfie said, touching his mother's shoulder.

"Well, it'll be nice to have another woman in the house again," Charley smiled at her mother-in-law giving a playful wink.

"How's Teddy coping?" Alfie's mother inquired, gesturing towards Alfie, signalling to Charley that he had shared everything with her.

"He's been better since Oscar has been awake. I think having a kid takes your mind off things doesn't it, but last night it was all so raw for him. I don't think he'll be feeling himself for a while," Charley explained, giving Alfie's mother a look of sympathy as she delved into Teddy's grief and trauma.

Alfie, glancing at his watch, recalled his morning meeting at the office. He quickly excused himself, giving Charley and his mother a kiss before heading back to his car. From there, he observed his mother and Charley walking into the house, their conversation about Teddy lingering in the air. Aware that his mother would have securely locked the door behind her.

Driving off, his mind was consumed with the words on both notes and the photos. He felt selfish dwelling on a looming threat, when his best friend had paid the high price for associating with him. He focused his thoughts on Teddy, so he didn't brew up another panic attack while driving.

Chapter 3

Entering the modern glass building, distinct from its neighbouring structures, Alfie marvelled at the towering walls of glass that surrounded him, reflecting the cityscape in their polished surface. The building's unique architecture featured large glass plates that extended seamlessly to the roof, adorned with rounded bricks. As he walked through the entrance, Alfie noticed the constant flow of workers, both entering and leaving the bustling office.

Approaching the front desk, Alfie was met with a warm smile from the receptionist. This friendly face belonged to Ronnie, who recently came to Alfie's aid during a paparazzi frenzy at the building's entrance. The media had swarmed the area, clamouring for photos of the man of the moment.

"Morning, Ronnie," Alfie greeted softly, with a warm smile. Ronnie, in turn, handed Alfie his mail while they engaged in conversation. Alfie had always treated Ronnie with respect not commonly extended by other bosses in the building.

What Alfie particularly admired about Ronnie was his exceptional work ethic. Despite the demands of a full-time job, Ronnie dedicated his evenings to studying business and marketing. Alfie had even offered him an opportunity to work and learn on the job, providing a chance to earn a good income. However, Ronnie, proud and self-sufficient, declined the offer, having paid for his night classes himself. Undeterred, Alfie promised Ronnie a job upon completing his studies, an offer Ronnie graciously accepted. This mutual admiration for each other's dedication to their respective endeavours created a good friendship.

"I think you have more fan letters than general mail, judging by the amount you have here," he joked, handing Alfie numerous white handwritten letters and a couple of brown envelopes. Alfie shuffled through them quickly, nervous of another taunting letter, he replied to Ronnie.

"I wouldn't be surprised. It's been a hectic week; I just hope it ends soon. Fame isn't for me," Alfie expressed, the exhaustion evident on his face. Assumptions were made as Alfie remained normal not burdening anyone with the true source of his weariness. Maintaining his usual demeanour, Alfie walked over to the elevator. As he pressed the button on the wall, the elevator doors slid open. He stepped inside, pushing the button for the top floor to reach his office.

When the elevator doors opened, Alfie stepped out, entering his expansive glass interior open-floor office. A fire exit door located a few feet away from the elevator had been left open. Suspiciously he inspected around him then walked over to the door. Pushing it open wider he stepped onto the landing, he cast a sharp glance up the staircase leading to the roof. Then, with a cautious look behind him, he checked the descending stairs that connected to every floor of the building. Disquiet played subtly in the back of his mind.

"Hello!" he shouted, his voice echoing down the stairwell. The only response to his call was the distant echo of his own voice travelling. Proceeding cautiously, Alfie went back into his office, ensuring to shut the fire door properly behind him.

Back in his office, Alfie halted midway in the room. The dazzling blue sky, splashed with white clouds, immediately caught his eye. As he took in the view, a profound stillness settled within him. His body, bearing the weight of recent anguish, was beginning to show signs of exhaustion. Back in his late teens during therapy, his psychologist used to advise him to focus on something still and peaceful. For Alfie, that always meant gazing at the sky. Subconsciously, he had repeated the action, seeking solace in the calming clouds swimming in the sky.

Thomas, a tall and slender man with chestnut-brown hair, approached Alfie from behind playfully whacking him on the shoulder. "The meeting's been cancelled today, Alf. They rescheduled it for next week," he announced, breaking Alfie's meditative gaze at the sky. Swiftly snapping out of his tranquil state, Alfie responded looking into his piercing blue eyes, "What was that, Tom?"

"The meeting with the new client got rescheduled for next week," Thomas repeated, studying Alfie's expression. "Are you okay?" he inquired. Alfie nodded and replied, "I'm fine."

"Good. By the way, Stewart and I just wrapped up the beer campaign we were working on," Thomas shared, leading the way toward a long white table at the centre of the room. Alfie followed closely. Stewart his expressive face brightened by his light ginger hair. His dark blue eyes reflected off the laptop screen. surrounded by scattered paper plans. As Thomas settled down next to Stewart, Alfie positioned himself behind them. Stewart stiffly sat as he played the campaign on the laptop. Alfie observed as a 45-second-long advertisement unfolded. Alfie nodded in approval; it perfectly encapsulated what the client had envisioned.

"Sorry I couldn't have been more hands-on with it this week and help you finish it, guys!" Alfie apologized, his tone laden with guilt.

"No worries, we had it covered," replied Stewart, still fixated on the laptop screen.

"Yeah, I mean, the interviews, everyone chasing you for the story, and you're moving house soon. Don't worry; we're partners; that's what we do," reassured Thomas, attempting to ease Alfie's guilt.

Alfie's eyes met the cloudy glass block opposite the table—his private office. Excusing himself, he casually walked toward his secluded workspace. Inside, he shut the door, the quiet click echoing his internal conflict, as he sighed in relief and dropping his act. Throwing his bag under the table, he placed his mail on the desk between his phone and lamp. Walking back to the door, he shrugged his shoulders putting his act of normality back on. Opening the door, he asked Thomas if he could speak with him privately. Thomas entered the room. Locking eyes with Thomas's piercing blue gaze, Alfie delivered the grim news about Teddy's mother and Eva's murder. Thomas in shock had the same horrific look on his face that his mother had worn when he had broken the news to her.

"It's not my thing to tell, but me, you, Teddy, and Lucy have been friends for a long time. So, I'm giving you a quick heads up when you see him on Saturday," Alfie said, avoiding reacting to Thomas's shock. He couldn't allow himself to be swallowed by the grief he buried, the pain that fought to surface every time someone reacted normally to such news.

Clearing his throat, he continued, changing his tone in an attempt to shift the subject. "Also, another reason I wanted to speak to you privately is that... you started this company with me. If it wasn't for you, I don't think I would be in the position I am now. So, once I've moved house and sorted all that stuff out, I'm signing half the business over to you! And this time, you're not saying no!" Alfie gestured to Thomas. Shocked, Thomas was left speechless. The weight of Alfie's words hung heavily in the air, and Thomas struggled to find an adequate response.

Eight years ago, when Alfie initiated the company, he extended an offer to Thomas, proposing a partnership that would entail each of them owning half of the business. However, Thomas, gripped by fear of the associated risks, was hesitant. He preferred working closely with Alfie but wasn't ready to have his name attached to the venture. Despite this initial reluctance,

Thomas remained fiercely loyal to Alfie over the years.

Now, Alfie felt compelled to rectify the past and make Thomas an official partner, acknowledging his unwavering dedication. This decision was reinforced by the pivotal role Thomas played in maintaining order during times when Alfie faced personal challenges. Six years ago, when Alfie's son, Oscar, was born, Thomas efficiently handled all aspects of the business, allowing Alfie to be hands-on while supporting Charley, who was experiencing postnatal depression.

It was also Thomas's influence that thrust Alfie into the limelight. Alfie, who had never aspired for fame, initially resisted every call and interview, aiming to keep a low profile. Nevertheless, it was Thomas who, through persuasive conversations, convinced Alfie to embrace publicity, ultimately raising the company's profile for the better. Alfie felt he owed Thomas for everything, now that he was financially secure, he was paying Thomas his dues.

Exiting the small private office, Thomas firmly closed the door behind him, sealing off any lingering sounds from within. Alfie, tired and uneasy, made his way to his chair, where his eyes immediately caught another foreboding brown envelope standing upright against a cherished photo capturing a moment with Oscar. Alfie's heart raced, a sense of impending dread settling in. Without hesitation, he examined the envelope with meticulous intensity, his hands trembling with a mix of curiosity and anxiety.

Suddenly, Alfie lunged toward the door, the envelope still firmly in his grip. He opened it with a mixture of nervousness and urgency. Thomas halted midway between the table where Stewart sat and Alfie's office. "Has anyone else been in here today?" Alfie directed the question at Thomas, ensuring his voice carried loudly enough for Stewart to hear as well.

"No, not that I have seen," replied Stewart sharply, his response accompanied by a confirming shake of Thomas's head and a confused frown. Alfie casually shut the door; his gaze fixed on the mysterious envelope. He locked the door, creating a barrier between the unfolding uncertainty and the outside world. Taking a deep breath, Alfie gradually opened the brown envelope, revealing its contents—a document he had personally placed on his desk. It was a proposal for another client, the meeting for which was scheduled for today.

Sitting on the edge of his desk, Alfie's hands pressed against his face, fingers rubbing down his cheeks as if trying to erase the unsettling reality. The weight of the situation bore down on him, and he felt as if he were on the verge of losing every ounce of his sanity. Turning away, he began to flick through the mail he had been handed by Ronnie, a futile attempt to divert his mind. Opening a couple of letters, he discarded them into the bin—short, frivolous declarations of love and business proposals from strangers seeking a piece of Alfie's success.

Amid the mundane contents, one business plan caught Alfie's eye. Encased in a bright blue envelope, the vibrant colours grabbed his attention. Unable to resist, he immersed himself in the preposterous proposal, laughing as he read through it. Superficially, it provided a momentary escape from the turmoil of the past few hours. Intrigued, Alfie stood from the edge of the table and nonchalantly strolled toward his chair. Pulling it out, his eyes were drawn to a thick, large white envelope on his seat.

Setting the humorous business plan on the table, Alfie picked up the white envelope, its weight noticeable in his hands. A sticky label with his name printed on it caught his attention. Slowly lowering himself into his seat, Alfie carefully opened the envelope. His hand explored its contents, revealing several separate items that fell onto the table—several photographs that sent him back into the reality he'd momentarily escaped.

The first photo sent a shiver down Alfie's spine. It depicted Charley and Oscar, their faces marred by red felt-tip pen scribbles. The faces were the only unmarked parts of their bodies, the threat Alfie recognised instantly. Holding the photo, Alfie ran his fingers over the other contents from the envelope, a sickening anticipation growing within him. The absence of a note heightened the eerie silence surrounding him. Turning the photo around, he discovered ominous writing on the back that sent a cold chill through his veins.

"You'll watch them die. He will feel the fear of what's coming as he watches his mother being ripped apart screaming for her life!"

An unsettling image of Oscar and Charley lifeless, drenched in blood, flashed vividly in Alfie's mind. Instead of succumbing to worry, a surge of anger welled up within him. His body burned from the inside out as he put down the photo, bracing himself for the next revelation.

The second photo depicted him and Teddy, but the disquieting details went beyond the initial distress. Flipping the photo, Alfie was met with words scrawled in a different handwriting.

"Will you tell him the truth before he dies?"

The question echoed in Alfie's mind, leaving him dumbfounded. Only he knew the secret he concealed from Teddy. The implications were chilling, and Alfie felt the weight of an unseen threat looming over him as he picked up the next photo.

This time, it showcased Thomas and Stewart alongside their friends, Alex, Ben, Jack, and Lucy. Turning the photo, Alfie confronted another cryptic message.

"Can you really trust your friends?"

Intensely scrutinizing their faces, Alfie was certain none of them had access to the secrets that haunted him. Discarding the photo, he picked up another—this time, a snapshot from a joyous party featuring Charley, Teddy, Eva, Thomas, Grace, Ben, Jack, Lucy, Alex, Jennifer, Stewart, Ella, and Ivy. However, the photo held a sinister twist, with a red cross over Eva's face. Turning the photo, Alfie read the same ominous line from the first note he received.

"Who dies Next?"

Putting the photo down, he picked up the final one—a picture of his mother, slightly torn. Turning it over, he was met with a chilling message.

"Mother's love started this!"

Alfie gathered the photos, carefully placing them back in the white envelope. Retrieving his bag from beneath the table, he dropped it alongside the two other ominous envelopes. Kicking his bag back under, he folded his arms on the desk, resting his head as he closed his eyes. The room's weight pressed upon him as he mentally sifted through everyone he knew, unable to pinpoint the mysterious sender. Closing his eyes, Alfie succumbed to a light slumber, lack of sleep and anxious shakes draining him to exhaustion.

Flashback/dream:

Alfie lay wide awake in bed, the silhouette of a young boy peacefully asleep in the adjacent bed. His gaze fixated on the ceiling, sleep eluding him. Suddenly, a shrill, high-pitched scream pierced the quietude, resonating through the entire house. The unsettling sound of wood snapping echoed, shattering the tranquillity of the small home. A series of forceful strikes assaulted the wooden door, its purpose to safeguard both the home and its occupants now under a relentless siege.

Present:

The phone on his desk suddenly rang, jolting him out of his nightmare. Lifting his head, his left arm swung, inadvertently knocking over the lamp on his desk, sending the phone and a cascade of mail to the floor. Letters covered the ground, the lamp shattered to pieces, its light bulb broken. His brief respite, interrupted by the intrusive ringtone. Bending down to retrieve the phone, he was startled by a sudden knock on his office door. Alfie stood turning his eyes toward the door.

"Alfie, are you alright?" Thomas asked with concern, having heard the commotion. He knocked again when Alfie failed to respond.

"I'm fine!" Alfie shouted disgruntled. The phone ceased its incessant ringing. Cautiously, he picked up the broken pieces of the lamp and the large shards of the light bulb, disposing of them in a bin in the corner. Leaving the scattered letters on the floor, he retrieved the phone, attempting to redial the caller, it was from a private number.

Rubbing his right hand through his hair, he looked out the window again. Moving closer, he took a momentary glance at the sky, then shifted his focus downward to observe the people going about their day. Inspecting every visible face, he tried to make out features, scanning the street. He spotted a man looking up at him. Concentrating hard to discern the man's face, he was met with a chilling gesture – a cutthroat motion. The man then pointed directly at him. Blinking, the man vanished from Alfie's sight.

The phone rang again, turning around, with composure he picked the phone up, sitting back in the seat. He took a pen from the side, as he began to flick it between his fingers. Greeting the caller, about to introduce the company name, he was interrupted.

"With all this success must come a price!" a shaky and croaky voice desperately whispered.

"Who is this?" frustration echoed in his voice as he spoke. Alfie heard a faint commotion before the mysterious caller replied to him.

"Alfie…I'm sor…" The voice was cut off, a different person came to the phone, the voice was older deeper and icily cold, but Alfie recognised it to someone he had spoken to before.

"Your little friend can't seem to take instructions," said the cold voice. Alfie confused, by the word friend. He stayed silent, trying to match the new voice speaking to people he had known. "She's very pretty, it's a shame she has to die because of you…" the voice eerily continued.

"You go anywhere near her you C---" the anger he had felt when he see the photo of Charley and Alfie consumed him, but he was cut off mid insult.

"Maybe we can find another use for her," the man insinuating something worse to further play games with Alfie's mind, as he laughed. A hoarse howl of pain pierced distantly through the

64

phone. Alfie listened to what sounded like a struggle happening at a distance away from the receiver. The voice came back to the phone. In the background, Alfie heard deep whimpers.

"He should have done as he was told, he wouldn't be suffering now if he did... Oh, Alfie, here's another one that's all your fault," the voice said malevolently with another eerie laugh.

"Who the fuck are you? What do you want?" Alfie careful not to be heard by Thomas and Stewart outside, said gritting his teeth, the anger overloading inside of him.

"I want you to beg me to stop just before I kill Charley, Oscar, and your mother, and then beg me to kill you quicker," slowly emphasising every word so Alfie felt the intent in every syllable that he spoke.

"Arsehole! Come for me instead of all these innocent people!" Alfie still speaking low in his pent-up rage.

"You have guts Alfie; I wonder if they'll be as strong when I rip them out of you!" the voice replied to him. Cutting off the call.

"Hello, hello," Alfie repeated into the phone, pushing the redial button on the office phone in an attempt to call the number back, but there was no number left to call. Pulling out his mobile from his pocket, he called his mother.

"Mum! Go somewhere private, please," he instructed with panic. He heard her moving around as she excused herself from everyone in the house.

"What's wrong?" she asked as he heard a door closing.

"I just had a phone call from whoever is doing this!" Alfie recounted the call, the background filled with the sounds of a struggle or something akin to it. She didn't know how to respond, worried for her son. Alfie, letting out his frustrations, could feel the anxiety amplified by his sense of helplessness. Hanging up the phone, he unlocked his door, walking into the open floor office. Thomas sensed something was amiss, gauging it from the expression on Alfie's face. Avoiding contact Alfie headed into the kitchen.

Alfie's mobile rang. Recognizing the number instantly, he answered the call.

"Hi, James, how are you?" Alfie spoke normally as he made himself a glass of water.

"I'm good thank you, I was just giving a quick call to let you know that the house is now vacant, and I have the keys for you to pick up," replied James, the estate agent.

"That's great news, I can swing by and pick them up today if you're around?" Alfie replied. A sudden shift of worry turned to delight as this couldn't have come at a better time. A new home that no one knew about other than his closest friends and family. Every person in the photos was staying with him this weekend, eliminating them as suspects.

"Yeah, of course you can. I will be in the office all day, so if you can come before closing," James replied.

"Great, I'll see you later on today then," Alfie replied, ending the call with the estate agent's final farewell.

Walking out of the kitchen, over to Thomas and Stewart, who were both seated at the table, he informed them he was picking up the keys to the new house. Thomas, getting up, disappeared for a moment, reappearing with three glasses and a bottle of champagne.

"Liquid brunch to celebrate," he gestured, grinning, popping the bottle and pouring the glasses until they were full. Stewart raised a toast, celebrating the completion of their latest project and to Alfie picking up the keys to his new home, or mansion, as Alfie called it. Just as they were about to drink from their cups, an abrupt collision interrupted their celebration.

The window caved in, glass shards erupting through the room, cascading down to shatter on the floor. Startled by the thunderous sound, Alfie and Thomas instinctively threw themselves backward, cups slipping from their grasp and crashing onto the ground. In the chaotic tumble, they both fell into Stewart, who went down beneath them.

Alfie, regaining his composure, leaned up with his arms behind him, only to be met with a gruesome sight. A bloodied, lifeless body hung, swinging back and forth, propelled into the room and then out through the shattered window. Alfie noticed the two ropes tied around the body - one around the neck, the other around the arms - blood dripping off the gruesome victim. It was evident that whoever had thrown him through the window wanted to ensure he was secure enough to crash into Alfie's office, leaving an enduring impact on the scene.

"Oh my God, it's Ronnie!" shouted Thomas, recognizing the bloodied, lifeless receptionist. Blood leaked from his legs and arms; his face painted in a gruesome display. The visible gashes in his body indicated he had been tortured before being put on this horrifying display. The shock and disgust were intense on Thomas's face.

Alfie, slowly got up, pacing toward the body, an undercurrent of fear colouring his movements. Despite the overwhelming dread, he felt compelled to see the body up close. As he analysed the blood-soaked body, he spotted hand marks around Ronnie's neck. The shock and disgust mirrored on Alfie's face, sending shivers down his spine as he worried about the horrors he would soon face.

Feeling sickly, Alfie took a step backward away from the corpse. Without hesitation, he turned sprinting away from the hanging body, escaping the gruesome scene through the fire exit door. As he burst out of the room, Alfie leaned against the wall, gasping for slow, deep breaths to steady himself. Suddenly, the sound of fast-approaching footsteps reached him.

Leaning over, he glanced downward, expecting to see someone running past. To his surprise, no one was in sight. Turning to look up the staircase toward the roof, Alfie came face to face with a figure dressed entirely in black, their face concealed by a black balaclava. In a swift move, the masked man delivered a quick backhand punch and forcefully pushed Alfie aside as he made his way downstairs to escape the building.

A surge of adrenaline fuelled Alfie's determination, as he gave immediate chase, believing that capturing this assailant would put an end to his torment. Jumping down the stairs, he tackled the masked man to the ground. Leaning over, Alfie attempted to yank off the balaclava, but the man retaliated by elbowing him in the stomach, momentarily winding him.

Crawling along a pillar, the masked man attempted to throw himself down the next flight of stairs to escape Alfie's pursuit. Undeterred, Alfie grabbed the masked man's leg, trying to pull him closer. In a desperate struggle, the masked man lifted his leg, curving his knee, and forcefully stamped the outsole of his boot into Alfie's face. The impact sent Alfie's head thumping into the wall, causing a momentary bout of double vision. Towering over Alfie, the masked man stood triumphant.

"It's not time yet," growled the same voice from the phone, carrying a rasp of fury. The masked man continued his escape, sprinting down the stairs. Alfie could only watch as the figure seemed to multiply, with two of him disappearing down the stairway.

Slowly, Alfie pushed his hands against the wall to steady himself. Standing up, he rubbed his head in slow, deliberate circles. The collision had given him a migraine, and he groaned, hands still holding his head, as he walked back up the stairs to his office. Inside, Thomas was on the phone with the police, urgently relaying the alarming events. Stewart, seeing Alfie walking as if he were drunk and holding his head, rushed over.

"Alfie, your nose is bleeding!" Stewart exclaimed with concern, leading him to the big table. He quickly emptied a box of tissues, offering them to him. As Alfie sat, staring at Ronnie's lifeless body, he blamed himself for the receptionist's death. Feelings of guilt surged through him, knowing he was the reason for Ronnie's death. His anxiousness temporarily disappeared as he reflected on what had just happened. Realizing that someone was coming after Charley, Oscar, and his mother, a blank rage coursed through his veins. Now fully aware of the impending threat, he knew what was coming and understood what he had to do.

Sitting in shock, faces of people he had upset or fallen out with flashed before his eyes. He just needed to know who was behind the mask. He considered his friends. So far, none of those close to him had been murdered, but he felt a looming threat. He needed to protect them.

The police swiftly arrived, efficiently separating Alfie, Thomas, and Stewart for individual questioning, ensuring consistency in their narratives. Despite Alfie's desire to divulge everything to the authorities, the fear of media attention held him back. He knew that exposing the masked man's threats might escalate the danger to those close to him.

Alfie recounted the phone call in the office but downplayed it, suggesting he initially considered it a prank. Regarding the attack on the stairs, he admitted not seeing the assailant. The intense questioning concluded, and the police escorted them away from the crime scene.

In the elevator, the trio maintained a heavy silence. Upon reaching the ground floor, Thomas and Stewart exited, while Alfie hesitated. Seeing a circus outside of news reporters, Alfie looked over to the receptionist desk devastated that the young boy was now gone. Thomas, showing concern, returned to the building to help Alfie get out.

"Come on, mate, we've got to go," Thomas comforted, gently nudging Alfie forward. As they stepped out, Alfie couldn't avoid the guilt washing over him. Outside, the darkened sky mirrored the sombre atmosphere. The flashing lights of cameras intensified as Alfie entered the view of the news crews. Overwhelmed, he lowered his head, shielding his face with his arm.

Exiting the building, reporters swarmed around Alfie. Thomas quickly stepped in front, acting as a shield against the intrusive cameras. Thomas glanced around for Stewart, who had mysteriously disappeared from the chaotic scene.

"Alfie, can you tell us what happened?" demanded a female reporter, thrusting a voice recorder into his face.

"He can't tell you anything!" Thomas shouted, forcefully moving the woman's hand away from Alfie.

"Did you know the victim, Alfie? Was he your friend?" inquired a male reporter, pushing through the crowd of journalists.

The reporters persistently shouted questions at Alfie as they all rushed towards him. Desperately, Alfie and Thomas manoeuvred through the chaotic crowd and reached Alfie's car. The reporters continued to hound them, blocking any attempt to leave, and capturing photos of the two inside.

Suddenly, seemingly out of nowhere, the police appeared. With authority, they intervened, swiftly moving the reporters aside, creating a path for Alfie and Thomas to drive away. The flashbulbs continued to flicker, capturing the tense moment as the car left the chaotic scene.

"It makes me sick! Poor Ronnie has just been murdered, and these people use his death as a commodity," raged Alfie to Thomas.

"I know," agreed Thomas. Alfie dropped Thomas off at his home, continuing to drive to get the keys to his new home.

While driving to the estate agent's, Alfie stopped at a red light. Gazing out of the driver's window, he saw a man dressed in black with a black balaclava covering his face, standing on the pavement, and staring at him. Anxious and enraged, Alfie quickly got out of the car, prepared to face this masked villain, but the disguised man had vanished. Tiredness started taking a toll on Alfie's mind.

The cars behind him impatiently and aggressively roared their car horns at him. Looking in every direction, Alfie tried to find where the masked man had run off to.

"Why are you doing this?" he shouted in the middle of the street. Continuing to search the street, but no one was there. Getting back in his car, he had to wait at another red light, with angry drivers behind him still roaring their horns. Lacking sleep, Alfie knew he was seeing things that weren't there. The masked man in the street was in his head, and the man earlier staring at him from the window must have been in his head too. He drove off as soon as the green light glowed, going as fast as he could to get to the estate agent's before it closed. His phone vibrated; he received a pop-up message from an anonymous sender. Intrigued, Alfie opened the message, and a video played...

Earlier that day,

Ronnie received a phone call asking him to take a package upstairs to the floor below Alfie's office. Picking up the parcel, he walked to the fire exit entrance so he could take the stairway. He had a phobia of elevators, so he always went up and down via the stairs, hurrying until he reached the fifth floor. There he saw a man wearing a black balaclava covering everything but his eyes. Startled, he asked the man what he was doing loitering there. The masked man never replied, staring at him coldly. Ronnie, feeling uneasy, took a step backwards attempting to slowly get away. The man had startled him, and he had a feeling of danger. Attempting to run back downstairs, the masked man instantly pushed him. Falling down each step hard, snapping his ankle on the concrete stair, he hit the pillar face first.

Crawling to the next staircase to roll down them, Ronnie pulled all of his weight toward the edge of the top stair. The masked man jumped on top of him, grabbing his hair and pulling him upwards, forcing him to stand on his broken ankle. Letting out a roar of pain, he cried as he struggled to get free, trying to escape when the masked man revealed a big sharp knife, putting it to his throat, forcing Ronnie to walk up the stairs. He struggled to keep his balance, buckling from the weakness in his ankle. Entering the rooftop, the masked man spoke, "I need you to call Alfie Sayers and repeat what I say in your ear," instructed the cold, aggressive voice. Ronnie nodded his head, agreeing.

Calling Alfie, the phone rang but no one picked up. The masked man, standing behind Ronnie, Ronnie took an opportunity, throwing his body weight onto the man. Swiftly getting back up, he began limping to the door to the stairs. The masked man tackled him to the ground, kneeling on top of Ronnie, wrapping his gloved hands around Ronnie's throat with severe pressure. Struggling, he fought to get free from the grip around his neck, with every struggle, the grip got tighter until there was a crack in his windpipe. Releasing his grip, Ronnie wheezed for air, coughing, defeated, he lay on the floor catching his breath, setting up a camera on the ledge opposite Ronnie.

Coughing on the ground, yanking Ronnie back to his feet, he handed him the phone and called Alfie again. "With all this success must come a price!" Ronnie's voice was hoarsely crackling, making it unrecognizable to Alfie. While Alfie responded, Ronnie attempted to escape again, dropping the phone, yet again the man caught him. He wasn't letting Ronnie escape. Wrestling on the ground, the masked man eventually stabbed Ronnie in the side of his stomach. Picking up the phone, the masked man placed the phone to Ronnie's ear while he lay holding his wound. "Alfie...I'm sor..." Ronnie panted, apologizing to Alfie. The masked man pulled the phone away and viciously began to stab him repeatedly, piercing his chest, arms, and legs, profoundly loving every strike, painting his body full of blood. He picked up the phone, moving out of view so the camera was solely on Ronnie, who was slowly dying, his breath slowly fading. When the conversation ended, the masked man revealed a rope, tying it around Ronnie's neck, walking over to the camera and shutting it off.

Present

Watching in horror, Alfie felt a tremendous amount of guilt as he observed Ronnie slowly dying on the video. His mobile's screen flashed back to the home screen. The video had ended. Searching his photos and then his messages, Alfie looked for the video to rewatch it, but it was gone, vanished like it hadn't been sent.

"Fuck! How? That's impossible!" he shouted, annoyed, and mystified. Enraged, he began to hit the wheel of his car, slapping the top half repeatedly. Looking toward the estate agents, Alfie got out, marching straight into the shop. James sat at his desk.

"Ouch, are you okay?" James asked Alfie, noticing a small bruise on his cheekbone.

"I'm fine!" Alfie snapped, drowning in his guilt and rage. Stopping himself as he heard his tone, he apologized. A large white envelope sat on James's desk, a sticky label with his printed name. Alfie spotted it instantly, noticing the similarity to the one he had received. Defensive and suspicious, his guard was up. James slid the envelope over to Alfie, who picked it up, feeling the weight of his new house keys in his hand. He folded the envelope up as small as he could, placing the keys in his jeans' pocket.

"I don't mean to pry, but it was on the news, and obviously I have your work address because of your documents, so, what happened earlier with that man who killed himself?" James asked Alfie, interested. Alfie scanned James' body language; something was off with him.

"I can't really go into it," Alfie replied sternly. "He didn't kill himself, though!" Alfie continued, still stern. He thanked him for the keys, hurriedly excusing himself. Leaving the estate agents, Alfie tried to match James to the masked man, but the voice, they weren't the same person speaking. Getting in his car, he carefully watched James inside the estate agents, hoping to catch him doing something suspicious.

Chapter 4

In the eerie stillness of his parked car, Alfie scrutinized James's every move within the dimly lit street watching the estate agent's office. Time seemed to stretch as he patiently awaited James's exit, and the tension heightened when James emerged, carefully locking the building. Slanting in his seat, Alfie ensured he remained hidden, a shadow in the darkness surveying as James climbed into his car.

Allowing James a mere thirty-second head start, Alfie initiated his pursuit, slipping into the role of an elusive shadow trailing its target. Precisely maintaining a safe distance, Alfie followed James's every twist and turn on the journey home, the anticipation thickening with each passing streetlamp. The night held its breath as James parked, disembarked, and disappeared into the safety of his own home.

Hovering at the end of the road like a phantom cloaked in darkness, Alfie bided his time until he was certain James wouldn't reemerge. Slowly, he eased his car down the deserted street, the quiet engine hum adding to the suspense. Suddenly, a chilling recognition gripped Alfie— the building James had entered loomed before him. Paralyzed for a fleeting moment, Alfie was haunted by an unwelcome flashback. **His mind thrust him back into the past, where the sensation of a knife in his hand, tearing into flesh, clawed at his consciousness.**

The revelation struck him with an unsettling intensity —what were the chances that James was now inhabiting his childhood home? A whirlwind of intense memories surged forth, assaulting Alfie's mind at the mere sight of the familiar structure. Overwhelmed by the gravity of the situation, he abruptly shifted gears, tearing away from the haunting spectre of his past, leaving the building and its memories behind in the rearview mirror.

Speeding down the unfamiliar roads, Alfie's mind raced in turmoil, leading him in the opposite direction of his familiar abode. Suddenly, the flashing lights of a police car appeared behind him, compelling Alfie to pull over. A knot tightened in his stomach, the imminent threat of a panic attack hanging over him like a storm cloud. The police officer approached, rapping on Alfie's window. Maintaining a facade of calmness, Alfie lowered his window.

"Sir, is there a reason you were speeding?" the police officer inquired sternly, eyeing Alfie with suspicion. As recognition dawned on the officer's face, Alfie could sense the pressure building inside him. The officer's tone softened, "Alfie... Alfie Sayers?" A false smile graced Alfie's lips as he confirmed his identity.

"I apologize for speeding; I had someone tailing me... It's been quite chaotic these past few weeks!" Alfie swiftly fabricated, seizing the advantage of his public figure status. The officer, seemingly sympathetic, offered assistance, "I can imagine life changes once you become are in the public eye... Would you like me to escort you home?" Gesturing with a helpful manner, the officer extended the offer.

Politely declining, Alfie insisted he believed he had evaded his false pursuer. The officer persisted, attempting to convince Alfie otherwise. Finally accepting Alfie's tale, the officer asked for an autograph before letting Alfie go. With a practiced smile, Alfie signed a piece of paper, and the officer gave thanks before driving off.

As the patrol car disappeared into the distance, Alfie succumbed to the impending panic attack. Trembling hands grappled with the steering wheel as a burning sensation surged through his body. Desperate for control, he unbuttoned the top two buttons of his shirt, struggling to regulate his breathing. Numbness spread from his hands to his arms, amplifying the sense of losing control. Palpitations in his chest intensified, leaving him immobilized. Leaning his head on the steering wheel, Alfie focused on deep, slow breaths, closing his eyes to empty his mind and ease himself out of the overwhelming overload of past reflections.

Taking his time, Alfie laboured to calm the storm raging within him. It had been ages since he grappled with such frequent intense suffering. The relentless pursuit and the unknown assailant had rekindled dormant anxieties, leaving him feeling defenceless against unknown threats. As a semblance of calm settled over him, he took a moment to regain his senses before steering his car homeward.

With deliberate ease, Alfie navigated through his street, each inch of the familiar surroundings scrutinized as if seeking hidden truths. The emptiness of the streets mirrored the void within him, and he parked in his customary spot, eyes fixed on the entrance to his home. A wariness settled upon him, knowing that once inside, he would face an onslaught of inquiries from Charley, Teddy, and his mother regarding Ronnie's tragic demise.

The news of Ronnie's connection to him had become a blazing headline, intensified by Alfie's own public proclamations of their shared workplace. The media buzzed with sensationalism, encapsulating his life in the spotlight. Double-checking that the car doors were securely locked, Alfie's gaze involuntarily gravitated to the spot where the shadowy figure had lurked.

His mind conjured images of James, attempting to overlay them onto the memory of the unknown presence. However, the mental puzzle defied resolution, impairing Alfie's unease. With a thoughtful pause, he leaned towards the passenger seat, retrieving his bag from the footwell. The worn leather under his touch held a sense of familiarity, a connection to tangible reality amidst the spiralling uncertainty. The weight of the bag, laden with notes and photos, became both a burden and a lifeline, grounding him in the midst of escalating paranoia.

Carefully extracting the envelopes from his bag, Alfie spilled the contents onto his lap, revealing a collection of notes and photos. His fingers flicked through the assortment, searching for a specific image. Finally, he pulled out a photograph featuring Thomas, Stewart, and their companions - Alex, Ben, Jack, and Lucy. Intriguingly, he flipped the photo over, repeating the cryptic question that secluded him: **"Can you really trust your friends?"**

Alfie scrutinized the photo, turning it back and forth as if trying to unlock its hidden secrets. The faces of his friends stared back at him, but a nagging sense of loyalty disrupted his suspicions. Despite his estimation, none of them seemed to align with the elusive figure haunting his recent encounters. A rigid line of thought took hold as he mentally listed individuals, delving into the realm of competitors and estranged acquaintances.

Swiftly dismissing competitors from suspicion, Alfie acknowledged the complexity of his past, shielded by a well-concealed secret. Only he, his mother and Teddy's now-deceased mother shared knowledge of this clandestine truth, bound by the burden to protect Teddy. No one could have any knowledge, and the tormentor's elusive taunting heightened Alfie's concern, especially since he couldn't identify anyone as the potential perpetrator.

Placing the photo on the passenger seat, Alfie delved into his past, determined to identify potential tormentors. He realized he needed to set aside the fear of his stalkers' knowledge and focus on uncovering who might have a motive for tormenting him. Remaining motionless, he stared out of the car window, mentally sifting through a list of names, recalling past conflicts.

First on the list was John Uptears, a friend from secondary school until the end of college. Their falling out occurred over Charley, whose popularity in college triggered Alfie's protective nature. One night at a house party Alfie witnessed John slip a Rohypnol into her drink, leading to a furious altercation, resulting in John never being seen again.

Next was Harry Plant, a university friend with whom Alfie had initially bonded over shared interests. During a student night out, Harry's disdain for Teddy, Alfie's close friend, escalated into insults and mockery. Alfie intervened, leading to a heated argument culminating in Alfie breaking Harry's jaw after a glass was thrown.

Hannah Dewsbury, a girl infatuated with Alfie, became fixated on breaking up his relationship with Charley. Despite her efforts, Hannah's actions led to isolation and hospitalization for mental health problems.

Searching for these old friends on social media, Alfie ruled out John and Harry. The absence of Hannah on social media raised suspicions that she might still be hospitalized. Two more names crossed Alfie's mind—Richard Gein and Ian Chapman, it was implausible for them to seek revenge on Alfie, which left Alfie speculating who would know to his involvement with them. Alfie concluded that the tormentor had to be someone unfamiliar to him.

Struggling to comprehend the absence of those no longer in his life, Alfie bent over to the passenger seat once again, retrieving the photo of his friends. Taking a deep breath, he gazed into the photo, desperately hoping that this was all a mind game, although if so, it had worked. Alfie scrutinized each friend individually, attempting to guess the motive that could drive them to attack him.

Thomas, his school mate since they were twelve, couldn't be the culprit. Known for his loyalty and trustworthiness, Thomas, like Teddy and Lucy, formed a rock-solid quartet. While Thomas had encouraged Alfie to pursue fame, there was no plausible motive. Even if he desired the company's profits, Alfie had always ensured equal payments, and both had achieved millionaire status.

Lucy, a friend since nursery and a member of the quartet with Teddy and Thomas, was like family to Alfie; he was closest to her of the other two. It seemed implausible that she would betray him, given their strong friendship. Besides, her love for Oscar eliminated any motive to threaten Alfie's life.

Thomas, Lucy, and Teddy were instantly ruled out of Alfie's mind which left the others.

Stewart, a recent addition to Say Advertising, had seamlessly integrated into Alfie's friend group effortlessly. A loner before joining, Stewart was a hard worker, but the only conceivable motive would be related to the business. However, he'd have to eliminate multiple individuals, including Alfie, Charley, Oscar, his mother, and Thomas, to gain ownership of Say Advertising.

Alex, a good friend with a penchant for asserting dominance and saving his own back, harboured a subtle rivalry with Alfie. Working in investments, Alex had initially discouraged Alfie from starting his own company, possibly sparking resentment at Alfie's unexpected success.

Ben, the quiet one in the group, easily led by Alex, seemed harmless at first glance. However, Alfie questioned whether there might be more beneath the surface, pressuring himself to find a plausible motive.

Finally, Jack, the unreliable member of the group, exhibited an elusive nature and kept his thoughts to himself. Alfie considered whether Jack's seemingly timid demeanour might be an act or if there was more to his character than met the eye.

Putting everything back into his bag, Alfie, frustrated with the unknown, felt his head pulsating with stress. He just wanted to know who was behind the killings and threats so he could end it all. His paranoia was growing. Knowing that he would be moving home earlier, he felt some relief that at least this new house would be better protected, and he could keep his loved ones safe. Getting out of the car and grabbing his bag, he took a slow walk to his front door, easing his mind from the disturbia. Opening the door, his hallway was stacked with cardboard boxes. Oscar ran over, jumping up at him.

"We finished packing, Daddy," he said with his childlike innocence, Bulldozer following behind him.

"I can see that," Alfie replied, picking Oscar up and closing the front door. Carrying Oscar into the living room, Charley, his mother, and Teddy sat in the living room eating a takeaway pizza. He held Oscar to his side, knowing none of them were going to talk about Ronnie while Oscar was in earshot.

"Looks like you were all busy today," he said playfully.

"Come and eat while it's still hot," replied his mother, getting up from her chair. Gesturing for her to remain seated, he dropped his bag by the corner of the door. Sitting on the floor, he set Oscar on his lap, and Bulldozer lay on the floor next to them both. Alfie took a slice of pizza, carefully eating it.

"Are you okay?" Charley asked, insinuating the murder of Ronnie. Alfie nodded, reassuring her that he was fine. He knew that she would have been worrying all day. Finishing his slice of pizza, he reached into his pocket, careful not to knock Oscar off his lap. He pulled the white envelope out of his pocket.

"Can you guess what's in here?" he whispered in Oscar's ear. Taking the envelope from his father's hand, Oscar shook the paper. Unfolding it, he took the keys out.

"Keys," Oscar said, showing his mother, grandmother, and Teddy.

"We move into the new house tomorrow!" Alfie declared.

"Can we get another dog when we are in the new house? Bulldozer needs another doggy friend," Oscar said, stroking Bulldozer's head.

"Oh, I think Bulldozer will need a little friend in this new house while you're at school, so definitely, and you can pick and name him or her," Alfie replied. Relaxing for the night, they all watched a film. Alfie seemly chilled but his brain kept repeating the events that had occurred within the last twenty-four hours. He fidgeted whenever snippets would pop inside of his head, glancing looks at his mother who knew the tension he was fighting. Oscar fell asleep on

Alfie's lap, carefully moving he stood up holding him.

"I'm gonna take him to bed and hit the sack myself, I'm shattered," whispered Alfie to not wake Oscar, picking him up carefully.

"I'm going to go to bed too," whispered his mother. Bulldozer stood up, following as Alfie carried Oscar to his bedroom. His mother grabbed his work bag by the door. Following behind Alfie up the stairs they both walked in silence. In Oscar's bedroom, Alfie put him to bed, tucking him in cosily inside the duvet. Bulldozer waited for Alfie to make Oscar snug before jumping on the end of the bed. His mother handed him his bag.

"What happened after I got off the phone to you?" she asked in a whisper. Briefly telling her what had happened with the masked man, she was stumped, also trying to work out who it was. Kissing his mother goodnight, Alfie left her to go into his room. Falling on the bed, Alfie immediately fell asleep, exhausted from the lack of sleep, overloaded with terror.

Dream/Flashback:

Thunderous, loud screams pierced through the house. Blood-soaked carpets absorbed the horror. The handle of the knife, wet with sweat from the intense grip, holding it tightly.

Blood dripped off the blade splattering to the floor. Heavy breathing echoed, the perpetrator gazing at the lifeless body sprawled on the floor. Unable to tear his eyes away from the damage he had inflicted, he didn't feel good, but a perverse sense of freedom consumed him.

Out of nowhere, a man materialized, forcefully pushing him. In a blank stare, his eyes focused on the thunderous scream emanating from the corner of the room. The woman turned her head, meeting his eyes... Charley was screaming, cradling a lifeless Oscar. The scene unfolded in a twisted dance of horror and despair.

Awakening in the early hours of the morning, Alfie grappled with the remnants of a haunting nightmare. As he reached for his phone, the dim glow revealed the cruel reality of having only slept a few hours. The room lingered in the stillness of predawn, a quiet canvas for his restless thoughts. Gazing at Charley, peacefully enveloped in sleep, he couldn't help but envy her undisturbed slumber.

A haunting image flickered in his mind's eye, replaying scenes from the unsettling dream. Charley's screams resonated, and the memory clung to him like a persistent shadow. Closing his eyes, he pressed his palm against his forehead, attempting to erase the vivid images. With a heavy sigh, he decided to rise, taking slow, deliberate steps toward the window.

Lifting a slit of the blind, Alfie directed his gaze to the emerging dawn sky. The approaching light mirrored the dawn of change, signalling the end of an era in a home filled with memories. Seizing the solitude of the early morning, Alfie walked into the passage, his steps echoing the quiet nostalgia of the past.

As he stood by Oscar's room, memories flooded in—a once-office transformed into a nursery, the joyous anticipation of impending parenthood, the playful moments that strengthened their bond. Yet, darker memories crept in, overshadowing the initial joy. Alfie recalled the sleepless nights, the weight of postnatal depression silently shouldered by Charley. The room, once a haven of happiness, now harboured bittersweet recollections.

A sudden scratching at Oscar's door diverted his thoughts. Opening it carefully, Bulldozer emerged, a comforting presence in Alfie's reflections. Fondly gazing at the walls that bore witness to his journey, Alfie found solace in the happy memories that this home had held.

Moving away from Oscar's room, he descended the stairs, memories of another tumultuous event resurfacing. The echo of Charley's fall down the stairs haunted his thoughts, a stark reminder of past struggles and unspoken pain. Alfie couldn't shake the guilt of his ignorance, unaware of the battles Charley fought silently.

Descending the stairs, Alfie cast a glance into the living room where Teddy lay peacefully asleep on the sofa. Taking deliberate steps, he reminisced about the past, recalling the initial days when he and Charley had moved in together. A flood of memories surfaced, the nostalgia of sleeping on a mattress on the living room floor, revelling in the freedom of their own space.

In the quiet of the night, Alfie couldn't help but recall the hardships he and Charley had faced, working tirelessly to build a life in this home. The echoes of the past resonated, reminding him of the time when Charley supported him in launching his own company. He reflected on the period when he leaned on her, acknowledging the strain it placed on her shoulders. The weight of responsibility weighed heavily on him, especially during the postnatal depression, an ordeal he felt responsible for.

Cautious not to disturb the sleeping Teddy, Alfie tiptoed into the kitchen. As he stood in the familiar space, a mix of emotions swept over him. The kitchen, witness to both joyous and challenging moments, held a pivotal memory. It was here that he had first discovered Charley's depression. Returning home from work when Oscar was merely two months old, Alfie found Charley on the kitchen floor, overwhelmed, tears streaming down her face, unable to cope with the solitude of caring for their child.

The memory struck a chord, and Alfie felt a pang of guilt for the burden he had placed on Charley during that challenging time. He silently acknowledged his own shortcomings. The kitchen had been the stage for the revelation of Charley's struggles, prompting Alfie to call for help. His mother rushed to their aid, recognizing Charley's distress and taking immediate action.

Charley was eventually taken away by doctors for a six-week recovery, a period that felt like an eternity for Alfie. When she returned, the bond between them had deepened, and her mental strength had flourished. Their relationship emerged stronger than ever, unbreakable in the face of adversity. The kitchen, once a witness to tears and screams, now stood as a testament to resilience and love.

Leaning against the cold kitchen sink, Alfie stole a cautious glimpse out of the window. A sudden shudder raced down his spine, his eyes locking onto a mysterious figure standing just outside his home. Clad in black and wearing the same balaclava as the man from his office, Alfie couldn't shake the ominous feeling that this might be the elusive figure from the shadows, patiently waiting for the perfect moment to strike.

With a sense of urgency, he reached to the side and yanked open a kitchen drawer. Keeping his eyes locked on the masked man, he fumbled through the drawer in search of a knife. To his dismay, the drawer was empty, holding only a couple of things left unpacked for the five occupants in the house. Hesitating to divert his gaze from the masked man, Alfie prayed this wasn't another trick his mind was playing on him.

Realizing that the man hadn't moved, he reluctantly broke their stare, leaving the kitchen as quietly as he could. Slowly, he opened the front door, Bulldozer following by his side. The protective Doberman growled at the masqueraded man standing still. Alfie made a shushing noise to prevent Bulldozer from disturbing the other sleeping houses. Both approached the motionless figure. Moving close enough, a wrath burned in Alfie as he swung a speedy punch; Bulldozer lunged at the masked masquerade latching onto their leg. The figure fell to the floor.

Bending down, Alfie pulled the balaclava off the man's face. "What the hell!" Alfie muttered to himself as he surveyed a mannequin lying on the floor. Bulldozer retreated from the dummy, standing guard by Alfie's side. Alfie checked the entire street, looking around to see if anyone was nearby. No one in sight; all he could hear was the passing night wind. He wondered who could have had time to place the mannequin there without being heard or seen.

Realizing that whoever was behind this was playing mind games with him, Alfie became more paranoid by the minute. "Everything okay?" asked Teddy. Turning abruptly, Alfie was startled by Teddy's voice. He looked at him suspiciously. Unresponsive, Alfie walked back into the house with Bulldozer, his mind racing with the unsettling reality that someone was orchestrating a sinister game with him at the centre.

Alfie walked back into the house with Bulldozer.

"What are you doing up?" asked Alfie, his tone caring but his mind suspecting.

"Been on and off asleep all night, keep seeing my mum and Eva's face." Alfie suddenly felt awful for his suspicion, especially after what had happened the previous night.

Back in the living room, Bulldozer curled up on the armchair. Alfie and Teddy sat down next to one another.

"Everything okay?" Teddy asked through a dubious yawn. Reassuring, Alfie nodded as he diverted the conversation back to Teddy.

"How are you feeling?" Alfie asked, empathetically, putting his attention of Teddy's wellbeing. An awkward quietness settled in as Teddy twiddled his fingers. He wasn't sure what to say to Alfie.

"I don't know… It's like an empty void in my gut… I just want them to catch whoever killed them… but… then… I want to make whoever is responsible suffer myself," Teddy gradually replied. Alfie felt responsible; would Teddy want to kill him if he knew that Alfie was being blamed as the reason they were killed? Sniffling, Teddy swallowed his emotions.

"I'm starting to think I'm cursed. Everyone around me has been murdered…. It's like someone's out to get me," Teddy confessed, holding back his pain with his head down, avoiding eye contact with Alfie. An urge to tell Teddy the truth paused him as he took in Teddy's defeat.

"I don't think so, Ted. If someone was out to get you, they'd have let you know…I'm sure," Alfie reassured, though knowing that he was being targeted.

Chapter 5

Early in the morning, Oscar jumped onto the sofa, abruptly waking Alfie and Teddy, who had fallen asleep there. Following closely, Charley and Alfie's mother descended the stairs.

"Moving day!" Charley enthusiastically announced, oblivious to the fact that Oscar had roused the two friends from their slumber.

"Yeah, moving day," yawned Alfie. Moving away from the sofa, he headed upstairs for a quick shower. As the warm water splashed over his skin, he closed his eyes as flashes of the death, threats and suspicion replayed in his mind. The only solace in his thoughts was the safety of Charley, Oscar, and his mother in the new home. Hastily donning a shorts and a t-shirt, Alfie descended the stairs again.

"Where's Teddy and Oscar?" he asked, a hint of panic in his voice. He didn't want anyone out of his sight.

"They've taken Bulldozer out for a walk," his mother replied, calming his nerves knowing Bulldozer would protect Oscar no matter what. In the living room, Charley sat, the news playing on the TV. Alfie and his mother stood behind the sofa, watching.

"We can now reveal that the suspected suicide of Ronnie Clay was, in fact, a murder. His body was discovered as he smashed into the top floor of this building, which is none other than Say Advertising. Police have assured us that Alfie Sayers, owner of Say Advertising, was not involved and has given a statement to help with the enquiry. Alfie, who has been seen a lot in the public eye, has yet to give anyone any public statement regarding his relationship with the victim, but..." Alfie cut off the news reporter switching off the TV.

"We haven't got time to watch this shit," he gritted, angered. Exiting the living room, he entered the kitchen to make a coffee, his gaze fixed on the window as he awaited Teddy and Oscar's return.

"Do you want to talk about what happened?" Charley asked sympathetically, standing in the doorway of the kitchen. Alfie shook his head, offering no verbal reply. Clenching his hand into a fist, he felt himself losing control, a simmering rage burning within him. Accustomed to dealing with issues head-on, the mounting anticipation was pushing him backwards. He refused to succumb to fear or the prospect of losing his loved ones.

Having already made him a coffee, his mother disturbed him, breaking the spiral of his distracted mind as he stared out the window. He turned to her, rolling his eyes, and shaking his head. She knew exactly what he was saying.

"You know she just cares and loves you so much. She just hasn't seen you at your very worst, and while you're trying to protect everyone and make out that you're fine, you're not... you're pushing her away. I've seen many stages of this with you... So, until we nail the bastard or bastards, you will be deteriorating into your anxiety, don't let them make you spiral... fight it;" whispered his mother instructing, concerned but stern. She touched his arm. "You need to keep level-headed as much as possible, which will feel impossible, but I know you can do it. Remember the tricks your therapist taught you all those years ago," she finished, pulling him in for a hug.

Charley had began moving boxes outside, feeling guilty Alfie took the box out of her hands, with an apology he gave her a kiss. Taking the box outside the front of the house. Just as Oscar and Teddy returned from their walk with Bulldozer, two journalists stopped Alfie as he placed another box on the floor. Knowing their reason for being at his house, Alfie turned his back, going back into his home. Camera clicks and some flashes repeated.

Picking up another box and placing it outside more photos taken.

"Excuse me, Mr. Sayers, can you answer a few questions?" asked the news reporter, pushing a voice recorder in his face. Alfie didn't answer and continued taking the boxes out of his house.

"Have you nothing better to do with your time?" enraged Charley, seeing the annoyance on Alfie's face. The journalist ignored her as he probed Alfie with more questions, which he ignored. At that moment, a large removal van pulled up outside Alfie's home. A tall man got out of the van, greeting Alfie and Teddy, a friend of his. The removal man began taking the boxes stacked outside and loaded the back of the van.

"Mr. Sayers, what would you like to say to Ronnie Clay's parents? Imagine if you had just lost your child," the reporter, desperate for a reaction, goaded. Alfie stopped dead in his tracks. Before he could react, his mother came charging toward the reporter, slapping him in the face.

"Do yourself a favour and get away from here; he isn't saying anything because there is nothing to tell, you cretin," an agitated, protective, motherly response, her hand raised and ready to slap the man again. Alfie calmed himself, knowing he couldn't react as his mother beat him to the slap and instructed the man to leave firmly. Infuriated that he hadn't successfully obtained any information from Alfie, the journalist stamped his feet as he and his colleague left the premises.

Alfie, Charley, and Teddy helped the man load the heavy boxes into the back of the van. His mother and Oscar put lighter and more delicate boxes into the back of Alfie's car. After placing the final box in the back of the van and giving the removal man the new address, Teddy jumped in the van with his friend, and they began to drive to the new house.

Alfie stared at the outside of his soon-to-be old home from across the road. He flashed back to the day he and Charley moved into the house, the excitement they both felt. He was devastated that he was leaving the house with fear rather than excitement. He walked across the road.

"We need a final photo of us all!" declared Charley, pulling out her phone as she instructed the four of them to squeeze into the frame for a selfie. Alfie's mother took the phone from Charley's hand, instructing them to stand outside the premises as she took a photo. Alfie walked to the front door, closing it for a final time. Alfie stuck the keys in his pocket. The house hadn't been sold just yet so was still Alfie's.

Going toward his car, Charley and his mother got into the back seats, as Alfie helped Oscar put his seatbelt on in the passenger seat. Bulldozer curled in the footwell beneath him. Alfie took another look at the house just before getting into the driver's seat.

"Are we ready?" Alfie asked his passengers, sounding more enthusiastic than he had since the devastating news.

"Yessss!" shouted Oscar gleefully as Alfie began to drive toward their new home. Driving along the road Alfie passed the van with his belongings wanting to get to his new home first. The drive was long, so to entertain they played car games to keep him entertained. Arriving on the street where his new home stood, Charley and his mothers mouths dropped as they looked at the houses they had passed.

Driving past thick brick walls at least fifteen feet high, Alfie stopped the car outside a thick metal gate. The cool summer breeze greeted him as he stepped out of the car, and walked over to a small box affixed to the brick pillar on the left side of the gate. Opening it, Alfie tapped a number sequence onto the keypad. Returning to the car, he pointed to the front gate, signalling to Oscar as the gates smoothly opened. Driving through, Alfie guided the car along the pathway, with Charley, Oscar, and his mother marvelling at the beautiful greenery on either side. Pulling up to the house, he parked at the side garage. Oscar was the first to burst out of the car, followed by Bulldozer, both running down the smooth grass at the front of the house.

"Stay on the grass and away from the big gates," Alfie shouted to Oscar, ensuring he remained in the safe zone while the removal man drove up the pathway. The gates automatically began to close. Charley and his mother exited the car, both speechless at the expansive exterior and the grandeur of the house. Alfie, having kept them all in the dark of the new home to surprise them. Teddy got out of the van.

"Now this is what I call home," he bedazzled, more upbeat than he had been since his loss. The removal man commenced unloading the boxes from the van.

"You ready to see this place inside?" Alfie said with excitement, feeling his tension ease with the safety of his new home. Unlocking the front door, Charley, his mother, and Teddy stood with their mouths wide open. Stepping inside, they found themselves in a spacious hallway, behind the front door, an entrance with a wooden door. Alfie's mother opened the door.

"It's a coat room," Alfie explained as she looked inside. She turned to look at him in disbelief, realizing it was spacious enough for more than just coats. Eager to explore the house, Charley brushed her hand on the soft wall as she walked through the open hole on the left, discovering a large dining room with a table centred in the middle. Cabinets were lined against the wall and the centre wall that looked onto the front of the house. Alfie led his mother and Oscar into the other side of the hallway, revealing a large living room. The room boasted a big core window with a beautiful view of the entrance of the home. It was massive, with sofas in the middle, fixed around a long glass table. A TV was mounted on the wall above an old-fashioned white mantel.

"I was thinking of moving the TV and sofas further up this room, rather than having them crowed together in the centre, I won't change it till after the weekend though," suggested Alfie as Charley finally entered the living room. "If we walk up to the end of the room, there's a second entrance to the kitchen," Alfie continued, pointing down the room.

They walked back into the hallway, standing opposite the staircase at the centre of the hallway that curved along the wall of the long hall, creating a smaller walkway toward the kitchen. A door blended into the wall on the right, next to the kitchen entrance, leading to the basement. Leading them to the kitchen, a wide island was in the middle of the room, surrounded by cabinets along the walls, with black tiling along the walls and white tiles on the floor. The sink stood opposite the garden window. On the other side of the kitchen was another door that Alfie opened, revealing a storage room already stocked with groceries and alcohol.

"Now, are you guys ready to see the garden?" Alfie gleefully teased as he led them through the glass door in the middle of the kitchen, taking them into the park-like garden. They walked along the perfectly cut grass, and further back, there was a large apple tree that provided shade during the summer's heat. They continued until they reached a fenced-off section, with marble flooring. In the middle, there was a blue swimming pool covered up to prevent leaves and bugs from overtaking. A bit beyond the pool, the bricks enclosing the house and its grounds featured a small arch intricately carved with an electronic door entrance. This led to a walkway adorned with a small brick wall, easy to jump over for access to a large open green field.

They ventured back into the house, eager to explore further. Ascending the staircase, they reached the first floor, where a short, straight banister lined the edge, ensuring safety and preventing anyone from accidentally falling below. Alfie's mother glanced over the banister's end, revealing another set of stairs leading upward. Along the hallway, they encountered five closed doors. Opening the first door revealed a room with a desk situated in the middle, prompting Alfie to designate it as his work-from-home office. The subsequent door they opened exposed a luxurious bathroom, complete with a glass shower and an oval bathtub that rivalled a jacuzzi. The next three rooms, already furnished with beds, awaited their discovery.

Ascending the next flight of stairs, they encountered a layout similar to the one below, featuring four additional rooms. The first room they entered was designated as Charley and Alfie's bedroom, complete with a spacious walk-in closet. Alfie guided them into the walk-in closet, neatly pulling a concealed shelving unit forward to reveal a hidden panic room. This particular feature held a special place in Alfie's heart, serving as his favourite aspect of the house due to its assurance of his family's safety. The hidden room was expansive, featuring a single bed nestled in the corner, a small sofa, CCTV with a medium-sized screen, and a couple of cupboards beneath the TV.

"Once locked from the inside, no one can open this from the outside," Alfie explained proudly, finding comfort in the fact that the panic room provided a secure haven.

They explored the other three rooms, each adorned with beds, temporarily leaving them as bedrooms. Oscar's room, situated opposite Alfie's and Charley's of course, was spacious and currently housed two single beds. Between the two rooms stood another staircase leading up to the attic. Although the attic's light wasn't functional at the moment, the daylight streaming through provided illumination. Alfie hesitated to let Oscar go up there, fearing for his safety.

After the comprehensive house tour, they descended the stairs and commenced moving boxes. Alfie carried a couple of boxes into the attic. While stacking them, he noticed a thick, solid wood baseball bat lying on the floor. After a quick swing, he placed the bat in a corner near the entrance. Returning downstairs, he grabbed another box and took it into his room. Upon opening it, Alfie extracted a tactical hunting bowie knife, a gift from his grandad for his 18th birthday. He tucked it between the bedframe and the mattress. Another find was a black slotted butterfly knife he had taken after his grandfather's death, which he placed in his back pocket. Engaging in the unpacking process, Alfie immersed himself in his belongings.

A sudden ringing noise reverberated through the house; this was the first time Alfie had heard his doorbell. Hesitant and pacing toward the intercom, he wondered who would be knocking on his door.

"Hello," he spoke politely, concealing his defensiveness. Two voices introduced themselves. Alfie wanted to see their faces before he let them enter. Fiddling with the intercom, Alfie tried to turn the camera on to see who they were, letting them inside by accident. Pressing his fingers against the knife in his pocket, he opened the front door, watching the unexpected guests walk up the pathway. Walking out of his house Alfie met them halfway between the house and the front gate.

"Welcome to the neighbourhood," a joyful woman greeted, offering a handshake. Alfie and Charley reciprocated the handshake. "I'm Alice, and this is Emerson," the woman introduced, still very cheery. Alice, with her curly brunette hair and plump face, exuded excitement in meeting her new neighbour. Emerson, her husband, a round-faced man with a thick short beard and shaved head, handed Alfie a familiar envelope like the white one from the estate agents.

"This was on the floor, just under your gate," Emerson explained. Alfie took it, thanking him, predicting its contents but refraining from opening it in the present company. Engaging in small talk, the four of them got to know each other.

"Tomorrow we're having a little get-together with some friends. If you two would like to join, it'll be dinner, some drinks, and maybe play some games or something, but plenty of alcohol for sure," invited Charley. As Alice and Emerson accepted the invitation, Alfie excused himself to find his mother.

Rushing back into the house, Alfie saw Teddy organizing items from the boxes in the living room. He ran upstairs, searching each room until he found his mother in Oscar's room, setting up his new bedroom. Realizing he hadn't seen Oscar in any of the rooms he checked, he asked in a panic, "Where's Oscar?"

"Wasn't he playing in the garden with Bulldozer?" she replied, jumping up to look out of Oscar's bedroom window. "Yes, he's outside… what's wrong with you… don't scare me like that," Alfie's mother said, infuriated as she turned from the window looking at Alfie. Alfie sighed as he closed the bedroom door, showing his mother the envelope. They both sat down on the bed.

Carefully opening the top, he placed his two fingers inside to pull out its contents. Unable to feel any notes or photos, he tipped it upside down. Nothing.

"That might not even be for you… It's empty," reassured his mother, putting her hand on his back. He was convinced it was a message, though unsure of its meaning.

"How would they send you another threat; they don't know where you have moved to?" she reassured Alfie, who seemed confused. "Maybe someone just dropped it as they went past, or the wind blew it out of someone's house; there's loads of reasons an empty envelope could be at your house." taking the envelope from his hand, his mother scrunched it up and placed it in her pocket.

Silent, Alfie knew his anxious mind was getting the better of him. "Yeah, you're right, Mum," he replied, not letting her in on his suspicions. He kissed her on the top of the head, thanking her for being there for him and helping him to stay grounded. He left Oscar's room, rushing back downstairs, he went outside to his car, and grabbed his work bag. Returning inside, he rushed to the first floor, opening the door to his office. Teddy had already placed boxes at the front of the desk. Closing the door, Alfie locked it. Sitting at the desk, he analysed each note and photo again. The photo of Eva startled him as he concentrated on the photo, taking notice of the knife impaled inside her, Alfie realised it was the same knife he'd just placed in-between his mattress and bedframe. A knock on the door Charley called his name. Startled he carefully placed the photos into a drawer on his new desk locking it.

Chapter 6

"I know what you did!" roared a voice, shattering the eerie silence. Alfie turned, his heart racing, and saw the man in the black balaclava, cruelly clutching Oscar by the scruff of his neck. Oscar pleaded, desperately trying to wriggle free. Alfie sprinted towards them, desperation propelling him to save his son. However, every stride he took, they effortlessly moved further away, tormenting Alfie with the haunting cries of his son.

Unexpectedly like magic, Charley materialized, an enigmatic figure standing defiantly in his path. He shouted at her, urgently pleading for her to move, pointing desperately to show that Oscar was being pulled away. Yet, she blankly glared at him, an unsettling indifference etched across her face. Suddenly, Oscar and the man vanished, evaporating into the darkness.

"You can't save him!" Charley's voice echoed; her stance eerily still. Alfie, frantically searching for Oscar, could no longer spot him in his field of vision. Panicking, he turned back to Charley, his voice trembling as he implored her to help him rescue their son. She remained unresponsive. Desperation consumed him, and he reached out, placing his hands on her shoulders, begging for assistance.

In a horrifying turn of events, Charley coldly stabbed him in the heart. "Do you remember how it feels to kill?" she said, her voice husky and deep, mirroring the haunting tone of the mysterious caller from the phone call in his office. Collapsing to the floor, Alfie lay clutching his chest, jolting with each heartbeat as he felt himself slowly fading into oblivion.

The scene shifted abruptly; now, he found himself in his grandad's house. A knife lodged in his heart; Alfie watched in agony as two menacing figures tortured a man before him. He pleaded for them to stop, and, for a moment, they paused. One of them marched over, delivering a brutal kick to Alfie's face. His life drained away, a desperate cry for help escaping into the void...

Awakening with a dull ache in his heart, Alfie clenched his chest, still feeling the throb from the haunting dream. Turning to the bedside table, he reached for a glass of water. As he drank, the lingering phantom pain gradually dissipated. Placing the glass back on the table, he rubbed his face, then cast a glance at Charley, who remained in peaceful slumber. Slipping out of bed, he paced to the bedroom window, drawn to the tranquil night beyond.

Peering outside, Alfie's gaze fixated on the stars that adorned the night sky. Their brilliance offered a stark contrast to the disquiet that seemed to persist in his life. The routine of waking up in the middle of the night, haunted by nightmares or memories of the past, had become a familiar pattern for years. Each time, he sought solace by gazing out of the window until his anxious mind calmed, only to return to bed for a restless sleep until morning.

In his quest for tranquillity, Alfie had hoped that a new, better-protected home would free him from the burdens that plagued his mind. Longing to forget the past and desiring a fresh start, he decided to try the solution he had constantly avoided as he got out of bed.

Stepping into the ensuite, Alfie opened the mirrored cabinet, rummaging through toiletries until he found an old bottle of prescribed medication – sleeping tablets. He felt secure in the knowledge that his new home was impenetrable, a fortress where his family could find safety. Determined to break free from the old cycle of nightmares and broken sleep, he swallowed a sleeping pill, washing it down with a sip of water from the tap.

Exiting the ensuite, Alfie returned to bed. As he lay down, he focused on clearing his mind, refusing to let his foreboding thoughts override the calming effects of the pill, as they often had in the past. Closing his eyes, he embraced the promise of a deeper and more restful night.

Opening his eyes, Alfie stretched out in his bed, glancing out of the bedroom window at the darkening sky. Realizing Charley wasn't beside him; he briefly panicked and grabbed his phone. Checking the time, he saw it was already past 5pm. The realization that he had slept extremely late propelled him out of bed. He hurriedly showered and dressed, crossing the hall into Oscar's room. The house felt so big; he couldn't hear anyone on the ground floor, a stark contrast to his old house where everyone was within earshot.

Taking a slow walk down the two flights of stairs, voices became audible as he neared the ground floor. Standing on the landing before the final three steps down, Alfie's heart skipped a beat as Lucy, with her angelic heart-shaped face and dark emerald, green eyes that sparkled with a mischievous glint, exuded a vibrant energy that captivated everyone around her. Descending the last three steps, Lucy ran into Alfie, her long dark brown hair cascaded down her shoulders, hitting Alfie in the face as they hugged each other.

"Haven't seen you for a couple of weeks, Alf. What's been going on?" she playfully teased, shoving him in the shoulder like an annoying sister. The warmth of her presence, combined with the lively charm reflected in her expressive gaze, made Lucy a captivating figure in any room.

"It's been a hectic couple of weeks!" Alfie replied with an awkward smile, rubbing his neck. Lucy knew Alfie well; he couldn't get a lie past her, making him eager to avoid conversations about recent events.

"Are you okay?" Lucy worried instantly, seeing his reaction. Alfie smiled and nodded. Lucy smiled back, playing along, but she knew something was up with him. "This house is absolutely beautiful," she continued, changing the subject not wanting to make him uncomfortable just yet. "So, when do I move in?" she joked, showing her playful sister side.

"Ha, well, there's room for you," Alfie said, still slightly awkward. Lucy was looking at him in that knowing way she always did when he wasn't telling her everything.

"Are you sure you're okay?" she asked with suspicion, placing her hand on his arm, reassuring him he could tell her.

"Yeah, it's because I've just woken up, I'm not fully with it yet," Alfie explained with an eye roll and a laugh. "And I'm a little all over the place from the events of the week and all the attention this week," Alfie's eyes darted to Teddy in the living room, insinuating the news of his mother. "Actually, I'm shocked you didn't come round mine after that," Alfie warily continued questioningly aware he'd brought up the subject he wanted to avoid.

"I did want to, but when I spoke to Charley, she told me to give him a few days, and then the stuff at your work happened. Thomas said you weren't your normal self before and after; you were distant," she was sympathetic in her explaining tone as she touched his arm, looking into his eyes. Instantly she put Alfie at ease, giving him inner guilt for questioning her. She drastically changed speaking sympathetically to caring and serious as she softly punched him in the shoulder, "you know me, and I know you, so stop being awkward… we'll get into all that next week, when it's just the two of us… this weekend we're having fun!... Which reminds me, you are very popular in my work, and some of the girls have asked me to either get a video message of you to them or to FaceTime them," Lucy spoke, pulling out her phone.

The doorbell rang as Alfie started making FaceTime calls to Lucy's co-workers. Charley waltzed through the hallway to the intercom, answering the door and letting the guests into the house. Lucy and Alfie moved into the dining room, sitting in the old-fashioned wooden chairs.

Thomas entered the house with his petite, black-haired, slim-framed, dark-eyed girlfriend. She looked tiny standing next to his tall height. Grace handed Charley a gift bag. Charley popped into the dining room, pointing to Thomas and Grace; they waved at Alfie as Thomas sniggered at the sound of Charley's co-workers fangirling over Alfie. After hanging up the call, Alfie said they'll continue later. Alfie walked out of the living room to give Thomas a brotherly hug. Charley took Grace into the kitchen to help her.

"Thanks for telling Lucy to leave me alone the other day… more or less," Alfie said, giving a grateful smile.

"I haven't spoken to Lucy this week, first time I've seen or spoke to her," denied Thomas as he looked at Lucy sitting in the dining room. Alfie went stiff with a shudder of coldness running through his body. He quickly brushed it off, changing the subject; there must have been a misunderstanding he thought.

"How are you coping after Ronnie?" Alfie asked, pacing his words as he didn't want to feel the guilt he had that day.

"I'm okay. Are you okay? You seemed like you went into shocked," replied Thomas. In that moment, Teddy came into the hallway, squeezing Thomas's shoulder. Thomas turned around as he began to focus on Teddy, Alfie walked into the living room, sitting on the sofa with his mother.

"Why didn't anyone wake me up?" Alfie asked his mother, just as Oscar came running into the living room with Bulldozer barking.

"You needed the sleep," his mother smiled. Oscar and Bulldozer dashed back out of the living room as Thomas, Teddy, and Lucy joined them. Small talk ensued until Thomas finally addressed the elephant in the room.

"So… there's been a lot happening this week… how is everyone feeling?" Thomas cautiously spoke, glancing at everyone. Alfie's mother checked on him, darting her eyes between her son and Thomas. The doorbell rang, cutting Teddy off as he was about to speak. Lucy volunteered to answer the door.

"To be honest, Tom, I'd rather not talk about it… it's all a rollercoaster… I just want to forget about the pain this weekend and focus on being with my friends," Teddy spoke, covering his face briefly before looking up at Thomas with a grateful smile. Alfie nodded, agreeing as he looked at Teddy, pursed lips biting the inside of his lip as he swallowed the burdens he carried.

"It's Alex, Ella, and Ivy," announced Lucy as she opened the front door, watching them walk toward the house. "Come on, you peasants, the rich and famous don't wait this long on people," Lucy taunted playfully. Walking back into the living room, Lucy pulled a face at Alfie. "I know Ella and Ivy are Charley's cousins, but they are so annoying… they're the definition of a basic bitch," she complained not discreetly.

"Be nice," Teddy warned mischievously. Lucy pulled a face at him. Alfie got up from the sofa, going into the hallway to welcome his new arrivals inside his home. Alex walked in, his rectangular head turning at every corner to catch the sizing. As he took in every detail, his expressive eyes met Alfie's, who was just slightly taller.

"Wow, this is huge," Alex said as he rubbed his brown stubbly beard, taking a second look around. Lucy came into the hallway, followed by Thomas and Teddy. She grabbed Alex by his prominent nose, shaking his head.

"Mouthy bollocks is lost for words; that makes a change," she mocked him as he pulled away from her grip. "Hello, girls," she turned to Ella and Ivy, who were twins with blonde, circle-faced features, slender frames, dark brown eyes, and little button noses. Alfie hugged them both and pointed them in the direction of the kitchen, where Charley and Grace were prepping food and having drinks.

"Where's Jennifer?" asked Teddy to Alex, looking through the still-open door.

"She had an emergency work thing going on this morning, so she's running late for everything today," Alex explained, making eye contact with everyone. "She's coming after with Ben," he finished. Oscar ran back through the house. Alfie quickly grabbed him, spiritedly lifting him in the air.

"Oi Oscar… you haven't said hello to Thomas and Alex," Alfie reminded him as he put him back on the ground. As Oscar started talking to his friends, Alfie's phone rang; it was Stewart. Answering the phone, he was met with silence. He listened intently as he repeated himself down the receiver. The call ended.

"Oh, before I forget, Jack isn't coming tonight… umm… he said he'll tell you all why when he gets here tomorrow," Alex explained to everyone. Alfie's suspicious mind instantly started accusing Jack as he was now going to be absent. His phone rang again.

"Oscar why don't you and Uncle Teddy show Aunt Lucy, Uncle Thomas, and Alex around the house," suggested Alfie sharply as he walked into the living room to answer the call.

"Stewart, where are you, mate?" Alfie answered normally, the familiar croaking noise that had been made when Ronnie was murdered made him fall silent. Placing a finger in his other ear, he listened intensely into the receiver – a wailing of pain and desperate pleas for help. He could hear Stewart begging for his life. Stunned, he slowly sat on the sofa stiffly next to his mother. Instantly she noticed dread on Alfie's face.

"Who is it?" she mouthed a look of defence and anger on her face. Alfie was non-responsive as his whole body began to stiffen and shake with worry. He began to tap his foot as he listened to get certainty of what he thought was happening. Tightly grabbing his knee, his mother tried to stop his agitated body from shaking. The call hung up; this time Alfie frozen in blame. Taking the phone from his hand, pulling it away from his ear, his mother looked at the number to see Alfie's home screen.

"Who was it?" she asked, trying to go to his call list, but blocked by the passcode. A vibration in her hand, a message appeared from Stewart. Concerned, she tried to open it, she tried putting in Oscar's birthday, but it didn't work. She then tried his, but that didn't work either. Impatiently she slapped Alfie, pulling him out of the iced condemning state.

"What is the passcode?" she asked, rushing him.

"It's your birthday," he replied. She was both flattered and surprised but quickly opened the message. A cold chill filled her head as she opened a photo, that disturbed her. She showed Alfie, who stiffened up again. Another ring on the doorbell sent Alfie's mother into a panicked frenzy. She attempted to awaken Alfie from the stiffened panic. The doorbell rang again.

"Can someone get that?" Charley shouted from the kitchen.

"I'll get it," she replied, dashing to the hallway where the intercom hung on the wall. With quick efficiency, she answered, allowing the guests entry. Swiftly, she returned to the living room and shook Alfie, still frozen in place. Frustrated mutters under her breath as she pleaded for his forgiveness. A second slap brought him back to reality, as she knelt eye level with him.

"You have a house full of guests, a son who'll be terrified if he sees you falling apart. Pull yourself together and stop acting awkward with people. Be the same Alfie they all know and love. Lucy is already onto you," she softly dictated, concerned for both Alfie and Oscar. She felt terrible for being harsh, but it was crucial that Oscar didn't witness Alfie in such a state.

"Okay," Alfie agreed, standing up and making his way to the hallway to open the front door. Jennifer and Ben had arrived, followed by Charley's brother Chris, whom Alfie never got along with. Jennifer possessed small but sharply defined features on her diamond-shaped face. Her flicky dark eyes and long, dark hair cascaded down her back, framing her face. Small, heart-shaped lips added a touch of elegance to her overall appearance.

Ben, on the other hand, was short and stocky, his square head accentuated by a bald crown. Greyish eyes peered out from beneath a prominent forehead, and a curved nose contributed to his distinctive facial structure.

Chris, of similar height to Alfie but with a slimmer build, had mousey-coloured hair complementing his big, sneaky dark brown eyes with a hint of red. His nose had a subtle kink. Alfie greeted him with a lukewarm welcome as he pointed him to Charley in the kitchen. Ben and Jennifer, like Alex, gazed around the house.

"This is bigger than the hotel I stayed in last week?" Ben said, impressed as he congratulated Alfie. Lucy, Teddy, Thomas, Alex, Oscar, and Bulldozer came down the stairs. Seeing his girlfriend, Alex rushed over to Jennifer, and they began a whispered conversation.

"Right, guys, Stewart isn't coming; he's sick," Alfie quickly lied, regretting it as he knew they would find out the truth soon. Following his mother's instruction to act normal, they engaged in conversation, and Alfie was doing well, especially as Lucy wasn't suspecting him when she looked at him.

"Seeing as everyone's here, can we eat now?" asked Lucy, looking at Alfie.

"Yeah, go in the kitchen, help yourself. I've just got to do something upstairs, and I'll be back down in a bit," Alfie told them, heading up the first three steps. Standing on the landing, he called his mother to come upstairs with him. They both went into his office, locking the door. Alfie pulled out his phone as they both inspected the photo that was sent to him – a slaughterhouse of blood and guts, worse than the photo he had of Teddy's mother and Eva.

127

"Look at Teddy's mother; does anything look familiar to you in this photo?" Alfie whispered, pointing at the gruesome scene. She looked at the photo intensely, taking a few minutes until it dawned on her. He then showed Eva and Stewart; she spotted it with Eva, not with Stewart until Alfie explained it to her, and finally, Ronnie.

"Who was killed the same way as Ronnie?" he asked her, it was a significant one he thought she'd see sooner.

"What the Fuck?... Alfie, I don't know who would know all this?" she confessed, a subtle worry in her voice.

"I don't know either, but I do know it's two people, one person couldn't," Alfie speculated, looking at her with increasing worry.

"Do you think it's someone downstairs?" she asked, looking back at the photos. Shrugging his shoulders, Alfie suspected but wasn't sure who it could be.

"If they are downstairs, the only thing certain is they will die as soon as they reveal themselves," Alfie spoke confidently, his tone edged with villainous resolve. "I need you to go to bed early; maybe when Oscar goes to sleep. If anything goes off, I need you to get inside that panic room. Before you argue, I know you will

128

keep Oscar safe, I know you'll keep Charley safe if I'm unable to. We both know in the moment I won't be overtaken by a panic attack, they come when the adrenaline goes. Friend or foe," Alfie meant every word as he smiled a reassuring smile at his mum, who was starting to show her own fears.

They descended back downstairs to mingle with the guests, including Emerson and Alice, their next-door neighbours who'd now arrived. Alfie observed every action and word spoken by his guests as they ate, played games, and even taught Oscar how to play poker, much to Charley's dismay. Oscar, drained from all the excitement, fell asleep on Alfie's lap just after 8 pm. As planned, Alfie's mother took Oscar upstairs with Bulldozer following. Alfie, after a brief moment in the kitchen, joined his mother in Oscar's room. Tucking Oscar in, he kissed the sleeping child on the head, expressing his love. Handing his mother, a knife from the kitchen, he kissed her on the cheek and reaffirmed his love.

"There's a huge chance we're both being stupid tonight, but just in case, you know what to do, right?" he handed his mother the code to the panic room. Leaving the room, he went back downstairs to everyone.

"Charley and Lucy suggested we should all get in the swimming pool," Thomas told Alfie as they all headed outside.

"Sounds like a plan," Alfie suspiciously watched everyone heading into the kitchen to go into the garden. Slowly, he paced behind, going to the pantry cupboard, where he pulled out an old bottle of whiskey. Pouring a quarter of a scotch glass, he shot the drink back. He'd only ever taken a shot of this whiskey once before.

"This one's for you," he said looking up at the ceiling before putting the bottle back. It would be his only drink of the evening; Alfie wasn't going to be caught off guard. Walking into the garden, he looked up to Oscar's bedroom, seeing his mother watching. He felt the cool night summer breeze hit him as he paced to everyone now in the pool. He watched them all fooling around and splashing water. Undressing down to his underwear, Alfie jumped into the water.

"Let's play chicken," suggested Lucy. Everyone cheered for the good suggestion, teaming up with their selected partners. Alfie, reluctant to lose his guard by getting lost in the fun, teamed up with Charley, Lucy with Teddy, Thomas, and Grace. Alex and Jennifer, Ben and Ella, Chris, and Ivy, and Alice and Emerson.

Ben and Ella were the first to fall; Lucy was too strong for Ella to take on. Next was Ivy and

Chris; Charley had knocked Ivy off quite cruelly. Lucy next pushed Grace into the pool in a matter of seconds. Alice and Emerson beat Jennifer and Alex; Charley and Alfie beat Alice and Emerson. In the final round, Lucy faced Charley. Entangled in a tight grip, neither female wanted to lose. Lucy and Charley were both as competitive as one another. Eventually, Lucy emerged as the victor. Thomas roared at Lucy and Teddy's success. Seeing Teddy wasn't his usual self, he wanted to encourage him and take his mind away from his pain.

They all got out of the pool individually, bombing back in with a splash. Alfie went third, but as the others began to jump in, water splashed into his eyes, the chlorine irritating them. Unexpectedly, he felt someone jump on his back. In defence mode, he fought to get them off, struggling in panic as he heard laughs around him. He felt a heavy breath of someone coming toward him as he kicked his feet off the floor, pushing the person behind him against the edge of the pool. He felt someone grab his feet as he swallowed water as he was being forced under the water.

Alfie struggled under the water. As he got himself free, he grasped for air, feeling someone duck him back under the water, this time putting their feet on his shoulders. Slowly losing his breath, suddenly he was free. He floated to the

131

top, coughing out water as he took quick breaths.

"Are you three dense? Could you not see Alfie wasn't fooling around; he was struggling to catch his breath? You idiots!" Lucy was furious at Alex, Ben, and Chris who had joined in adding a spiteful intent at drowning Alfie.

"I think we should leave," Alice said to Emerson as the two excused themselves and left through the garden's exit. Clearing his eyes of the chlorine pain with a towel, he looked at everyone in the pool.

"Who stood on my shoulders, when it was obvious I was losing my breath?" demanded Alfie, agitated with a sinister vengeance. Ben got nervous as Alex tried to joke it off.

"It was me; thought it'd be fun to make it look like an accident!" replied Chris, giving a cruel smile. Getting satisfaction from taunting Alfie. He had no idea the mind frame Alfie was in and he'd just marked his card.

"Get out of the pool!" demanded Alfie! His face had changed; No one had ever seen the angered killer instinct Alfie had, this was a small glimpse, and everyone noticed a change warily.

"Alfie, please don't," begged Charley, getting out of the pool and running over to him, "you know what he is like, he does stupid things, he's an idiot, you're going to really hurt him if you do this," Charley begged, the fear in her face made Alfie hesitant. He didn't want to upset her. Chris laughed noticing the reluctance from Alfie at Charley's plea. Infuriated, a curled fist connected into his kinked nose. He covered his face as the impact of Lucy's punch caused his nose to bleed instantly. Winking at Alfie, Lucy let him know that she had his back.

Leaving the pool area, Alfie was the first in the house. He went straight upstairs and had a shower to rid himself of the bleachy smell from the pool. He changed into fresh comfortable clothes as he checked on his mother and Oscar. Bulldozer slowly got down from Oscar's bed, sniffing Alfie as he could smell the anger and caution, he was hiding. Alfie left the door slightly ajar as he took a slow walk back downstairs.

Barefoot, Alfie felt the chill of the wooden hallway floor beneath him on the ground floor. Observing everyone gathered in the living room, he noticed they were engrossed in hushed murmurs, unaware of his presence. A sense of foreboding urged him forward, as he approached, the muted sound of his footsteps went unnoticed by the gathered group. Upon entering the living room, he sensed an explicit tension as his friends turned their eyes toward him.

"Alfie, what's going on?" Charley questioned; her face etched with terror, confusion and disappointment. Alfie glanced at the contents on the glass table, not experiencing the dread he had anticipated, but instead a surge of fury. He questioned in his mind how his friends had discovered the photos and notes in his office. Silently scrutinizing each of them as suspects.

"Is everything alright, Alfie?" Lucy attempted to diffuse the tension; her concern was evident. Meanwhile, Chris smirked, relishing in the isolation he perceived Alfie to be in.

"Why didn't you tell me about this, Alfie?" accused Charley, joining the others in assumptions. Ignoring her, Alfie felt annoyance escalating, especially considering the experiences they had been through together. She repeated her question, and Alfie's annoyance surged.

"Because I wanted to keep you safe!" he shouted with anger, she should know the reason, scanning the room. Thomas responded more calmly than the others, understanding the seriousness of the situation.

"Tonight was because of you, Alfie. Who is this referring to?" questioned Teddy through gritted teeth, Alfie's defensiveness easing as he looked at him knowing he was caught in a whirlwind of emotions. Hesitating to answer, Alfie looked at

134

Thomas, who had positioned himself between Alfie and the others. Sensing Alfie's inner turmoil, Lucy swiftly grabbed his arm.

"Come with me, Alf," she said, pulling him out of the living room, and into the dining room, where they both sat at the table. Lucy began asking questions, but Alfie remained silent, staring at her like he was in a catatonic state. Thomas walked into the dining room, checking on Alfie.

"Why did you lie?" Alfie asked Lucy, staring aggressively into her eyes.

"Lie about what?" Lucy replied in shock, eyes wide open in disbelief as Alfie begun to interrogate her.

"You told me that Thomas told you not to bother me after Ronnie was murdered," Alfie continued, turning his gaze to Thomas. "You told me that you never spoke to her?"

"I did speak to you!" Lucy abruptly responded, pulling her phone out and showing Alfie the call log and the time, they spoke. "I left my phone in the office that night; it wasn't me you spoke to!" Thomas revealed, looking back at Alfie.

"Seriously, what is going on?" Lucy asked worried her eyes on Thomas then desperately looking at Alfie.

"DO YOU REMEMBER WHAT IT FEELS LIKE TO KILL!" Chris shouted aloud, antagonizing Alfie, and adding fuel to Teddy's fire.

"Fuck off, Chris! Before I hit you harder," Lucy shouted as she leaned into the hallway, going back to Alfie she kneeled in front of him squeezing Alfie's hand. Certain that Lucy and Thomas were not behind this, Alfie could hear Charley and Chris arguing in the hallway. Hearing the siblings argue Alfie jolted out of the chair; Lucy could see his intent as she pushed him backwards. Charley and Chris's voices shouted louder; storming past Lucy Alfie stamped into the hallway grabbing Chris's t-shirt by the shoulder he shoved him to the floor.

"Ooh, big hard Alfie, you going to kill me," Chris mocked looking up at Alfie as he slowly stood up.

"Leave him alone, Alfie! He's not wrong; we deserve to know what's going on!" demanded Ivy, positioning herself between Alfie and Chris. Angered, Alfie turned his back, looking at Charley and Lucy behind him. From behind Ivy Chris leaned over slapping Alfie in the back of the head. Alfie spun round enraged as Chris laughed in his face.

"NO!" roared Ivy, defending Chris as Alfie pushed forward to retaliate. Lucy's fury surged,

136

provoked by the disdainful tone and treatment Ivy had directed at Alfie. With a swift and determined stride, Lucy stormed past Alfie, seizing a fistful of Ivy's hair with an immovable grip. The sudden force yanked Ivy away from Chris, disrupting the momentary control she had asserted. Swinging Ivy round till she hit the floor, Lucy began a cascade of resounding slaps that echoed through the hallway. To defuse the situation Thomas and Alex grabbed Lucy, Thomas picking her up as Alex put himself in front of Ivy.

In response to Ivy's abrupt removal, Alfie seized the opportunity, swiftly grappling Chris before delivering a forceful punch; the impact sending him spiralling back to the floor. Closing in, Alfie then leaned down, grabbing Chris by the throat, tightening his hold in an intuitive display of escalating tension being released.

"I think I remember exactly how to kill; keep pushing me prick!" Alfie spat into Chris's ear maliciously. Startled Charley gasped, Alfie could hear the upset in her breath, releasing Chris who rubbed his throat giving Alfie a murderous look. Teddy, with tears in his eyes, walked into the hallway. Everyone looked at the agony unfolding in his face. Alfie turned around looking at each other. Alfie could feel the frustration in Teddy's glare.

"What secret are you hiding from me?" Teddy asked, confused, angry, and grief-stricken. Alfie stood silent, the urge and want to tell Alfie the truth pulsating through him, but he knew he couldn't not now. Alfie shook knowing the damage the truth would do to Teddy, he didn't want to taint the memory of his mother and didn't want to send his friend spiralling.

"I don't know, Teddy; I have no answers for any of this, I'm sorry," Alfie lied convincingly, as he looked at Teddy with an apologetic face.

"So, my mother and Eva are dead because of you, and you don't know why?" Teddy looked Alfie in the eyes, watching his reply, Alfie shook his head denying his knowledge. A cold sweat broke from Teddy's face as he watched the shaking of Alfie's head. Teddy flew into a rage, ramming Alfie into the wall and pushing his hands twisting his arm around his back. Holding his head to the wall with all his might. "You're lying; tell me, please just tell me!" Teddy begged desperately just wanting the answers. Alfie struggled to get himself free as Teddy threw him to the other side of the hallway. Grabbing him Teddy began to bounce him back and forth off the floor. Alfie felt defenceless, unable to react knowing Teddy was releasing the pent-up emotions he'd had for the past three and half days.

"Teddy, it's Alfie; when has he ever hidden anything from us?" Lucy said, putting her hand on Teddy's arm, leading him to let go of Alfie. As Teddy's hands reluctantly released their grip on Alfie's top Alfie lay on the floor taking a deep breath. Alfie stood up; he could see everyone's eyes on his as Teddy turned around. A torrent of grief surging through him, transforming into a searing rage that fuelled his next move. Without a moment's hesitation, he unleashed a powerful punch aimed directly at Alfie's stomach, the force of his sorrow and frustration manifesting in the blow. Alfie doubled over in response to the unexpected strike, momentarily taken aback by the intensity of Teddy's emotional outburst.

Driven by a mix of anguish and fury, Teddy swung his fist for a second blow, determined to unleash his pent-up grief. However, Alfie, recovering quickly from the initial hit, displayed an unexpected agility as he instinctively sidestepped the incoming punch. The dance of combat unfolded inadvertently, with Alfie evading Teddy's relentless onslaught. Desperate not to fight with him, Alfie pushed him away when he couldn't evade the attack. Teddy was relentless throwing attack after attack Alfie's way.

Suddenly Bulldozer thundered down the stairs, his jaws clamping onto Teddy's leg. Alfie relaxed as he watched Bulldozer attacking Teddy. It wasn't that he wanted his friend to be hurt, but he knew that if the mysterious tormentor was in his home, they now just witnessed a taste of what they will have to face.

Everyone stepped back not wanting to intervene as the dog viciously attacked. All but Charley who knew how to control the dog swiftly intervened. Demanding the dog stop, she pulled him by his collar off Teddy.

"Look everyone, Tonight has gotten a little heated, maybe we should all go to bed and start a fresh tomorrow, and we'll talk about it rationally," Thomas instructed taking the lead in the chaos.

"You mean give Sayers the opportunity to get his story straight? He just attacked me!" Chris shouted arrogantly to the room, locking eyes with Alfie.

"Get out of my house, Chris! There's too much going on to have you stir the situation too," Charley commanded, still holding Bulldozer. Chris tutted, laughing as he walked past Charley and headed upstairs to grab his bag before leaving. Charley led Chris out of the front door and down the pathway, opening the gate for him to leave.

Outside, Lucy and Thomas guided Alfie into the garden, engaging him in conversation.

"I feel terrible hiding this from all of you, but I don't know what the messages mean, and I don't know who's doing this. I also feel terrible for Teddy after all he's been through in the last few days," Alfie explained in a panic, revealing a vulnerability none had seen before. Lucy sensed there was more to the story but refrained from prying, considering everything that had transpired.

"Who did you kill?" Lucy asked, staggeringly, her face pleading for Alfie to trust her as he had so many times before.

"His name was Richard Gein; I hit him with my car," Alfie fabricated a confession. "Look, the only thing I can assume is that at least one person inside is involved. I trust you both. Can you two sleep on the same floor as mine and Oscar's room? Oscar has been threatened too, and I need people I can trust around him," Alfie informed, being more honest than he had been all night. Thomas and Lucy nodded in agreement.

Alfie went inside, calling Bulldozer as he ascended the stairs. Checking on his mother and Oscar, Alfie instructed the dog to stay in the room. After closing the door, he entered his room, locking it securely. Opening the panic room, he attempted to find footage of who had entered his office, but the cameras weren't recording, only observing. He stayed awake, monitoring everyone on the cameras until he was sure they were all in bed.

Chapter 7

"I didn't mean to; I didn't mean to kill him!" cried teen Alfie as an older man took the bloodied steel out of his hand. The older man grabbed Alfie by the shoulders, looking into his eyes his mouth moving without producing any sound. Alfie gazed at the man, understanding every word he was silently mouthing; he nodded, following the instructions. The older man looked around the room, taking in the carnage. Alfie began to convulse, his airways closing as he was consumed by the horror of the night. Trembling, he fell to the ruined carpet, shaking as he curled up in a ball. He felt death looming as his breath grew heavier as if it was about to be cut off. The given instructions soon faded from his memory; the older man panicked, realizing Alfie needed to comply. The young woman, in streams of tears, held the lifeless young boy on the floor, oblivious to what was happening behind her.

Teen Alfie, lying on the floor, slowly stood up, transforming into his present adult self. Still shaking, barefoot on the cold grass in front of his home, he called out for his friends, for

143

Oscar, and then his mother. No one responded. Turning every corner in search of someone, he ran toward his home. The door was locked. Banging and pushing, he attempted to open it, scanning the sides of the house. Approaching the living room window, he saw his friends lying in a line dead. Smashing the window, he watched as a masked man walked into the living room, with Charley by his side, holding Oscar close to them.

"Jack! I know it's you!" shouted Alfie, as Charley revealed a piece of rope. She wrapped the rope around the child's neck, choking Oscar. Alfie yelled, attempting to run toward his son, but he was stuck on the spot. Charley laughed, joined by the masked man. Mocking Alfie, the masked man pulled off his mask, revealing himself to be Thomas.

Alfie awoke once again, drenched in sweat, his eyes filled with tears. He glanced over at Charley, peacefully asleep. Slipping out of bed, he entered the ensuite, closing the door behind him. Studying his reflection in the cabinet mirror, he confronted the older man from his past staring back at him.

"Sorry," Alfie whimpered, meeting the gaze of the old man. Splashing cold water over his face, he peered back into the mirror. His eyes betrayed him, haunted by the memories of the man. His clothes clung to him, damp from the night sweats; Swiftly, he entered the shower to refresh. Contemplating his dream, he'd recognized the first part, a recurring memory that had become almost routine. However, the second part was entirely new to him.

Years ago, during Charley's post-natal depression, Alfie had dreamt of her abandoning Oscar, but never had he envisioned her causing harm. Considering recent events, he assured himself it wasn't real or even plausible.

"It's just a dream. It's just a dream," he whispered, allowing the cascading water to rinse away the beads of sweat clinging to his skin. "Come on, pull yourself together," he muttered, stepping out of the invigorating shower. Leaning against the cool porcelain sink, he found his mind entangled in a labyrinth of thoughts, unable to untangle the web of suspicions lingering over everyone in his house, including Charley. Murmuring a desperate plea to break free from his dream, he pushed away from the sink and exited the ensuite, the air heavy with the residue of his unsettling dreams.

Returning to his bedroom, he checked on Charley, still peacefully asleep. Taking a moment to stare at her, he wondered why his dreams were casting her as the villain. Stealthily, he entered the walk-in wardrobe, swiftly changing into a black vest and grey jogger bottoms. His scruffed-up jeans from moving day fell to the floor, and as he picked them up, he felt his Grandad's black slotted butterfly knife tucked in the back pocket. He took it, placing it in the pocket of his joggers.

Despite his efforts to forget, thoughts of Thomas as the masked man lingered. Alfie questioned whether his dream was a warning, though his cynical nature resisted such beliefs. Thomas was the least likely suspect in his eyes, but now he found himself challenging that assumption.

Getting back into bed, he lay there, lost in thought. He knew he couldn't go back to sleep, surprised that his mind had even allowed him to fall asleep after all that had happened a few hours prior. Looking at Charley, he was sceptical about his dream and her reaction to him earlier. Gripping the duvet, he felt his adrenaline surging. He pushed himself up and quietly left his bedroom.

"Standing in the hallway, he stared at the opposite door, checking on Oscar and his mother. They were both peacefully asleep. Bulldozer got down from Oscar's bed, nudging his head against Alfie's leg. Alfie stroked him before they both left the room. Bulldozer accompanied him as he quickly peered into the other bedroom. Thomas and Grace were fast asleep; he was relieved, as his mind was telling him that Thomas would be up, killing the guests in his house. He hated suspecting them all. Opening the last bedroom on the second floor, he checked on Lucy, who was wide awake.

"You're awake?" Alfie whispered, initially suspicious, but the tension eased as Lucy responded.

"Of course, I'm awake. I'm worried about you," she whispered, looking at him with genuine concern. "Those photos and messages, they're a lot for you to have held to yourself," she acknowledged sincerely, tapping him on the shoulder.

"I know, Lucy... I just wanted to figure it out, find out who it was, and end it without stressing any of you out," Alfie replied with genuine care, placing his hand on Lucy's arm and giving her a soft squeeze.

"By the way, when you came up here earlier, Ivy was having a right bitch about you, so I kind of beat her up... again... she didn't seem to understand the first slap," Lucy giggled, explaining quietly to Alfie.

"Really? What was she saying?" asked Alfie, wondering why she had so much to say when his own friends, who it concerned most, were saying less. His face screwed up in suspicious thought, listening to Lucy share the gossip.

"Well, she started off saying that you were obviously guilty, she never liked you, you were bullying Chris… she was basically talking a lot of bollocks. So, I pulled her backwards by her hair, slapped her—I didn't punch; she's a girly girl, she couldn't take a full blow—and then I warned her to keep her mouth shut!" Lucy explained while delicately mimicking the actions.

Alfie gave a proud and satisfied smirk, knowing Ivy had faced consequences deserved, but he couldn't help but wonder why she was so invested in making him the bad guy. Paranoia began to take the lead. To distract himself, he changed the subject of the conversation. "I'm going to check on everyone. Do you want to come with me?" he asked her, tilting his head to the side in a gesture to go downstairs. She accepted the invitation as he, Lucy, and Bulldozer went to the first floor. They checked each room, finding Alex and Jennifer in one room, Ella and Ivy in another, and Ben, who was on his own.

"Did Teddy leave?" he asked Lucy in a whisper as he shut the last bedroom door, shaking her head indicating no to Alfie's question.

Checking the rest of the house, Lucy took a slow walk down the stairs with him, scrutinizing Alfie's face as they engaged in small talk, detecting a worry involuntarily reflected in his eyes. Alfie could feel her gaze, but skilfully avoided any attempts she made to press him on the matter. Standing in the ground floor hallway, Bulldozer gave a low, aggressive growl as Lucy and Alfie spotted the outline of someone in the dark. Walking into the living room, Alfie turned on the light, and Teddy turned, looking at them with hostility. Bulldozer growled again, and Alfie snapped his fingers at the dog, instructing him to stop.

"Please leave me alone," Teddy breathed in defeat as he turned his back and sat down on the sofa. Lucy walked into the living room and sat down with him. Alfie, staring at the back of Teddy's head, felt a terrible ache knowing the turmoil his friend was going through. Cautiously, Alfie eventually walked in the living room taking a seat with them, Bulldozer sitting by his side on guard.

"I'm sorry, Ted," Alfie confessed, the most truthful thing he'd said to anyone all night. His hands entwined together as he hunched over his elbows on his knees, desperate for Teddy to forgive him.

"What secret have you been hiding from me?" Teddy asked assertively, piercingly gazing into Alfie's eyes, watching his every movement. Alfie paused for a moment, debating Teddy's reaction. Could he handle finding out that four people in his life had lied to him, making him believe something that was never true? Alfie couldn't bring himself to tell him, not yet.

"The secret is, whoever killed your mum and Eva is blaming me, and I really don't know why! All I know is they were killed. I have this note, this warning, with no clue what it means. Then, a guy in my building is murdered, and I'm blamed again!" Alfie vented, letting his frustrations out without revealing too many details. His eyes were desperate, begging for Teddy to accept his words. Lucy leaned over to Alfie, putting a hand on his combined hands.

"We'll work it out together," she comforted with a smile. "We've always had each other's backs since forever ago. No one's going to get any of us," Lucy reassured. Turning to Teddy, she tried to pull him closer to Alfie, but he pulled away.

"Alfie, I don't believe you. There's something you're not telling me, and I can't forgive that! My mum and Eva are dead because of you. You're responsible for this, and whatever it is you won't tell me, it's cost me my mum and my girlfriend. I can't forgive that," Teddy spoke brokenly, as if Alfie had literally stabbed him in the back. The look of betrayal on Teddy's face said everything he hadn't said. "I'm going to go and stay with my cousin tomorrow, and when you do decide to tell me the truth, we can try and sort things out from there," his voice softer and vulnerable but his face serious and hurt.

"Come on, Ted, that's not fair," replied Lucy, trying to resolve the tension between the two. Just as she was about to continue her attempt to repair the boys' friendship, Teddy interrupted.

"No, Lucy, what's not fair is you always taking his side! I've lost my mum and my girlfriend, and still, it's 'come on, Teddy,' like I've done something wrong! You lose the people important to you, your mum, or your sister or even your precious Alfie, and see how you feel," Teddy's voice raised slightly as his fury deepened. Bulldozer hunched forward, but Alfie grabbed him quickly, preventing his attack. "I know this is your house, but as soon as the sun's up, I'm gone. Can you just leave me alone till then?" Teddy pleaded. Lucy and Alfie looked at each other, standing up and leaving the living room.

Taking a slow walk to not wake anyone up, Alfie and Lucy made their way back to the second floor. Opening Oscar's bedroom, he led Bulldozer back onto Oscar's bed. Lucy stood in the hallway as she watched the loving father making sure his son was comfortable. Carefully leaving the room to not wake his mother or Oscar, he met Lucy back outside.

"Are you okay?" Lucy asked with concern. Alfie nodded with a tight, grimaced smile. Lucy hugged him, reassuring him that everything would be okay. Not wanting to talk about it, Alfie hugged Lucy back and said goodnight as he went back to his bedroom.

Less than an hour had passed; Teddy's words weighed heavily on Alfie's mind, making it impossible for him to go back to sleep. Checking the time on his phone, he noted it was 2:11 am. Tossing and turning, he struggled to clear his mind of the blame he held. Glancing at Charley, who was deep in slumber, he carefully got out of bed. Exiting his bedroom, he entered the passage. He considered going into Lucy's room, but he knew she would want to talk about what he was trying to avoid.

Pacing toward the staircase, closer to his bedroom, Alfie decided to seek solitude in the pitch-dark attic. Standing at the doorway, the full moon beamed a light into the centre of the attic. Steadily, he walked across the rough wooden floor, being careful to avoid tripping over the boxes he had placed there. Standing at the large square window, gazing up at the moon,

Alfie appreciated the beauty of the night and his new neighbourhood. The streetlights glowed, reflecting off the metal gates that protected the homes. The peace of the night was abruptly disturbed by a white van passing through the street. Alfie focused on the van until it disappeared from his sight. Suddenly, Teddy's words pierced through his brain. Alfie fought the regret he felt, only to suddenly see Ronnie standing on the roof outside the attic window.

Frightened by the sight of Ronnie, mimicking the bloodiness of his death, Alfie took a step backward, tripping on his feet. A splinter embedded into his foot, but ignoring the pain, he looked back at the window, seeing Ronnie had vanished. Using the moonlight to see, Alfie pulled out the fragment of wood; a tiny dent that dripped a couple of drops of blood on the floorboard. Getting up, he took another look out of the window.

Peering near the front of his house, Alfie noticed a masked man between the gaps of the gate. Assuming it was just his imagination after what he had just seen, he rubbed his eyes. Looking back down, the masked man was still by the gate. Squinting his eyes to get a clearer look, hoping the man would vanish from his view, he noticed the mask the man wore wasn't the same black as the unknown murderer in his office; this one was a bright orange. He rubbed his eyes again, believing it to be a hallucination until the gate slowly began to open.

Sprinting through the attic, his footsteps heavy with dread, Alfie's worst fears had materialized. Hurdling across the uneven floor, he collided with cardboard boxes, crashing onto them with force. Despite the fall, his feet continued their rapid motion, propelling him toward the attic door. He lunged down the stairs, desperately throwing himself forward.

Bolting into Oscar's room, he picked Oscar up from his bed. Bulldozer, sensing his panic, started barking relentlessly, awakening Alfie's mother. Instructing his mother out of bed sharply and commanding the dog, they rushed into Alfie's bedroom. His mother scurried, rattling Charley out of her slumber. Opening the panic room door, Alfie called for his mother and Charley to get inside quickly, laying Oscar on the single bed. His mother grabbed his arm, pulling him to face her.

"Who is it? What's going on?" she asked with panic in her voice and aggression on her face.

"I don't know. Someone's gotten into the house. I need you to stay in here," Alfie said urgently as he hastily started edging out of the panic room. "Just let me back in! Once you lock it, it won't open from the outside," Alfie reminded his mother, realizing Bulldozer was following him out of the panic room.

"Stay!" commanded Alfie as Bulldozer sat down, watching him leave.

Leaving the panic room, Alfie was met by Lucy, standing in the door frame between his room and the hallway.

"I heard shouting, what's going on?" she asked, sensing the urgency, her hand on the side of the door frame squeezing.

"Someone's just let themselves through the gate, we need to get everyone to safety!" he instructed her, "Go in the attic; there is a baseball bat by the door, grab it!" He instructed her, pushing past her and storming through the door where Thomas and Grace slept Alfie abruptly woke them.

Thomas, scared in the face of Alfie's fast aggression, jumped out of bed.

"You and Grace need to wake everyone up and tell them to hide. Then you and Lucy come back up here. Me, you, Grace, Lucy, and Teddy are going into my panic room. I can't trust the others!" Alfie explained rapidly before dashing away.

"Panic room?" Thomas asked dumbfounded, Alfie disappeared away from the bedroom door.

Charging down the stairs, Alfie came to a halt on the landing before the final three steps, finding his front door wide open. Outside, the white van he had seen drive by was parked in the middle of the grass. Revolving toward the living room, Teddy wobbled toward him. Moving down a step toward him, Alfie, in shock, froze on the stair. Soaked in blood, his attire dark and wet, Teddy held his hand around his neck as blood gushed out between his fingers, internal damage suffocating him as he watched his friend fall to the ground.

"No!" Alfie anguished, seeing his friend. Alfie took another step towards Teddy as tears began to fall from his eyes. Collapsing to the floor, Alfie went to bend down toward him as the murderers caught his eye. He slowly backed up the stairs; his eyes fixed on them. One figure wore an orange balaclava, its slits concealing mirrored eyes and a covered mouth. Another donned a pink balaclava with the same mirrored eyes and mouth covered, while the last person wore a black balaclava with mirrored eyes and a concealed mouth. They were clad in all-black attire, complete with matching combat boots and black gloves. Their silent and menacing stance unnerved Alfie as he caught his reflection in their mirrored eyes.

Leisurely, the orange intruder paced toward Alfie as he backed up the stairs, blankly tormenting him with a stare as Alfie twisted his body and retreated onto the steps leading to the first floor. Instinctively, adrenaline surged as Alfie turned, attempting to ascend the stairs. With a vindictive grip, the orange intruder grabbed Alfie's leg, dragging him down the steps. Alfie clung to the banister to avoid becoming prey, his face scrunched in a mix of fear and rage, clenching his jaw as he tried to kick the intruder off. The pink intruder glided forward, revealing a hunting eight-inch blade with a black handle. Raising her arm to stab Alfie in the leg as he struggled to break free from the other's grip.

Stampeding down the stairs, the pink intruder glanced over Alfie's head as the thick wooden bat collided with her hand. Lucy nearly toppled forward due to the intense force she exerted into her swing. Startled by Lucy's sudden appearance, the orange intruder became distracted. Alfie seized the opportunity, stomping the sole of his foot onto the orange intruder's face, leaving a speck of blood from the splinter embedded in his foot.

Lucy and Alfie hurriedly ascended the stairs. In their panic, they collided with Thomas and Alex, the four of them tumbling to the ground. Alfie and Lucy quickly crawled past them, standing up in haste.

"We need to hide!" shouted Alfie, knowing it was too late to get anyone in the panic room. Terrifyingly slow, putting all their weight on each step, the stairs creaked as the intruders made their way upstairs. A loud, pitchy scream filled the house as Jennifer, Grace, and Ella screamed in sync. Seeing the big hunting knives in their hands fuelled urgent panic in everyone. Everyone started scattering into rooms. Thomas and Grace attempted to run into the closest room on the left. The pink intruder caught Grace by her hair, yanking her backward; Thomas attempted to free Grace as the pink intruder plunged her knife into his arm. Grabbing the wound in his arm, Thomas let go.

Alex, Jennifer, and Ella hid in the opposite room as Alfie and Lucy hid in the room further down the hall. Alfie pulled out his grandfather's butterfly knife, ready to stab anyone on entry.

A roaring gunshot made everyone jump as the bullet from the gun penetrated the wall. Silence filled the house as Thomas stood helpless, the pink intruder holding Grace at knife point, the black masked intruder holding the gun he had fired.

"Please don't hurt her," begged Thomas, helpless to save his girlfriend. Alfie and Lucy looked at each other in the other room, both contemplating what to do next. "Come out, everyone, or they are going to kill Grace!" pleaded Thomas loudly. Alfie debated what he should do. He didn't want anyone else to die; he didn't want Thomas to be the next friend he lost, but he didn't want to be helpless either. Alex, Jennifer, and Ella came out of hiding. The black and pink masked intruders marched the others downstairs. Enjoying power over their victims, the pink intruder kicked Alex down the stairs.

Their hearts pounded in unison; Alfie's hands clenched involuntarily, and Lucy's breath caught in anticipation as they listened intently, bracing for someone to enter the room where they hid. Carefully searching every room, the orange intruder prowled the hallway, knife at the ready to plunge into their victims. Lingering in the hallway opposite the last unopened room, the intruder took his time, well aware of the instructions he planned to disobey.

Alfie readied the butterfly knife, pressed against the wall, as the doorknob began to twist. Alfie's nerves steadied, knowing what he was about to do, his mind blank from compassion. Kicking the door, bolting it open, the room looked empty. The intruder cautiously walked inside. Before Alfie could attack to kill, Lucy swung the bat, striking brutally into the orange intruder's face, creating a small crack in the mirrored right eye. With a swift motion, Lucy skilfully leaped over the intruder, her agile movements allowing

159

her to avoid any immediate danger. Alfie, instinctively reacting to Lucy's escape, followed suit, ascending the stairs to the second floor.

Inside Alfie's bedroom, they closed the door. As Alfie grabbed his phone from his bed, he removed the false shelf for the panic room, banging on the door. His mother opened the door, letting him and Lucy in. Locking it from the inside, he dropped to the floor.

Burdened by the guilt of secrets and the last conversation he had had with Teddy; he felt a gut-wrenching pain inside his stomach that made him feel nauseous. He held his pain in his throat, preventing himself from crying. Collapsing to the floor and dropping the butterfly knife, Alfie was consoled by his mother and Lucy as they rushed to his side.

"They killed him," he trembled as his mother embraced him tightly, forcing the wailing pain inside to stay.

"Daddy?" Oscar awoke, yawning after he spoke, wiping his face. "What's wrong, Daddy?" he asked, sensing the distress.

"Daddy's okay, Oscar. He just needs a Nanny hug," replied Alfie's mother. Alfie started sorting himself out. Going over to Oscar, he cuddled his son, a moment of safety and peace as he held his son. He debated his options in his head, knowing what he had to do, but also knowing that he didn't want to leave his son without a dad.

"Alfie, what do we do now?" Lucy asked, not wanting to disrupt the moment with his son but realizing there wasn't time for him to play father. Charley took Oscar from Alfie and sat with him as Alfie approached his mother and Lucy. Instructing his mother to call the police, Alfie handed her his phone.

Walking over to the screen, his mother had put them on and watched what he could. A large chunk of the cameras were not working, which puzzled Alfie as he'd been watching them a few hours earlier.

"How? Those cameras are so small; there's no way someone has cut them off!" Alfie assured, trying to get them to work. He fiddled with the screen showing the stream from the first and second floors; however, only the hallways and Alfie and Oscar's bedrooms were working.

"Who have they got?" he asked his mother. She began to list the names of those taken downstairs.

"I think that was Ella, so where's Ivy and Ben?" he asked her, inspecting.

"I didn't see them anywhere," replied his mother, meeting his suspicion. "Do you think?"

she began to ask, but Alfie cut her off, telling her he wasn't sure. His concentration on the screen deepening as he put all his personal turmoil behind him for now...

"I don't know how I'm going to handle them," Alfie confessed, looking at his room on the camera and in the hallways, trying to map out his attacks. He looked to Lucy, still holding the bat in her hand. "You're staying in here; I'm not risking you too," he told her.

"The fuck I am!" argued Lucy, lifting up the bat. "Look, Sayers, you've got your secrets that you've kept from me, whatever... But we have always had each other's back when trouble was on the horizon, so I'm in this with you... Plus, someone needs to help make sure Oscar's not fatherless!" Lucy replied sternly and protective, pointing the bat toward him to convey that he wasn't pushing her out to protect her.

"Have you ever killed anyone before?" Alfie asked her. She shook her head in response, with a confused look on her face.

"I have... and this, going out to this, it's not pulling Ivy's hair or punching idiots; this is kill to survive... and that never leaves you once you touch it!" Alfie confessed in a frustrated tone. Charley sat watching coldly, covering Oscar's ears. She was annoyed, and Alfie, seeing her face, couldn't understand her anger, especially

162

with what was unfolding in their house, and the risk it bared.

"Deliberating survival strategies in his mind, Alfie pictured unseen rooms... Catching quick glances of Charley as she sat with Oscar, she seemed cold and distant. It confused him; she had no reaction and seemed motionless to what was happening. Alfie's phone rang; an icy dread flushed through his body. His mother seeing the name that appeared handing the phone back to Alfie. Teddy's name appeared big on his phone screen.

"What do you want?" Alfie demanded, glancing at his mother and Lucy.

"You," a deep, disgruntled voice replied, the caller's voice disguised to prevent Alfie from identifying them. Turning the speaker on, Alfie walked to a corner, putting as much distance between him and Oscar, in the room as possible so he wasn't in earshot. He turned the volume down as he, his mother, and Lucy crowded around the phone.

"Let everyone leave, and you can have me. I'll come downstairs freely, but only after you let everyone go," Alfie tried to negotiate, looking at his mother, who nodded in approval at his attempt.

"NO!" the voice hissed in reply, "No one leaves! You come downstairs now, or we start killing your friends without you... and they will die knowing it's because of you," the voice teased. "Poor Teddy, did you tell him the secret!" The voice teased before hanging up the phone.

Biting his lip, Alfie looked at his mother, then at Lucy. His mother shook her head disapprovingly, knowing her son was going to leave that room and give himself to the slaughter. Alfie's eyes darted around the room; he wished he could be selfish and hide until the police came, knowing he would see his son when the sun rose. He spotted the butterfly knife he'd dropped on the floor; bending down, he folded it up, putting it in his hand. He looked around the room, finding a first aid box. He opened it, cutting a white bandage enough to tie the knife to the back of his leg.

"I've got to go down there, or they will start killing them all," Alfie explained to them all, keeping Charley in earshot.

"Just go! This is all your fault anyway," Charley replied coldly turning her head refusing to look at Alfie. Alfie's mother jumped to defend her son before Alfie pointed to Oscar, who was soothingly resting in Charley's lap.". "Just keep an eye on the camera; if I can get back up here and bring anyone with me, I'll need to run in as

164

fast as possible," Alfie instructed his mother. Swiftly, he opened the panic room door, leaving as Lucy followed behind.

"Please stay in there!" Alfie begged, pointing toward the panic room door as it closed behind them.

"I have no choice now; we're in this together," Lucy replied as they walked out of the walk-in wardrobe and into Alfie's room.

"Drop the bat," Alfie instructed; she dropped it in the centre between the bed and door. "We need to be defenceless... for now," Alfie whispered as they left the bedroom and made their way downstairs.

"How are we going to get them?" Lucy asked, whispering as they slowly went downstairs. Confessing he wasn't sure, with no fear on his face, Lucy was puzzled trying to figure out what Alfie had done to cause all of this.

Standing on the landing, Alfie diverted his eyes to avoid Teddy's body. Pacing to the living room, Alfie saw the three intruders standing waiting for his arrival. All his friends sat on the floor, Thomas covered in blood from the gash in his arm, Grace's hair mangled from the grip, Alex had a cut on his chin, Jennifer and Ella looked like the only untouched victims.

The black-masked intruder pointed his gun at Alfie, as the pink-masked intruder grabbed Lucy, dragging her into the living room, pushing her toward the others. She tripped and fell on top of Thomas and Ella. The orange-masked intruder grabbed Alfie by his black vest, pulling him into the living room, making him sit opposite the others.

The pink intruder, her laughter echoing malevolence, revelled in Alfie's apparent defeat, a wicked satisfaction painted across her masked face. That same deep disgruntled voice spoke, "Now the games can begin!"

Chapter 8

Fear permeated the living room; Alfie sat across from his friends, observing the terror drawn on their faces. His head leaned against the sofa, hazel eyes scanning the surroundings, analysing the three intruders—their height, their movements. The pink intruder, impatient and eager for the kill, paced around the room, waiting for the signal to strike. The black-masked intruder, nonchalant, stood against the wall, gun at the ready. The orange intruder appeared to be the weak link, agitated with a knife at the ready; Alfie sensed an eagerness to finish the plan fast.

Teddy came into Alfie's sight, and his heart raced, pounding against his chest. It was difficult, but Alfie knew he couldn't acknowledge Teddy's death in this moment. Suddenly, a kick landed on Alfie's thigh; he refused to react. The pink-masked intruder's mirrored eyes stared down at Alfie, reflecting his emotionless face. Annoyed by Alfie's lack of reaction, the pink intruder attempted another kick but was halted by a distorted, deep voice. The pink intruder marched over to the black-masked intruder, muttering into their ear.

"Fucking kill me if that's what you want but let them go!" Alfie fumed, jumping up pointing to his friends. The black-masked intruder nodded, gesturing to the other two. From behind, the orange intruder kicked Alfie's legs away, causing him to fall to the ground with a thump. The orange intruder began to repeatedly kick Alfie, who didn't fight back.

Lucy and Thomas tried to move forward to help, but the pink intruder emitted a loud, muffled grunt, slashing the knife to give a subtle warning. Lucy and Thomas slid backward, avoiding the blade.

"No hero acts today, Alfie," the pink intruder's disguised voice intoned deeply, stroking the knife slowly across Alfie's face and neck.

Alfie pulled away from the knife as the pink intruder grabbed the back of his hair. An eerie silence hung between them as Alfie gazed into the mirrored eyes. The intruder's intense grip on his hair and desperation to instil fear made Alfie wonder how personal this vendetta could be.

"Your friends are loyal, but they don't know you, do they?" the pink intruder taunted. Though the voice was disguised, the intention behind the words felt clear. Letting Alfie's hair go, standing up and inspecting the victims on the floor, the pink intruder pointed the knife at the intended

168

victim as a silent instruction to the orange intruder.

Loud screams from the crowded victims filled the air. Alfie lay on the floor, eyes closed, aware of what was coming from the screams, praying it wasn't who he feared. A plea from Thomas sparked a response in Alfie; he heard the panic in Thomas's voice. A high-pitched squeal from Grace echoed as the orange intruder dragged her between the living room and hallway, standing in front of Teddy's lifeless body.

The pink intruder grabbed Alfie's face, forcing him to open his eyes and turn around. Alfie resisted.

"It'll be worse for her if you don't comply," the black-masked intruder warned. Alfie gave in, turning to Thomas first and mouthing, "I'm sorry," with no sound. He gritted his teeth, watching Grace struggle in the clutches of the orange intruder.

The pink intruder ambled over to the orange intruder, who was holding Grace captive. In her struggle, Grace received a slap from the pink intruder, causing her to freeze in fear. A distorted cackle merged from the pink intruder relishing in the helplessness of their victim. Placing a gloved finger over Grace's mouth, then a gloved finger to their mouthless mask the pink assailant made a shushing sound, taunting Grace with their power. Slowly sliding the blade of her knife inside Grace's mouth. Feeling the sharpness of the blade against her cheek, Grace froze, hoping to avoid injury. The pink intruder held the knife in such a way that any movement from Grace would cut the side of her face. Alfie didn't want to watch, diverting his eyes elsewhere, but Teddy's body was all that caught his sight. He fought the urge to surrender to the grief Teddy's death brought him.

From behind, the orange intruder plunged his knife into Grace's stomach. Quickly, the pink intruder withdrew the knife from Grace's mouth, cutting one side of her face creating a false smile. The orange intruder threw Grace to the floor, causing the pink intruder to tense up, revealing a fury in their body language, furious with the orange intruder for ruining their fun.

Thomas lunged forward, as Alfie grabbed a hold of him swiftly, understanding his reaction. Alfie felt guilty, knowing this was all his fault. Thomas struggled to get free, intent on a fight, but Alfie had no choice but to prevent his friend's death as long as possible. In that moment, a haunting thought dawned on Alfie: holding Thomas to the floor, he looked round at the intruders and his friends, knowing that if he survived, most of them were going to die. Thomas crawled on the floor, fighting for his freedom, as Alfie intensely held him down.

Whimpering on the floor, begging for her life, the pink intruder kneeled over Grace. Watching the tears fall from her eyes the pink intruder basked tilting their head so Grace could see her reflection.

"Please," Grace sobbed holding her wounds. The pink intruder revealed her bloodied hunting knife, wiping a tear on the tip of the blade. Looking at the side of Graces face with its faux smile.

"Smile pretty," distorted and cold the pink intruder ruthlessly plunged their blade repeatedly into Grace.

"No stop, stop!" Thomas screamed as he struggled under Alfie's restrain. Crying pitiful pleas his girlfriend's life. Forcefully whacking his head backwards, he caught Alfie on his chin, causing Alfie to loosen his hold. A stiff elbow into Alfie's chest, Thomas turned round pushing Alfie off him. Startled the pink intruder ceased her attack on Grace as they stood up alerted by Alfie and Thomas's struggle.

"This is all your fault!" Thomas screamed in Alfie's face, spitting saliva. Rushing over to Grace who was making a creaking noise as she breathed. The pink intruder raised their knife at Thomas but was deterred by the black masked intruder. Cradling Grace as he desperately apologized for not saving her, his white t-shirt soaking up her blood as he placed his hand on the side of her ripped open face. Devastated he begged to fight to stay alive as his eyes streamed tears.

The black masked intruder nudged their head at Thomas, indicating to the pink intruder to put him back with the others. As the pink intruder grabbed Thomas's arm to pull him away, he pushed them away from him. Quickly the orange intruder grabbed him by the scruff of the neck, as the pink intruder pointer their knife near his jugular, which forced him to begrudgingly move Grace's body slowly and lay her on the floor before the orange intruder marched him back with the others.

Alfie sat anxious thinking Thomas was going to attack and seal his fate, but he didn't. Pushing him into the group, Thomas sat back down as Lucy consoled him, trying to calm him down discreetly. Alfie and Lucy caught each other eye and they both silently conveyed an urgency to escape.

"Pick!" instructed the black-masked intruder suddenly, his disguised voice annoying Alfie as he looked at the gun pointed toward him. Visualising ways to get the gun out of the intruder's hand, but no route led to anyone surviving. Turning his head to his friends, Alfie looked at them all, this guilt increasing as he looked at their fearful expressions. He scanned them all pretending like he was going to choose, hoping that he could drag this out as long as possible. Catching Lucy's eye again then looking at Thomas's devastated face.

Catching his gaze at Lucy and Thomas, the black-masked intruder pointed his gun at Lucy. The orange intruder attempted to grab her, but she fought back fiercely. Falling onto her back, she power-kicked the orange intruder with both feet. Falling backwards, Alfie sharply seized him, pulling him on top of himself, one arm around his neck, the other holding his wrist to prevent the use of his weapon.

Rushing toward Lucy, the pink intruder plunged the knife downwards, just missing as Lucy pushed herself further back until she hit the living room wall underneath the window. Thomas and Alex sharply grabbed the pink intruder as they pulled their knife out of the wooden floor. Thomas spitefully grabbed and pulled their wrist, compelling the pink killer to drop the knife on the floor. Lucy made a leap for the knife as a loud gunshot fired amidst the chaos, startling everyone. Jennifer screamed, a high-pitched yelp...

Releasing the pink intruder, they quickly snatched their knife off the floor. Alex pushed his hand on Jennifer's shoulder, applying pressure to her shoulder, which had been penetrated by the bullet fired. Alfie still holding the orange intruder, his hold around their neck tightening to try and choke them to death. The black mask intruder pointed the gun at Alfie, indicating for Alfie to let the orange killer free. Alfie refused as he shuffled the orange intruder to cover him from any bullets fired. The pink intruder's mirrored eyes focusing on Lucy took slow steps towards her, seething for the kill.

In a panic, and seeing the intruders distracted, Ella seized the opportunity. Crawling along the floor, she aimed to escape. Her hands touched the floor between the living room and hallway as she propelled herself forward, her legs sprinting in a desperate bid for freedom. Another bullet flew through the room, hitting the living room wall, as the black mask intruder fired to stop Ella in her tracks. Panicked, the black mask intruder stepped near Alfie as he held the orange intruder. Kicking Alfie in the side of the head, jolting him to release the orange intruder.

"Get her!" The black mask intruder instructed in his distorted tone. The orange intruder quickly raced out of the house to catch the escapee.

Outside, Ella ran, sprinting as fast as she could, charging down the long path with her eyes fixed on the open gate. The orange intruder chased behind, clasping at the neck of her top, pulling her toward him. She screamed another blaring shriek, whacking her hand on his, freeing herself from the killer's grip, as she pushed her bare feet to slap against the ground faster.

"HELP ME!" she screeched, her voice filled with pain, calling out to the street, hoping someone would hear her as she neared freedom. The orange killer sped up and tackled her to the ground. Kicking her feet, she dug her fingers into the grass, desperate to escape the killer's grasp. The orange intruder grabbed her leg and pulled Ella back toward him. Squirming, her leg still kicking for freedom, the intruder rammed his knife into her calf. Another helpless scream escaped from her throat.

Aggressively flipping her around to face him, her terror-stricken reflection stared back at her. The orange intruder sat on top of her, pinning her to the floor. She attempted to scream again, but the intruder covered her mouth with their gloved hand. Ella bit down as hard as she could, forcing the intruder to remove their hand. Flinching away, Ella quickly grabbed the top of the intruder's mask, pulling it off and revealing their face.

"You!" she shrilled in shock, the intruder startled by Ella seeing their true identity panicked as the intruder intensely punched Ella knocking her head off the ground. Dropping the orange mask, the intruder sharply grabbed it placing it back over their face. Holding her bleeding nose Ella sobbed as she begged for her life.

The intruder hesitated knowing he couldn't take Ella back into the house alive, the intruder raised the knife over Ella readying themselves to make an impactful plunge. Shuffling her body Ella tried a doleful attempt to getaway. The intruder let Ella shuffle free, looking at the orange mask in shock as they remained on the floor kneeling. Standing up Ella turned around limping closer toward the open gate as the intruder suddenly sprang forward penetrating the knife from the back of Ella's neck. Rapidly pulling the knife out, the intruder watched as Ella fell to the floor, panting for her life. Standing over her the orange killer watched as her body began to convulse on the floor. Unable to watch her suffering the intruder rammed the knife into Ella's chest bursting her heart killing her instantly.

Back in the house, the other two intruders were unnerved. Ella attempting to escape wasn't part of the plan. Alfie watched the pink intruder first, noticing there was an eagerness to hunt and kill the escapee. The knife held tighter in their hand as they fidgeted. Lucy had scooted back to the others; she sat holding onto Thomas's wrist, trying to comfort him secretly. Her and Alfie's eyes kept meeting, Lucy's dark emerald eyes

176

widened, signalling to Alfie that they needed to think of something quick. The pressure was getting to Alfie; he knew that he had to act fast. Lucy was now in their sight as the next victim, and he couldn't let her die; he had to save the others.

Outside, the orange intruder stared over Ella's dead body, closing her petrified open eyes. He grabbed her legs, dragging her back inside the house. Back inside the house, he dragged her, dropping her legs between Teddy and Grace. Alfie glanced at the body, seeing all three lifeless. He sharply turned his head away. He couldn't allow himself to get caught up in the chaos he was burying inside. Turning his head, Alfie closed his eyes for a second, a second too long, as the intruders noticed he was hitting his breaking point.

The pink intruder walked toward Ella's body, taking in the art the orange intruder had created. The orange killer handed their knife to the pink intruder, stomping over to Alfie. Alfie tried to push the intruder away as the orange killer grabbed his wrist, pulling him up. Twisting Alfie's arm behind his back, the orange intruder grabbed Alfie by the vest's neck, marching him toward the three dead bodies. Alfie fought to get free as the intruder shoved him to the floor, falling onto Grace and Ella's corpses. His eyes instantly met Teddy's still and bloodied body, flashes penetrating his mind's eye as he relived seeing Teddy holding his throat and the blood gushing through his fingers. Pushing himself up, Alfie needed to get away from the bodies as he began to shake with anxiety. With their black boot firmly on his back, the orange intruder stamped on him, forcing him back to the ground.

"Look what you've done!" The distorted voice roared. Alfie looked away from Teddy, his eyes swaying to Ella. A rage began to burn inside him.

"Stop!" cried Lucy, unable to control the impulse to protect Alfie. Mirrored eyes reflected on her as she put her head down, terrified she'd now sealed her own fate. Handing the orange intruder their knife, the pink killer marched toward Lucy. Thomas shuffled, putting himself in Lucy's way. Hearing Lucy's voice, Alfie tried to get up, but the orange intruder placed his foot back on Alfie's back, holding him on top of Ella and Grace. As he listened to the footsteps getting closer to Lucy, he rolled his body to the side, pushing the orange killer out of his way. He jumped up, looking at Lucy.

"No!" Alfie shouted, a hint of anger flushing through. His shout distracted the pink intruder, who stopped as she stood opposite Teddy. Looking at Alfie, then to her colleagues, then back at Alfie.

"No, you tell me no?" the deep voice spoke, mocking him. "You want us to spare her because you care for her?" the pink intruder continued, edging forward to him. "Do your friends know of your actions?" questioning him, the room fell silent. The pink intruder walked closer to Alfie, grabbing him by the hair again, dragging him across the floor and pushing him into his friends. "Tell them what you've done!" The pink intruder demanded. Alfie took a deep breath, frustrated.

"What have I done?" Alfie questioned the intruder, wanting to know the connection and cause once and for all. He looked at the pink intruder, refusing to break his gaze.

"Tell them, tell us… It can end this, Alfie, just fucking tell them!" Alex erupted with panic as he pleaded with Alfie to do what they were saying. He didn't want to die, and he didn't want Jennifer to die either.

"It won't!" Alfie gritted through his teeth; his eyes still fixed on the pink intruder. Alex slowly stood up. His hands in the air cautiously showing his defencelessness.

"Look, I don't know what he's done, and Alfie, I'm sorry, but I can't risk this for you, especially when I don't know what I'm going to die because of. Jennifer is pregnant; she's only just found out she was pregnant. So please, please let us go. We were never here, we don't know anything about what happened here, please just let us go, please," Alex desperately threw Alfie under the bus as he tried to survive. The pink intruder let go of Alfie, pushing him backward. Turning to face Alex, the pink intruder tilted her hand in the air, gesturing for Jennifer to stand up. Jennifer slowly stood, standing next to Alex. Getting closer to them both, the pink intruder's mirrored eyes reflected each of them. Jennifer sensed danger, taking a slow step backward.

Abruptly, the pink intruder pushed Alex to the floor. Jennifer tried to run, but the pink killer pushed her into the wall. Colliding from behind, the pink intruder smashed her head harder into the wall. Alex attempted to jump up to save her, but the orange intruder rushed, pushing him back down as the orange killer kicked Alex in the face, stunning him on the floor. The pink intruder clenched her hand over Jennifer's shoulder, squeezing where the bullet had penetrated her flesh; Jennifer squealed louder than before. Indulging in Jennifer's tears of pain, the pink intruder stood still, savouring the ecstasy. Frightened, Jennifer began to pee on the floor, her body shaking from the severe pain. Releasing Jennifer's shoulder, the pink intruder wrapped their arm around her neck, pulling her into an embrace. Muttering something in her ear, the pink killer speared their hunting knife into Jennifer's stomach.

The pink intruder let Jennifer fall to the floor. Holding her belly and crying, the pink intruder walked away. Disoriented from head to foot, Alex crawled over to Jennifer as Alfie slid to Lucy and Thomas. The orange intruder attempted to separate Alfie from the group, but both Lucy and Alfie reacted swiftly. Lucy pushed the intruder, and Alfie swept his feet away. As Alfie and Lucy were making an escape attempt, a knock on the front door distracted everyone.

"Hello?" A man called from the door. "Is everything okay in here, Alfie?" he asked, his shadow large on the wall as he carefully stepped inside the house, instantly noticing the three dead bodies on the floor. The man gasped, taking shorter and cautious steps inside the house.

"What the fuck?" he exclaimed startled, as his shadow slowly began backing away. Noticing him leaving, the intruders panicked as the pink and orange killers tried to catch him stealthily. Alfie noticed the concentration on the black masked intruder as he aimed the gun, watching the other two. Carefully putting his hand up his jogger leg, he pulled the butterfly knife from the bandage. Slyly moving closer to the black balaclava intruder.

Dragging the man into the living room, the intruders stood him in full view of the living room, the black masked killer still aiming his gun. Sharply, Alfie stabbed the sharp steel into the intruder's thigh. Startled, the intruder fired the gun, knocking Emerson on the floor. Swiftly pulling the knife out of the killer's thigh, Alfie rapidly swept the invaders' feet off the ground, collapsing to the floor. Agilely, Alfie climbed atop the intruder. The room echoed with the scuffle of bodies colliding on the floor. Alfie, fuelled by urgency and determination, latched onto the intruder's gun-wielding hand trying to take it from him.

The pink intruder grunted with venom as she lunged forward to help her partner, readying to stab Alfie in the back. Lucy injected herself into the pink killer's lunge, tackling them to the floor. Struggling for the knife, their hands locked in a fierce battle for control. The orange intruder attempted to intervene as Alex grabbed the orange killer from behind and Thomas grabbed the intruder from the front, bending down to bite his wrist, forcing him to drop the knife. The orange intruder kicked Thomas away.

"Help!" Jennifer cried on the floor, hearing the commotion. Thomas caught a glimpse of her, hoping Alex didn't as the gash on his arm made his grip weak; he needed help holding the killer.

Wrestling on the floor, Alfie and the black masked intruder both holding onto the gun with an intense clutch. A bullet fired from the gun, traveling down the long living room. Alfie glared into his reflection as he looked the masked assailant in the eyes, slamming the side of his fist into their face.

Lucy, overpowered by the pink intruder, held the killer's knife at bay with her adrenaline and fear as she struggled to subdue the pink assailant. Thomas, leaving Alex to deal with the orange intruder, rushed to help Lucy, grabbing the pink intruder from behind and throwing them across the room.

Startled by Alfie's fist, Alfie overwhelmed the intruder but could not get the gun from their grip. Alfie began to crash the intruder's arm against the floor, trying to force them to let it go.

Helping Lucy off the floor, Thomas turned around as the pink killer ran toward him, plunging her knife into his shoulder. Lucy screamed, instantly reacting to Thomas being harmed. Pulling out the knife, Thomas fell onto the sofa. Rapidly, Lucy grabbed the pink intruder's knife-wielding hand, trying to wrest the knife from them. The pink intruder swiftly grabbed hold of Lucy's hair, yanking her head backward as she slowly edged the knife toward her throat.

Distracted by Lucy's scream, Alfie stopped struggling with the intruder for a second too long as the intruder returned his punch into the side of Alfie's face. Flinching slightly, Alfie loosened his grip on the gun as the intruder shoved him off. Jolting up, Alfie was still on the floor when the black masked intruder kicked him hard in the gut.

Another bullet fired in the house, causing everyone to pause. Seizing the moment while Lucy's hold weakened, the pink intruder got behind her, holding her at knife point. The intruder kicked Alfie again, but he reacted swiftly, sweeping the intruder's legs away once more and stamping on their face. Releasing the gun, Alfie kicked it away from the intruder, and it glided under the sofa.

"Stop!" an aggressive distortion roared. Alfie looked in its direction, seeing Lucy held helplessly. Alex released the orange intruder, who pushed Alex to the floor. Thomas slanted on the sofa, holding his arm and shaking from the pain.

"Can't say we didn't expect this?" deep and distorted, the black mask intruder said. Alfie heard a slight hint of the killer's real voice as he kicked him. Grabbing Alfie by the back of the vest, the intruder pulled him up, unveiling a knife identical to the other two intruders' weapons. Standing behind him, the intruder placed the knife to Alfie's throat. Alfie and Lucy both helpless, gave each other looks of apologies. Alfie took a quick scan of the room, noticing Thomas bleeding, desperately wanting to check if he was okay. Alex was now with Jennifer, holding her hand as she cried. Darting his eyes to the dead bodies in the living room and at Emerson not moving.

He looked at his friends with remorse, knowing he was the reason they were going to die. He felt bad for suspecting them; he felt worse that they didn't know the reason why they were all going to die. Alfie closed his eyes for a moment, asking for forgiveness in his head.

From a distance, sirens sang, growing closer and closer. Suddenly, blue lights began flickering, brightening up the night sky. The sirens got louder as they turned into the front gate of his house. The room froze, as an instant relief filled Alfie until he realized what desperation in these killers might mean.

Chapter 9

Lucy's eyes were intense on Alfie as the pink intruder's knife drew closer to her throat. Alfie's palms were sweating as he deliberated ways to survive. His eyes darted to the window as the blue lights from police cars beamed up his driveway, getting brighter as a single car approached. With the brightening police lights, Alfie began to panic, less police were not a threat to these murderous animals. His mind racing as his sight swayed between his friends wondering who would live to tell the tale.

The pink intruder hurled Lucy to the floor opposite where Thomas sat on the sofa. Leaning over the sofa Lucy check over Thomas assuring his injury wasn't fatal. Rushing the pink intruder grabbed Alex by the scruff of the neck pulling him away from Jennifer. Alex tried to fight to stay but was swayed by the cold wet blade to his neck. Shuffling over Alex sat next to Lucy his eyes fixed on Jennifer , his heart racing as he watched the intruder hovering near her. Jennifer's whimpering cries were a risk of exposure which unsettled them all.

"Get rid of them!" demanded the black-masked intruder, balancing the blade under Alfie's chin, pushing his masqueraded face into the side of Alfie's.

A knock on the door; the intruder looked through the window checking that the police weren't looking inside the house. Knife to Alfie's throat marching him through the living room to the hallway, muttering threats of motivation to make Alfie do as he was told. The black masked invader pushed Alfie toward the door, as they positioned themselves behind the door, close enough to make sure Alfie didn't try anything.

Alfie opened the door at a slant, revealing only his body to the officer. The police officers looked him up and down, as Alfie smiled at them.

"Evening officer's how can I help you?" Alfie asked with a fake smile, he was trying everything he could to remain composed, so the other two intruders didn't hurt the others.

"We had a call from a Ms. Sayers reporting a disturbance at this address," spoke the first policeman, standing muscular and tall, strong lines on his jaw moving as he spoke.

"A disturbance?" Alfie questioned, his gaze switching between the two officers. The second police officer noticed Alfie's stiffness, raising suspicion. Keeping his eye on the second officer, who looked at him suspiciously, Alfie inspected his shaved head, small questioning eyes, and athletic shape, hoping he'd be the one. "There's no Ms. Sayers here, officer," Alfie continued, as the officers looked at each other. His posture awkward, subtly he moved his eyes toward the door, trying to signal to the officer.

"Could you tell me why there's a trail of blood leading up to your door?" the second police officer interjected before the first police officer could ask his next question. Alfie's eyes moved from the door, catching the dark red blood trail on the concrete. Alfie's heart began to pound as he felt the intruder touch his hand on the back of the door to remind him that he was still there.

"You're going to have to come with us down to the station," the second police officer instructed as he leaned forward to pull Alfie out of the house.

"I can't do that?" Alfie replied, as he shifted backwards resisting the officer. Exasperated Alfie knew he couldn't leave the house, he couldn't risk his friends or family in the panic room.

"Is there a reason you can't come with us?" the first police officer responded looking at Alfie with less interrogation. The mask intruder pressed harder on Alfie's hand motivating Alfie to lie.

"My son's upstairs, and there's no one else here to look after him," Alfie replied staggered as he looked at the police officers with desperation.

"You can bring your son with you, and we'll get someone to pick him up from the station for you," the second police officer replied with a stern, assuming voice. Knowing where this was heading, Alfie could feel a tightness in his neck and chest. Through gritted teeth, he forced himself to breathe, his mind racing, overthinking every scenario that could unfold. He had only one choice if he wasn't to succumb to the pressured anxiety fighting for freedom.

The second police officer grabbed Alfie by the shoulder with a hard pull, trying to get him out of the house. In an explosive outburst of disquiet, Alfie kicked the second officer with intent, knocking him backwards and causing him to fall to the floor. The first police officer tried to grab him, but Alfie kicked him backwards too. In a desperate, explosive outburst, Alfie released his hand from the door's corner. He threw all of his body weight into the front door, causing it to swing backwards and collide into the hidden intruder.

Aggressively, Alfie grabbed the side of the door again, repeatedly shoving it backwards into the intruder, who had dropped their weapon. In the depths of desperation, Alfie forced the door into the intruder with intense aggression, delivering vigorous attacks. The intruder grunted as a crack formed in the back of the door. Dropping to the floor, the intruder tried to push their knees in front of them to prevent getting hit in the face.

Both police officers stood up from the floor, grabbing Alfie by his arm and the back of his vest. The second police officer threw him on the floor outside, restraining Alfie while looking inside the house. The sight of the three bloodied bodies and Emerson caught his eye instantly. The first police officer took hold of Alfie as the second pulled out his gun, edging inside the house.

"You idiots, you fucking idiots!" Alfie screamed, struggling to free himself as the first police officer put a handcuff on his right wrist. Shifting his left arm, refusing to be bound, Alfie took a quick look as the officer paced deeper into the house. "They're going to die, get off me, you've killed them!" Alfie shouted hysterically, fighting the first officer's grasp.

Approaching the bodies, the second officer aimed his gun as he turned his focus into the living room. "Drop the weapons!" The police officer shouted, aiming at the pink and orange intruder. The first police officer looked away from Alfie, pausing for a second as he saw the other policeman.

"Behind you!" Alfie shouted in warning as the second police officer turned around, the black masked intruder in his shadow, plunging the knife into the second police officer. The first police officer let Alfie free as he watched the black masked killer savagely attack his partner. A gunshot erupted as the second officer tried to shoot the intruder. Another impactful blow from the intruder's knife caused the policeman to drop the gun.

Outside, the police officer pulled out his own gun, holding it steady as he headed toward the house, aiming. Alfie quickly jumped up, yanking the police officer away as the black mask intruder picked up the police man's gun, firing at the first officer. Firing his gun blindly, the officer aimed inside the house; the black masked killer jumped back into the living room, taking cover. As Alfie and the police officer hid at the side of the door outside.

"How many are inside the house?" the officer asked Alfie in a panicked breath.

"There's three killers, four still alive but two injured and four dead, there's another three hidden in a panic room, my son, mother and my fiancé," Alfie explained fast as he put emphasis on the people upstairs.

The police officer looked at Alfie, who raised his aim gesturing the handcuff on his wrist. The officer handed him the key, letting him free himself. Unlocking the bracelet, the officer peered round taking aim inside the house, but the black masked intruder fired first. Jumping back, the officer knocked the key and handcuffs out of Alfie's hand.

"I need to radio for back up but I can't get to the car," The police officer explained, looking at his car right opposite the open door.

Inside the house, the black masked killer listened intently for movement from the outside, holding the gun ready to fire and kill the burden that had interrupted their night. Lucy squeezed Thomas's leg as she watched the pink and orange masked intruder watching their partner. The pink intruder stood at the front of the sofa as the orange stood closer to the hostages. Alex, keeping his focus on Jennifer, deliberated how he would get to her and get her out of the house.

Lucy started to feel agitated; she couldn't just sit here helpless waiting for someone to rescue her. Turning her head slightly, she looked at the orange killer, disguising her sizing with her hair over her face. Placing her palm on the wooden floor, pressing down to test if it was squeaky. Taking her time, she moved her eyes around the room, watching all three intruders in her sight. Leaning her head onto Thomas's leg, one hand holding him, the other feeling underneath the sofa. Feeling the cold metal touch her fingers, she slowly pulled it with her fingertips closer to her, pacing to not make a sound.

Catching a glimpse of Lucy, the orange intruder, suspicious of her, tapped her with their foot. Panicked, Lucy quickly pulled the gun into the palm of her hand, clutching it with a tight hold. Leaning her hand under the sofa, keeping the gun out of sight; she turned, looking up at the orange mask. Noticing her hand under the chair, the intruder tilted their head to get a better look. Fixed eyes scurried at the distance in the room from the sofa to the living room's door to enter the kitchen. Impulses surging, Lucy looked around the room one last time, with only the orange intruder in her way squeezed the gun, pulling it from under the sofa quickly, as she whacked it into the orange intruder's groin. Dropping their knife, Lucy shoved it across the room as she jumped up, running for her life through the living room, barging into the kitchen.

Her escape hadn't gone unnoticed as the pink intruder caught the sound of Lucy's footsteps.

Inside the dark kitchen, Lucy sneaked around, as she peered through the kitchen's main door seeing the legs of Teddy's body, snappily she debated to take a shot at the intruder. Hearing footsteps in the living room, Lucy with meticulous steps made her way to the garden door. Amplified by survival, she pulled the door handle down slowly, avoiding any clicking noises to draw attention. The stomping feet were approaching louder as the door unlocked. The night's breeze hit her face as she swallowed the fresh air which tasted like freedom.

Rushing into the kitchen, the pink intruder saw the garden door wide open. In a fit of rage, the pink killer tightened their grip around their knife as they sought their next victim.

Inside the house, Alex rushed to Jennifer's side, holding her hand, and using his other hand to hold her stomach. He reassured her that everything would be okay. The orange intruder stood at a distance, knife in hand, not knowing what to do next. Thomas remained on the sofa, holding his shoulder that was still seeping blood.

In lightning speed, Lucy ran around to the right side of the house, her feet slapping against the grass. Passing the dining room, another eruption from a gun rumbled. Lucy dived to the floor, taking cover on her stomach as she crawled along the house, using the walls as her guide. Twisting around the corner of the house, she felt relieved to see Alfie and the policeman.

"Alfie," she panted, breathless from her escape. Startled, Alfie turned around in defence. Lucy kneeled up as she moved closer to him. "It's me, calm down," she whispered in heavy breaths as she put her hand on his fist.

"How'd you get out of there?" Alfie asked in a whisper, looking over her to check for injuries.

"I took a chance and ran," Lucy replied, showing Alfie the gun she had collected from the living room. Seeing the weapon that matched that of the invaders, Alfie grabbed it from Lucy's hand, tapping the police officer who was covering.

"I've got this, keep him distracted. I'm going to catch him from the side," Alfie explained. The police officer didn't like the plan; he had questions, but Alfie hadn't given him a chance to reply as he crept around the house.

Stopping underneath the dining room window, Alfie peeked up, catching the black-masked intruder in the hallway, awaiting the officer to get in their view. Taking a shot, the window smashed, shattering shards inside and out of the house. The intruder moved forward as they fired a shot at the same time. Removing themselves from the line of Alfie's fire, the intruder turned their attention to the dining room. Alfie peered his head, taking a look at the intruder's location as a shot fired just missing Alfie as he ducked. Blindly firing in their direction, the intruder retreated into the living room for cover.

Alfie shuffled back to the front of the house, a plan in motion. Tapping Lucy on the shoulder, she was covered in blood. Looking behind her, the police officer was no longer in position, now slouched on the floor, lifeless with a bullet in his face, unrecognizable.

Gawping into the officer's disfigured face, Alfie felt a burden of guilt. He hadn't even known the officer's name, and he died for him. Shaking off the regret, Alfie removed the gun from the officer's hand, passing it to Lucy. Directing her to follow him, hunched over, they shimmied around the house undetected. Passing the smashed dining room window, they stood up, making their way into the garden. The kitchen door still wide open, they sneaked back inside the house, pointing to his mouth and tilting his head to Lucy's gun. Alfie gave her an unspoken instruction to fire as soon as they see the killers. Aiming their guns, they both burst into the living room from the kitchen, catching the black-masked intruder off guard. Both fired three rounds in sync as the intruder made his escape back into the hallway, falling on Emerson, who shrieked from being awoken. The black-masked intruder made a hasty exit from the house.

Cautiously inspecting the room, Alfie stepped slowly deeper into the living room, his heart pounding with anticipation, his eyes focused on the potential threat. Lucy followed behind as

Alfie, oblivious to his friends around him, scanned the hallway and quickly closed the door. Emerson lay on the floor with eyes open, Alfie offered a hand to pull him up. Lucy gasped in horror as she noticed Alex cradled over Jennifer, blood leaking on the floor. Alfie walked back into the living room, looking at Lucy, who stood stiff. Turning his head at Alfie, Alex took a step toward him.

"Get away from her, this is your fault!" Alex cried with rage. Alfie noticed the blood over his clothes and face.

"What happened?" Lucy asked, distraught, as she took a step closer to him.

"What happened? When they realized you were gone, the pink one went to look for you… when the pink one came back, the orange one held a knife to my throat, hand over my mouth, and made me watch as the pink one tortured her! Look at what they've done," Alex spat fury and blame as he stood up revealing the carnage inflicted on her. "This is your fault… both of yours!" Alex shouted, looking at Lucy, who flinched, then at Alfie, who remained motionless.

"Where did they go?" Alfie asked, ignoring Alex's pain. He couldn't get emotional; he knew where that would lead him.

"I don't know... My girlfriend, who's carrying my baby, is dead! BECAUSE OF YOU! I didn't exactly ask them where they were running to," Alex shouted agitatedly, his glazed eyes burning through Alfie. Intoxicated with anger and loss, Alex ran at Alfie. Lucy jumped forward to prevent it but was pushed aside, as Alex threw a punch in Alfie's direction. Grabbing Alex's wrist, preventing a connection, Alfie pushed him to the floor.

"I'm sorry Jennifer's dead, I really am! But we do not have time to deal with how you're feeling about it!" Alfie asserted aggressively, firm in his stance. Bending down, Alfie placed the gun into Alex's cheek. "I didn't want this, any of it, so I'm going to make this simple: if you want to dwell on the now and blame me, I'll put a bullet in your head now. Or, if you want to survive, then you can blame me when this is all over, so swallow your feelings and fight, or take a bullet in the head and join the others we've lost tonight," Alfie continued, his words laden with frustration and aggression. Lucy looked at Alfie in shock; she'd never seen him act so coldly.

"I want to live," Alex said, fragile, taking the gun away from his face. Alfie stood up and walked over to Thomas, checking him over before helping him up from the sofa. Lucy walked over to Alex, helping him up off the floor. Alfie's eyes flashed to Emerson, who stood idly in the living room.

"Why did you come over here?" interrogated Alfie, analysing Emerson.

"I heard screaming, I wanted to check if you were all okay," Emerson replied with hesitation, caught off guard by Alfie's inquisition.

"So, you see the gate wide open, a van in the front, possibly blood on the floor outside, and you must have seen the dead bodies on the floor with the door wide open, and you still chose to come inside?" Alfie continued investigating, scrutinizing every ounce of Emerson's body language, which became fidgety.

"Me and Alice were woken up by the screaming. After the argument at the pool, I thought there might have been another argument or a fight, so I came to check if everything was alright," Emerson replied firmly, feeling his uneasiness taking over. "Where's Alice?" asked Alfie, easing his pressured interrogation.

"She's at home," Emerson replied with a slight pause before continuing, "Shit, I left the gate open." Making a run for the door, Alfie quickly gave chase grabbing him, preventing him from leaving.

"You're not going anywhere, walking out there you're risking your life," Alfie explained,

Emerson's reaction put Alfie at ease for a moment seeing the desperation to get back to Alice convinced his suspecting mind.

"There's a dead police officer on the floor, and you're interrogating me like I'm a suspect... so my guess is leaving my gate open with my wife home alone puts her in danger," Emerson replied, trying to push past Alfie pushing him back. Lucy, Thomas, and Alex walked into the hallway.

"You can't leave now. You could put Alice's life in more danger by going that way," cold and hostile, Alfie replied as he walked past him. Thomas's head turned looking at Grace as tears fell from his eyes. Seeing the sadness in Thomas's face gave Alfie even more guilt. Emerson attempted to leave the house again, but Lucy clicked the gun in her hand, making him stop in his tracks.

"Everyone follow me upstairs," Alfie instructed as he began walking up the stairs. On the first floor, Thomas, Alex, and Emerson waited in the hallway, while Alfie and Lucy thoroughly scanned each room, ensuring there were no lurking intruders.

As they explored the three bedrooms, the aftermath of chaos unfolded in one—a bed overturned, clothes scattered. The second bedroom remained untouched, an island of calm in the storm, while the third mirrored the serenity. The luxurious bathroom held no shadows or threats.

Their search led them to Alfie's office, a space cluttered with boxes stacked at the front of the desk. A subtle gasp ruptured the silence as Alfie kicked one of the boxes, prompting both him and Lucy to tense. Communicating silently with a gesture, Alfie directed Lucy to stand guard as he cautiously maneuverer around the side of the desk. Pushing it forward, he backed up, gun at the ready.

A low, desperate voice shattered the tension. "Please don't shoot!" cried Ben. Alfie, still poised, lowered his gun, exchanging a perplexed glance with Lucy, who mirrored his confusion gave him a questioning look.

"What are you doing in here?" Alfie asked, gun midway between his legs but ready to aim and fire.

"I ran in here when Thomas said someone had broken in," Ben confessed sheepishly. "After the photos and everything earlier, I… I just didn't want to die," he confessed embarrassed for abandoning them.

Alfie lowered the gun, looking back at Lucy; both still holding suspicion. Helping Ben stand up, he took him outside with the others. Ben, unnerved by the blood covering Thomas and Alex took a nervous gulp.

"Where are the others?" Ben asked cautiously, looking at them all, but none of them responded.

"Dead!" Alfie spoke coldly, deflecting all the inner turmoil fighting to escape. "We need to get upstairs," he said softer as he began walking up to the second floor. Repeating their checks from the first floor, they examined all the rooms except the attic and Alfie's room. Lucy had grabbed her phone from the room she had been in. All was clear and empty. Heading inside Alfie's bedroom, Alfie noticed Charley's phone on the bed. Bending over the bed, he grabbed it and put it in his pocket.

Alfie's mother swung open the panic room door upon spotting them on the camera footage entering the room. They filed in, except for Alfie, who halted his mother at the door.

"Who was or is it?" Asked his mother in a whisper. Alfie shrugged his shoulders shaking his head still in the unknown.

"Do you still have that knife?" he whispered. She nodded, a puzzled look on her face. "Be on guard. I still don't trust any of them," he continued, briefly filling his mother in on what had happened. Moving aside for Alfie to come inside the safety room, Alfie shook his head, showing his mother the gun. "I'm going to get those bastards and end this!" he told his mother, stepping backwards.

"Oi, Sayers! Where are you going?" Lucy spoke up, annoyance evident, the panic room door closing behind her.

"Lucy, just stay in there and keep them safe, please," Alfie pleaded with irritation.

"No, as I said before, I'm with you on this!" Lucy declared, her annoyance rising. Walking back downstairs, Lucy by his side, they were silently cautious for the intruders. In the silence, Alfie reflected on Lucy's friendship, the loyalty she gave him with no questions. He knew she was a true friend, but the past few hours amplified it.

Downstairs, both waved their weapons around, ready to shoot at first sight. Avoiding facing their friends' corpses, they carefully walked into the kitchen. Alfie checked the large cupboards in the kitchen before both of them went outside, extra cautious as they paced through the garden. Stopping by the pool, Lucy turned to Alfie.

"The one in the black mask—he just ran away, but he had a gun too, and the other two had already gone. Do you think they just gave up; they're gone?" Lucy asked, puzzled as her eyes narrowed on Alfie's.

"I don't know," Alfie confessed as he continued, "But they've gone to all this work to get me, and now they're gone, and on the whole— Ivy's missing, Ben was hiding in the best hiding place—conveniently, Emerson walking into the house, Charley seems offish with me since last night. I'm not sure who I can trust apart from you, my mother, and Thomas... now," Alfie confessed, finally letting some of his burdens out.

"Ivy's just a bitch. They probably didn't know Ben was in the house. Charley might just be in shock," Lucy replied, trying to ease his suspicious mind. "Alfie, I know you. There's more to this than you're letting on. Who did you kill?" she asked. Just before Alfie could reply, the pink intruder, knife gleaming with menace, sprinted toward Lucy. She fired the gun, missing, as the intruder came closer. The world blurred as Lucy, on impulse, dropped her firearm to the ground, grabbing hold of the killer's arm before the knife could penetrate her chest. The assailant, vicious and determined to deliver a fatal blow, pressed with all their might, but Lucy refused to succumb to the killer's will. As the struggle ensued, Lucy took a step backward, trying to redirect the path of the knife. Standing on the precipice of the pool, Lucy could feel the water hitting her heel.

Swiftly aiming his weapon, Alfie tried to get a steady shot of the pink killer. He was unable to get a clear shot as the pink killer and Lucy danced around in front of him. Intently watching as Lucy approached the edge of the pool, Alfie fired as the two splashed to the bottom. Unsure if he had hit the killer, he lowered his gun and moved to the edge of the pool.

Sinking to the swimming pool's depth, Lucy refused to release her hold on the pink killer's knife-wielding hand. Kicking her feet off the watery ground, Lucy repositioned herself, so she was above the killer. The impact reverberated through the water, sending ripples to the surface. Alfie aimed his gun, trying to get a clear shot through the shaky water.

Hovering in the water, Lucy pulled her body closer to the pink killer, leaning into their arm. She clenched her teeth into the killer's arm, swallowing water as she bit down as hard as possible. Lucy held on until the intruder dropped the knife. Watching the knife fall and submerge to the marble floor, Lucy swam to the surface to catch her breath.

Coughing and spitting water out of her mouth, then taking a deep breath, Alfie ran around the pool, attempting to get close enough to pull her out. With a grip on her leg, Lucy was pulled beneath the water. As she struggled, the pink killer ascended to the surface. Alfie, resolute, aimed his gun, but the shifting aquatic battleground defied his precision. The pink killer then descended back into the pool, holding Lucy under them.

Momentarily ceasing her strain, Lucy relaxed her body, conserving her precious breath. Reaching her hand up, she grabbed the intruder's wrist, pulling the killer down as deep as she could. Catching the killer off guard, they went into a panic as they fought for release. Rotating to position the pink murderer beneath her, Lucy released the intruder's wrist, maintaining a firm hold on the intruder as she ascended back to the surface.

Pushing the killer underneath her, Lucy wrapped her legs around their neck. Swallowing a fresh breath, she placed her hand on the intruder's head, holding the killer underwater. Thrashing wildly beneath Lucy's crushing hold, water splashed, leaving puddles on the poolside. Holding her breath, Lucy pushed her body down to sink the pink intruder deeper, waves of desperate attempts at freedom rippling over the pool.

Feeling the intruder's body lighten, Lucy kicked them deeper as she swam over to Alfie, who helped her out of the pool. Breathless and panting, Alfie handed her the gun she had dropped.

"Are you okay?" Alfie asked, concerned, as he looked over Lucy for any wounds.

"Yeah, I'm good, just need to catch my breath properly," Lucy replied, panting, as she turned to see the pink killer floating in the pool. Alfie's eyes were fixed on the killer's body, eager to find out their identity.

"We need to see who that is," Alfie stated, not taking his eyes away from the disguised body. He felt a rush of relief knowing one of them was dead.

"They're not going anywhere; let's just get the others first!" Lucy replied, still breathless, twisting her white t-shirt top to get the water off her as much as possible. Scrunching up the legs of her navy shorts, Lucy looked at Alfie, who was fixed on the killer; she could see his eagerness to unmask them. There was a moment of silence as Lucy thought to herself.

"Alfie, I've got a plan. You won't like it, and it's probably going to be really stupid, but I think it'll work," Lucy said, her face serious, with stubbornness in her voice. Taking his eyes away from the killer, Alfie looked at her, without saying a word. Lucy could see on his face that he was waiting for her to tell him.

"We don't know where the orange one went, but we know that the one in the black mask went out the front. Your neighbour was worried about his wife, so let me out the back here, and I'll go over there. One, we can make sure she's safe; two, if he is in the house, we can corner him and kill him, or if they are both over there, we can still corner and kill them," Lucy explained as Alfie instantly refused to let her fly solo.

"It's stupid to split up, it puts your life in danger, and I don't want you to die," Alfie replied, anxious about what could happen to her.

"Look, the gate's there, just let me out and go back to the panic room, and I'll call you when I'm there. It's the best plan we have right now, and yes, it is stupid to split up, but it's also smart because they won't expect it," Lucy stated, determined to make Alfie agree. Walking away from Alfie toward the garden exit gate, Alfie didn't like her plan, fueling him with worry as he played different scenarios of how this could play out in his head. Turning around, he watched as Lucy uncovered the spare set of keys hidden in the false brick. Lucy began to open the gate as Alfie rushed to stop her.

"I don't want to risk you," Alfie confessed, just as Lucy was making her way out of the gate.

"I'm not risking me, just go wait for my call," Lucy replied, disappearing through the gate.

Sighing with an anxious breath, Alfie shut the gate, leaving it unlocked. His brain was erratic, hoping he hadn't just let Lucy walk into a trap, guilting himself that he should have gone with her. Pacing with caution back through the garden, Alfie's heart began to race fast as he gazed upon the pool; the pink killer was gone! Carefully, as he made his way back to the house, his ears listening intensely, his eyes focused vividly on every detail around him.

Back inside the house, he was wary as he entered every room. Closing the kitchen garden door first, he locked it so no one could get inside. Gun aimed, he looked through the hallway, closing the first kitchen door. Using the door between the kitchen and the living room, Alfie entered inside, closing the door behind him.

Startled with disgust and an ice-cold chill as he stood at the end of the living room. Staring down toward the big window with the view of the front of the house, Jennifer, Ella, and Grace's bodies had been positioned underneath the window so they were sitting upright, staring at him.

He was vigilant as he strode through the room, his weapon aimed and ready to fire. He avoided looking at the three dead girls but could feel them watching him as he strode through the living room. Diverting his gaze away from the bodies, he faced the hallway; Teddy and the police officer were left as they were. Alone and catching sight of Teddy, tears silently fell from his eyes. He was angry, and he was sad, which for Alfie was a deadly combination. The ground floor of the house was clear, so he made his way up the rest of the house until he was back in his bedroom. His mother already had the panic room door open, having seen him in the hallways on the CCTV.

Inside the panic room, his eyes darted to Oscar, who was asleep. He looked at Charley sitting with him, giving her a smile which she turned her head away from. Bulldozer jumped off the bed, running over to Alfie, sniffing him. Thomas stood up from the long chair near the CCTV, his arm and shoulder bandaged up by Alfie's mother. Alfie went and sat next to him, Bulldozer sitting by his feet.

"Where's Lucy?" Thomas asked, with a look of worry on his face. Alfie banged his head on the soft cushioning of the chair as he explained Lucy's plan to him. Alex, who had been sitting on the floor against the wall with Emerson and Ben, stood, walking over to Alfie with a passive posture. He kneeled opposite Alfie, apologizing for what had happened downstairs.

"It's fine, Alex, I get it. I would have been the same, and I'm sorry, and you were right, this is all my fault," Alfie replied understandingly as he tried to make amends.

"No, Alfie, it's not, but you do have to tell us what this is all over or what you think it might be over because I need to know why they killed my girlfriend and baby. I want to help you kill them, but we all deserve to know the truth now, we've all lost something tonight!" Alex continued, looking Alfie in the eye. Knowing he was right, Alfie looked over to his mother who nodded her head, giving him the freedom to release the burden.

"Fine," Alfie replied as everyone's eyes fell on him.

Chapter 10

In the depths of winter, rain tapped against a small-framed window. Thirteen-year-old Alfie Sayers sat alert on a younger boy's bed, gazing through the open door into the hallway, fixating on the towel cupboard door opposite. The echoes of shouts emanated from the stairs below. Surveying his bedroom, Alfie discovered a Walkman cassette player and a headset. Placing the headphones over the younger boy's head, he pressed play on the cassette, witnessing the calming effect of the music on him. Leaving him alone, Alfie stepped into the hallway, then proceeded into the carpeted living room. The shouting downstairs grew louder, prompting Alfie to descend the stairs discreetly, hiding from the view of the front door, and eavesdropped on the escalating argument.

"Fuck off!" his mother's anger punched through the air, a chilling prelude to the thunderous slap that resonated through the hallway. Alfie advanced, his young hazel eyes widening at the sight of a distinct handprint etched on the bearded man's face. The assailant's baseball cap tumbled to the floor, revealing his brown shaved head. Ignoring Alfie's presence, the man swiftly seized Alfie's mother by the throat, a tight grip forcing her against the wall.

"Get out now!" Alfie warned with false confidence, staring defiantly at the man. Unfazed by Alfie's words, the man's anger showed no signs of subsiding. After pushing Alfie's mother against the wall, he picked up his cap and walked out of the house.

Quickly, Alfie's mother locked the door, shooing Alfie back upstairs before rushing into the kitchen and securing the window. Alfie lingered, watching his mother, who seemed visibly shaken by the man's aggressive reaction.

Turning toward the kitchen door, Alfie's mother instructed him to go back upstairs as she rushed around the house, securing all windows downstairs. Alfie's mind was racing with the revelation he'd discovered in the adults' argument, burdening his little head.

Alfie took the headphones off the young boy, placing them on the chest of drawers. Walking over to the bedroom window, Alfie watched the rain slapping against the glass. His mother, now in the living room, was on the phone. Alfie could hear her talking, explaining the conflict, catching only snippets of the conversation. He was too shocked from what he'd discovered downstairs to really take anything else in.

Staring at the boy in bed, Alfie hoped he had eased his anxiety from the conflict. As he remembered what that childhood worry was like inside, he was still scared, but he was getting older. He couldn't show that; he had to stand up to his fears. Alfie laid down in his bed, closing his eyes. He listened to his mother still bitching and complaining on the phone. Tuning the world around him out of his hearing, he focused on the rain to clear his mind until he drifted asleep.

Awakening in the early hours of the morning at 2:11 am, the house was still. Getting out of bed, Alfie paced across the passage, glancing into the living room. His mother was fast asleep on the sofa. Walking past the living room, he headed toward the towel cupboard and entered the bathroom. After using the bathroom, he flushed and washed his hands. Feeling thirsty, he went downstairs into the kitchen, pouring himself a glass of water. Placing the glass on the sink when finished, he took a quick glance into the downstairs bedroom before starting to walk back upstairs to go to bed.

The disconcerting sound of wood snapping echoed through the confined space of the small home, a grim symphony of destruction. Aggressive strikes reverberated throughout the house as the security of the house was slowly dismantling with each pounding strike.

The noise abruptly stopped, freezing Alfie midway on the stairway as he swiftly turned to head back downstairs, feeling the vibrations of the attack on the door. Sprinting up the stairs, Alfie collided with a man, pale-faced with dark blonde hair, rushing out of the living room. Alfie fell to the floor, looking up at the man who shot past him and headed downstairs. Swiftly regaining his feet, Alfie observed his mother's erratic movements as she pulled a baseball bat from the side of the sofa, ready for the looming fight. With urgency, Alfie rushed back into his bedroom.

"Oscar, wake up!" Alfie said in a low voice, trying not to awaken the boy in a panic. He shook his younger brother, attempting to rouse him. Young Oscar didn't stir, so Alfie carefully lifted him out of bed, gently placing him under the bed. Surveying the room, Alfie began to arrange objects in front of the bed, creating a cluttered appearance to deter anyone from looking underneath.

Loud strikes, akin to crashing blows below, relentlessly battered the wooden door that had once stood as a barrier of protection for the occupants. The pounding bore the weight of aggression, a relentless force seeking entry. With each successive strike, the door trembled under the ferocious assault, its structural integrity pushed to the brink. Every strike was fierce, growing more savage, leaving no room for doubt about the intruder's determination.

The first lock succumbed to the relentless onslaught, shattering into fractured pieces that littered the floor like broken promises. The metallic clang as it hit the ground mingled with the haunting echoes of each strike.

As the man got downstairs, a collision was heard, with aggressive grunts from two men roaring. The sound of wood snapping and glass smashing filled the house as chaos escalated downstairs. Alfie rushed through the hallway, seeing his mother armed with a baseball bat ready for a fight. He ran toward the bathroom, hiding inside the towel cupboard.

Listening intently, Alfie focused on the scuffle in the living room. He urged himself to be brave and help, but a crushing worry held him back. Footsteps pounded against the stairs as someone began to ascend. Alfie hoped it was the pale-faced blonde-haired man. Peering through the holes of a vent in the door, he watched as the man his mother had earlier altercation with stood gazing into the living room. Alfie could feel his body beginning to shake as he continued to listen. He heard the man grunt as his mother swung the bat, inflicting pain, but then the sound of the bat dropping on the floor. His mother screamed as a deafening slap echoed. Fearfully,

Alfie shifted his gaze into his bedroom, hoping his little brother hadn't awoken and moved the objects he'd placed to hide him.

"What is he doing here?" Disgruntled, the man shouted, sending worry through Alfie's veins as he heard the sound of his mother's helpless pleas. Another loud thump resounded through the house, causing Alfie to flinch as he heard the sound of someone falling to the floor.

Peeping through the vent, Alfie watched the man searching, going into his bedroom. His heart pounded as he placed his hand over his mouth to prevent the sound of his panicked breathing from revealing his hiding place. Observing the man standing near Oscar's bed, his heart pounded even harder. Frustrated, the man stormed out of the bedroom, prowling through the hallway, heading toward the bathroom. Alfie could smell his sweaty odour as he got closer to the towel cupboard, holding his breath to avoid making any sound that might reveal his location. He sensed the man linger before he disappeared downstairs.

Hesitating, Alfie debated leaving his safe space to check on his mother and brother. His heart pounded so fast that he could feel it against the bones of his chest. Placing his palm on the door, he hesitated to push it open; he knew he needed to get to the landline and call for help, but his body was frozen, not allowing him to push his way out.

Gritting his teeth, Alfie took a deep breath, finally leaving his hiding space. He tiptoed through the passage as he heard the man walking around downstairs. Creeping into the living room, he saw his mother lying on the floor, out cold. Bending down, the floor creaked as he touched her face. She was okay, just knocked out. Alfie sharply got up, rushing to the house phone. Picking it up, Alfie dialled a number.

"Alfie!!!" A deep, penetrating voice roared aggressively, its resonance echoing through the corridors. Turning his head, Alfie locked eyes with the man, his small frame trembling under the weight of intense fear. In that moment, the air seemed to thicken with oppressive terror that clung to him.

"Drop the phone!" instructed the man forcefully. Alfie's breaths became rapid, each inhale a struggle against the suffocating grip of panic. The man's eyes bore into Alfie's, an abyss of menace that sent shivers down his spine. The terror held him captive, rendering him helpless in the face of impending danger. Alfie thought about his options; fear told him to comply, but the caregiver in him urged defiance. A voice murmured through the phone. Alfie stared at the man, noticing his eyes deranged with intent; Alfie could read his intention clearly on his face.

"Help!" Alfie shouted down the phone. Infuriated, the man lunged across the living room, grabbing the phone out of his hand as he shoved him into the wall. Ripping the phone from the wall, he threw it across the room. Backing away towards his mother, he tried to wake her as the man walked toward him. Alfie's breaths became rapid, each inhale a struggle against the suffocating grip of panic. The man's eyes bore into Alfie's as he got closer, grabbing him up from the floor. A cold, fleshy fist, remorseless and solid, collided with Alfie's tender cheek. The impact sent shockwaves through his young body as the man let his top free. Alfie stumbled, the bearing making him giddy as he collapsed to the floor beside his mother, out cold.

Head pounding from the impact to his face, Alfie's eyes opened, blurry. He attempted to touch the side of his bruised face until he realized he was tied to one of the kitchen chairs. Glancing to the side, he saw his mother bound as well. He shrugged around, trying to get loose, but it was no use; the bindings were tight. Alfie's eyes darted beyond his mother, and he spotted his little brother tied to the chair next to her. Three chairs in the centre of the living room, three victims tied up. Alfie pushed his bare feet off the dark grey carpet, attempting to free his legs.

"It's no use, Alfie boy. You aren't going anywhere now," the man said, standing unhinged opposite them, a thick, long kitchen knife in his hand. He tapped the blade on his knuckles.

"Just let them go, Freddy," Alfie's mother begged, trying to lean forward. The man laughed at her desperation, with a menacing smile, shaking his head in refusal.

"This is the way you have made it, Diane. You wouldn't give me a chance!" The man said to Alfie's mother deranged and delusional his eyes refusing to break from his penetrating gaze upon her. He moved a little closer, getting on his knees so he was eye level.

"And why was Eddy here?" he continued.

"Please, just let them go. They are children," Alfie's mother begged, fidgeting in her binds. Dismissing the man's question.

"Stop asking me. The answer is no," Freddy gritted with venom sadistically, holding the point of the knife to her nose. Oscar began to cry, a fearful sound echoing through the room as the reality of the situation sank in. The man mimicked his cries, mocking the child before telling him to shut up.

Wandering back and forth in the room, the knife jittering in his hand, Alfie focused his eyes on the living room window. Rain still splashed down as he gazed through the wet night sky. This was the first time his mind had taken him to the possibility he was going to die prematurely. All the panic he'd felt throughout the night amplified inside him. With gritted teeth, he swallowed his pain, focusing on the beauty of the raining night to distract himself from revealing his fear to the man before him.

The man turned around, walking away from his bound hostages, and placed the knife on the sofa's arm. Interrupting Alfie's focus on the night sky, Alfie watched the man's movements, wondering how long he had until he would be killed. His chest heavy with dread as his body battled the fear inside. The sobs of his little brother tormented him, making it a harder fight to defeat the turmoil inside of him.

Alfie's mother soothed her younger child, slowly stopping his cries. The room became silent as Alfie watched the man's face; his features had been overtaken by rage, making him almost demonic. The man turned away from Alfie, his mother, and younger brother, turning to the window, standing in front of Alfie's view. Looking to his mother, Alfie tried to pull his arms free from the binds. He and his mother looked at one another, communicating with their expressions.

"I'll be back in a second," the man stated, sweeping the knife from the sofa's arm, leaving the living room. Alfie panicked, thinking that the man was playing games and planning to stab him from behind so none of them could see his attack coming. Alfie began to struggle even more, trying to loosen the ties.

Hearing a creaking from the stairs, Alfie suddenly felt a tugging on the ropes around his arms. Flinching, Alfie winced, thinking the man had made his attack. A low shushing noise in Alfie's ear; he turned his head around, seeing Eddie behind him, freeing him from his binds.

"You're a brave kid," Eddie whispered to Alfie, sensing his fear. Freed, Alfie turned around, seeing the man standing behind Eddie. As Eddie turned around, the man stabbed the kitchen knife toward him. Grabbing the man's hand, Eddie whacked his hand against the wall, forcing the man to drop it.

Quickly grabbing the knife from the floor, Alfie sharply cut his mother's ties, freeing her. As Eddie and the man began to fight, scuffling toward the living room door, the man grabbed the side of Eddie's face, colliding his head into the frame of the door repeatedly until he dropped to the floor.

Taking the knife from Alfie, his mother began cutting the bounds around Oscar. Smashing into Alfie's mother, the man grabbed a vicious grip on her hair; a loud scream erupted as she dropped the knife on the floor. Diving to the floor, Alfie grabbed the knife, going toward his brother, whose chair had been knocked backward as the man collided into his mother. Alfie gazed upon his brother as he lay still, all the panic inside of him burned away as an intoxicating wrath took over him.

The man threw Alfie's mother to the floor. Bending down, he sat over her as she attempted to turn her body to crawl away. Turning her round to face him, he held her down as he slid his hands from her shoulder, slowly wrapping them around her neck.

Tightening his grip around the blade of the knife, Alfie lunged forward. The blade sliced through the air with swift determination, thrusting it into the man's side just above his hip. Instantly, the man yelled, feeling the blade penetrate through his flesh. Letting go of Alfie's mother's neck, the man slapped Alfie with the back of his hand. Consumed in rage, the slap didn't faze Alfie as he yanked the knife out of the man's side.

Sharply, the man placed his hand over his wound as he moved toward Alfie, trying to take the knife from him. Reaching his hand forward to grab the knife from him, Alfie plunged the knife through the man's hand. The man cried out in pain as Alfie pulled the knife out of his hand.

Standing up, Alfie's mother kicked the man in the side of the head before rushing to check on Oscar.

Falling to the floor, Alfie climbed on top of the man, plunging the blade into his chest. Begging and pleading for Alfie to stop, he coughed up blood. Tearing the blade from his chest, Alfie brutally repeated the stabbing motion as blood poured into the living room.

"Just fucking die, you bastard!" Alfie shouted as he looked at the man slowly dying with every penetration of the blade. Blood splattered onto Alfie as his frenzy continued, every stab more intense with aggression. Tears began to fall from Alfie's eyes down his cheek, leaving a line down his face. Alfie had lost all control as the killer inside of him had emerged.

Chapter 11

Hands clasped together, Alfie's gaze remained fixed on Thomas and Alex, though he could sense the entire room staring at him in disbelief. With a heavy heart, he cast his eyes downward, overwhelmed by the horror etched on his friends' faces, unsure of how they had received the news.

"I had no choice; it was him or us," Alfie concluded, feeling the weight of judgment bearing down on him. His mother approached, but Alfie rose to his feet, offering her the seat, yet she remained standing beside him. Surveying the room, he was met with a thick silence and judgmental stares, causing him to swallow hard. Glancing back at Oscar, who was still asleep, Alfie caught sight of Charley's angered expression. "You never told me you actually killed him… you told me…" Charley began to question before Alfie's mother interrupted her.

"I told him to never tell anyone," Alfie's mother sternly responded to Charley. Pointing to Oscar, who was asleep, she pressed her finger to her mouth, demanding Charley lower her voice.

"Some mother you are," Charley muttered under her breath, her words piercing the awkward silence in the room. Alfie glanced at Charley, taken aback by her rudeness towards his mother, unsure of how to react.

"The mother who knew how to look after her son when he was born," Alfie's mother retorted, her tone laced with spite as she responded to Charley. Hurt and filled with regret over how things had transpired that night, she stood her ground.

"Right… not the time or the place," Alfie interjected with a warning look to Charley. Grabbing his side in pain, a tingling sensation shot through Alfie's body. His mother noticed his wince, showing her concern. Alfie lifted the side of his vest, revealing a bruise from the earlier barrage he'd received.

"It's fine, I just caught it as I moved," Alfie reassured his mother. "Don't worry about it, it'll be fine. It's just a bruise," he continued, shrugging away her worry. He walked over to the corner of the room, worried about Lucy.

"I never knew you had a brother," Thomas spoke, causing Alfie to turn and look at him.

"Yeah, after everything that happened, Lucy and Teddy never mentioned it because they knew I couldn't talk about it," Alfie replied, stuttering as the memory of his brother overtook his mind. He could feel his body begin to shake; noticing his mother walked over to him, placing her arm around his shoulders.

"So how come you were never arrested for killing that man?" Alex asked with curiosity.

"Because someone else took the blame. They even made the news for it, didn't they?" Emerson answered before Alfie could. The image of his brother in his head faded fast as Alfie turned, looking at Emerson with even more suspicion. Taken aback, Alfie hesitated to respond as Emerson continued. "In Uni, I studied criminology and wrote a paper on it, and if I'm correct, it wasn't one murder that night; it was three, wasn't it?" Emerson pressed. Feeling the pressured glares around him, Alfie began to breathe heavily, his mind rattling with ways to respond.

"No, that's wrong," Alfie's mother replied sternly, her voice carrying a warning tone. "Anyway, I don't think now is the time for questions. Save your inquiries for when you get out of this house alive," she continued, effectively distracting everyone with the gravity of the situation they faced.

Alfie and his mother gave each other a look of weariness. As Alfie removed himself from everyone, heading toward the door, he slid down the wall to sit on the floor. Taking out his and Charley's phone, he looked at them both, hoping for Lucy's call any second now. Every second the phones weren't ringing, Alfie panicked if Lucy was still alive. He was annoyed with himself for letting her go alone, but then he looked over at Oscar, the only reason he stayed in the house. He should have made her stay, picked her up, and brought her back into the house to wait in the panic room with the others. He feared her death riddling him with guilt.

Sitting and waiting didn't suit Alfie; it allowed his mind to wander to the worst-case scenario. Taking his mind off Lucy, he began thinking about the night, the killers, asking himself questions.

- "How did they know the code to the gate?"

- "Why didn't they search the house for Oscar, his mother, and Charley?"

- "Was this to do with his father?"

- "Was this to do with Richard and Ian?"

- "Why didn't they kill me when the police arrived?"

- "Why was Emerson unharmed?" he muttered in a whisper to himself as he bit his thumbnail to muffle his mutters. Looking around the room, Ivy's absence played on his mind, but would she

228

be able to kill her own sister. Overthinking was driving Alfie a little crazy, but he needed to distract himself from falling into an attack of anxiety.

Charley, leaving Oscar's side, walked over to Alfie. He was agitated, fretting with his hands and mumbling. Bending down she grabbed his arm, stopping his fidgeting to focus on her.

"Why didn't you tell me about any of the letters and threats?" Charley interrogated, her face hostile.

"Not now, Charley. There's too much going on to go into it all," Alfie replied, dismissing her, looking at his phone, eager for it to light up with Lucy's name.

"Don't dismiss me, Alfie. You've put mine and Oscar's lives in danger," Charley responded with blame as she folded her arms.

"Sorry? I've done nothing but try to protect you!" Alfie raised his voice, slightly irked at her accusation. He put the phones into his pocket as he met her eyes.

"Well, you seem to have done a great job of that. We're stuck in here waiting, while your best friend is now dead. All this death around you, maybe I should get Oscar as far away from you as possible," Lucy Venomous in her words, trying to keep her voice low, but everyone had already heard, tension in the room making everyone feel awkward. Alex, Ben, and Emerson didn't know where to put their faces.

"You bitch!" Alfie's response was laced with anguish, the thought of Oscar being taken away from him and the trauma of Teddy's death thrown in his face. Her words cut into him like a knife in his heart. He felt his hand trembling as he struggled to contain the anxiety bubbling inside him. Alfie's mother turned around watching the altercation, while Bulldozer leaped off the bed and approached Alfie. As Charley's hand connected with the side of Alfie's face, delivering a stinging slap, instincts urged him to react, but Alfie restrained himself, unable to strike the woman he loved. Bulldozer growled menacingly, positioning himself between Charley and Alfie, issuing a warning to Charley.

"Down!" Charley commanded, making a grab for the dog's collar. Bulldozer knocked her attempt away, showing his teeth and growling once again.

"At least someone in this house is loyal," Alfie quipped in response, looking down at Bulldozer before turning his gaze back to Charley. Marching over, infuriated—evident in every stomping step—Alfie's mother pushed Charley out of the way, positioning herself in front of

Bulldozer. She placed her face close to Charley's.

"If you ever put your hands on my son again, I promise you I will fuck you up. You just found out Alfie killed someone; wonder what his mother is capable of. Be grateful that my grandson is in this room and saved you this one time," with her warning, Alfie's mother spat fury, emphasizing every word with her finger poking Charley on the nose. Rolling her eyes, Charley walked away back to the bed where Oscar slept. Alfie and his mother silently looked at each other, frustration written on their faces.

"I need to get out of here, like now," Alfie said urgently to his mother, panic evident in his voice. Placing his hand on his forehead, he ran his fingers through his hair. His words were heard by the others, who instantly volunteered to come with him. Thomas, getting up, moved his arm, wincing in pain.

"Thomas, I'm sorry, but I need you to stay here," Alfie said gently, his concern evident in his voice. He appreciated Thomas's loyalty more than words could express, but he couldn't bear the thought of risking his friend's safety any further.

"We'll come with you," said Alex, volunteering Ben's assistance. Emerson remained quiet, his face avoiding Alfie's expectant gaze, while Charley death-stared at Alfie.

"So, do you want to stay up here, Emerson?" Alfie asked, putting him on the spot. Facing towards the floor, Emerson nodded, confirming he didn't want to leave the safety of the panic room. Two things crossed Alfie's mind as he looked at Emerson with fury. One, he wanted to stay in the safe place even though earlier he was rushing to get out of the house to save his wife. Second, why was he so adamant to stay in the panic room with Alfie's loved ones? His decision put Alfie at a crossroads: does he leave his mother, child, and Charley alone with a potential killer, or does he stay in the room?

Awakening, Oscar looked over at his dad, calling to him. The call from his son forced him to push aside his suspicions as he reassured Oscar he'd be back soon, forcing him to make a quick decision to leave and hunt out the other intruders. Alex and Ben quickly followed him out into his bedroom as his mother shut the door, watching Charley and Emerson closely. Bulldozer remained at her side, fixed on Oscar.

Standing in the walk-in wardrobe, Alfie took in a deep breath, holding his face in his hands. He was consumed with emotions: despair for leaving Oscar again, anxiety and anger over the whole situation, and an increasing amount of guilt over Lucy.

"What's the plan, Alf?" asked Alex cautiously, sensing the amount of pressure Alfie was feeling. Him and Ben stood behind Alfie as he sucked in his emotions and regained control of himself.

"We need to arm ourselves," Alfie replied, pulling the gun from his joggers' waistband. Leaving the bedroom, all three of them guardedly walked through the house, with Alfie taking the lead and stealthily listening around them, until they got back down to the ground floor. In the hallway, Alfie tried to avoid looking at Teddy's body. Concentrating to look elsewhere made his eyes glimpse at him quickly. He could feel the lump in the back of his throat building but gulped it down with a deep breath and clenched teeth.

"What the fuck happened here?" Ben asked, gobsmacked by the hallway's blood-painted floor.

"Pretty obvious, isn't it, dipshit!" Alex replied to Ben, as he saw the trauma on the side of Alfie's face that he so desperately tried to fight. Alex noticed that Ella and Grace's bodies were missing, so he walked into the living room. The sight of them sat upright beneath the window, as if they were watching something, made him feel

233

sick. Sharply leaving the living room, he placed his hand on Alfie's shoulder.

"Let's make these motherfuckers pay for this," Alex said with harsh intent, his words meant on his face. Nodding his head, Alfie agreed and pushed his legs forward as he led Alex and Ben into the kitchen. On the countertop, Alfie pulled a twelve-piece knife block toward him. Grabbing a chef's knife, he took it by the side of the blade, handing it to Alex. Taking the straight-edge steak knife, he handed it to Ben in the same manner. Making his way to the sink, he opened the cupboard beneath. Rummaging through, he pulled out a small bottle of drain cleaner and placed it on the island.

"Whoever wants to take this, throw it in their face; it'll burn through their masks and onto their face," Alfie informed. Ben reached over, grabbing the bottle.

"Where are they? How do we find them?" asked Alex with anticipation an eagerness in his voice to avenge the death of Jennifer.

"I don't know, but we need to get to Lucy. It's been nearly an hour since she went to the house next door, so we're going to start there," Alfie replied, his adrenaline surging at the thought of Lucy's potential death. "Are you both ready?" Alfie asked as he got past them, heading out of the kitchen.

Stopping in the narrowed hallway opposite the basement door, Alfie's heart raced as a phone began to ring urgently. Desperate to hear Lucy's voice and fulfil her plan, he reached for the phones, pulling both his and Charley's from his jogger's pocket. Just as he saw Lucy's name appear on the screen of his phone and moved to answer, the attic door swung open from the inside. With a gasp, Alfie turned his head, only to find two gloved hands gripping his vest tightly, dragging him forcefully through the door.

Chapter 12

Tumbling down the thick, hard wooden stairs, Alfie gasped as the bruise on his side struck the corner of a step. With a sigh of pain, he hit the floor, his head smashing against cold concrete wall. The gun dropped from his hold sliding across the dark room, disappearing into the unknown with a loud scraping. Alfie looked up, watching as the orange-masked intruder shut the basement door and promptly locked it, sliding a wooden plank under the handle as an extra precaution to keep Alfie trapped.

Taking each step tauntingly slow, the orange killer watched Alfie as he squirmed on the floor, trying to regain his senses. Blurred vision, two hazy outlines of the orange intruder approaching. Alfie felt around the floor near him, hoping to feel the gun. Squinting his eyes with all his focus, Alfie stared at the killer, concentrating to watch their movements.

"Alfie, Alfie, Alfie," the disguised voice said slowly in monotone. A sudden loud kick on the door upstairs caused the intruder to look behind them, giving a mocking laugh at the attempt of Alex and Ben trying to kick the door open to help Alfie. The intruder pulled a knife from their black trousers. Sitting on the second bottom step, they gazed at Alfie, their mirrored eyes reflecting Alfie's vulnerability. Leaning forward, the orange killer began playing with the knife in their hand, warming the blade for the impact they'd planned.

"These are the moments you just want to catch on camera to relive over and over," the disguised voice said in monotone. Alfie pushed his hands against the floor, trying to sit up. He squinted and closed his eyes repeatedly, attempting to regain his full sight. Another laugh from the intruder made Alfie feel vulnerable, reminiscent of how he felt when he was thirteen. He knew he couldn't attack the intruder without his vision; doing so would only put his life at risk.

"It's a shame you seem so weak… it's hardly fair," the monotone voice continued, watching as Alfie struggled to steady himself to sit upwards. The intruder tapped the blade of the knife into the palm of their black glove, full of eagerness to use it.

"Who the fuck are you?" Alfie asked, disgruntled, as he swallowed saliva, still trying to focus his eyes in the darkened room. His eyes darted from the intruder to the pitch-dark room behind the staircase, catching a glimmer of light from a small window at the top of the wall. The coldness of the flat concrete floor seeped through Alfie's grey joggers and onto his skin.

Closing his eyes, Alfie listened to the silence, waiting for the sound of movement. This was the first-time all-night Alfie felt uncertain and terrified.

Hearing a creaking, Alfie opened his eyes. His hazy vision caught the silhouette of the orange-masked intruder as he lunged off the step, pouncing toward him. Rolling to the other side of the room, Alfie placed himself beneath the window, which dimly lit the room. He listened intensely for approaching footsteps, placing his hands on the floor to feel vibrations. Charging footsteps slapped against the cold, flat floor. Squinting, Alfie caught the outline of the killer as he awaited their approach. Using all of his body weight, Alfie pushed out both of his legs, kicking the orange killer away. Their blade barely scratched Alfie's leg before they stumbled backwards, hitting the ground with a loud thud. Pushing himself sideways against the wall, Alfie disappeared into the darkness of the room. Getting on his hands and knees, he crawled away from the wall searching for the lost gun while hidden in the darkness.

Feeling around the floor, Alfie came to the end of the room and felt the wall. Quietly using the wall to guide him, he stood up with his back against it. Silently shuffling to the corner of the room, he released paced breaths as he listened for the intruder to begin the hunt. Squeezing his eyes shut, he hoped his vision would stabilize when he saw light again.

Each footstep was painstakingly slow, the knife swooshing as it cut through the air in the room. Alfie could sense the tables turning as the intruder was now in a desperate state of worry. The rustling of the knife was regular and fast. Alfie slowly hunched down to avoid being impacted by the knife when the intruder got slightly closer.

With his eyes now open, Alfie could vaguely see the shading of the orange balaclava approaching, his head still feeling giddy. Hands firmly against the wall, Alfie positioned himself. As another footstep got closer, Alfie tackled the intruder by his legs. Jumping on top of the killer, Alfie grabbed his arm with the knife, wrestling for the weapon. In a battle for the knife, Alfie bashed the side of his elbow into the intruder's face. With the impact, the intruder loosened his grip, and Alfie attempted to grab the hunting knife but accidentally pushed it across the room instead.

Repeatedly punching the intruder, Alfie launched into a vicious assault, hoping to knock the intruder out cold so he could strangle them to death. In the darkness, Alfie couldn't see the counter as the intruder punched him in his side, adding intense pain to the injury he'd sustained earlier that evening. A second of hesitation, and the intruder threw Alfie off them, causing him to roll toward the light from the window. His vision returning, he noticed a light switch on the wall near the bottom of the stairs.

On guard, slowly stepping against the wall, Alfie braced for another pursuit from his attacker. Switching the light switch dimly lit the room, which still left corners of the basement in darkness. The orange-masked killer charged at Alfie with knife in hand. Alfie grabbed his hand, using all his might to prevent the knife from penetrating him. The orange killer swept Alfie's legs, tripping him to the floor. Holding onto the intruder's arm, Alfie took him down with him.

The tip of the blade edged into Alfie's shoulder, cutting a small line into him. Blood started to trickle down his skin. Moving his body to the side, Alfie let go of the intruder's hand as the knife stabbed into the floor. Throwing a quick jab into the side of the intruder's face and biting into the intruder's gloved hand, Alfie bit down until he could feel his teeth sinking into the flesh. The intruder dropped the knife again, slamming the side of his fist into the side of Alfie's head, forcing him to let go.

Rapidly grabbing the knife, Alfie released his bite as he stabbed the sharp blade into the intruder's hand. Rolling from underneath the killer, standing up and kneeing the intruder in the face; Alfie gripped the top of the orange balaclava, pulling the mask off.

"You!" Alfie exclaimed with fury as he looked at the face behind the mask. Another knee to the face, and Alfie yanked the knife out of the man's hand, kicking him backward to the floor. Chris began to laugh at Alfie's blatant anger.

"You murdered your cousin; you threatened your own sister and nephew?" Confused and annoyed, Alfie had many thoughts, but the idea of Chris being a murderer wasn't one of them. Chris laughed again looking up at him.

"Charley was never in danger," Chris replied sarcastically, holding his hand, as blood seeped out onto the floor.

"You killed Ella, she was your family, why is Charley any different?" Alfie interrogated, standing at a distance with the knife in his hand.

"Oh Alfie, you really are… thick, aren't you," Chris stated still looking up at him on the ground, with a gloating smile on his face. "This… This was all Charley's idea," Chris continued, still smiling. Alfie felt the walls close in on him; his heart felt broken at the mere thought she could have betrayed him like this.

"You're lying!" Alfie defended with intense eye contact, studying Chris to find the bluff.

"Am I? Did you tell Teddy your secret?" Chris asked, eager to break Alfie as much as he could.

"There isn't a secret!" gritted Alfie intensely, stepping forward.

"Sure, there is, but I'm guessing he didn't tell you, his secret?" Psychologically teasing, Chris taunted. His smile wider as he watched the confusion on Alfie fight with the hatred on his face.

"What secret?" Alfie continued, gritting, clenching the knife in his hand tighter.

"He should be the one to tell you, really…. Oh wait…. He can't…. because I slit his throat!" Chris teased, watching the angst spread across Alfie's face. Alfie moved closer to Chris, who backed away.

"Fucking tell me!" Alfie roared, getting closer and grabbing Chris's hair, yanking his head backward and holding the knife to Chris's throat. "Tell me, or I even the odds for Teddy," Alfie promised with no hesitation.

"Charley fucked Teddy behind your back!... That's why he had to die and why you have to die," Chris replied with cockiness arrogant that he would destroy Alfie one way or another.

"You liar," Alfie gritted through his teeth, pushing the knife's edge into Chris's neck.

"I'm not. That time when you disappeared, they slept together, and Teddy stopped it when he started seeing Eva… she doesn't love you!" Chris gleamed speaking slowly to make sure Alfie caught every word.

Alfie's head was spinning from this revelation, his mind blurred as he pictured Charley and Teddy together. The thought made him feel sick; he'd risked his life to keep the mother of his son alive, and she would be the one to betray him. In a fit of rage, Alfie began stabbing Chris mercilessly, letting out every frustration he'd had over the last couple of days. He delivered repeated blows into Chris's stomach, letting his body fall to the ground, the knife still intact in his stomach.

Breathless, Alfie looked at the bloody mess he'd made, his mind going wild. He couldn't fathom Charley being the mastermind. How would she know about Teddy? He could feel his body begin to shake as he debated what he had to do. Could he actually kill the mother of his child?

Shaking the intense thoughts out of his mind, he began searching the dimly lit basement for the gun that had slid across the room. Alex and Ben were still banging to get inside. Ignoring the noise from upstairs, Alfie's mind reflected on what Chris had told him. He didn't want to believe it to be true, but then he thought of how

Charley was so mad at him for trying to protect her and Oscar. Replaying the antics of her slapping him in the face, and the rudeness to his mother, it was out of character for her. Searching under the stairs, he touched the cold metal handgrip hidden in the dark. He pictured the look Charley gave him before he left the panic room, then regrettably imagined shooting her as he held it; he didn't want to take any of Oscar's family away from him.

Stepping over Chris's body, Alfie debated what he was going to do, ignoring his friends trying to save him. He took a deep breath and sat on the bottom step, touching the back of his head, feeling a bump from where he had hit his head.

Inhaling deeply drawing long breaths, Alfie, still unsure what to do, held the gun firmly in his grasp as he stood up to walk upstairs. Suddenly, two hands grabbed around his ankle, causing Alfie to fall face down on the step, the gun firing a shot into the wall. kicking his free foot Alfie tried to get Chris off him, but Chris pulled him down the stairs causing him to drop the gun. Laying on the floor, Alfie turned his body as Chris climbed on top of him. Wrapping his hands around Alfie's neck he began to strangle him. Blood slurped out of Chris's mouth; his body painted red as Chris vigorously put his dying weight onto his hold on Alfie's neck. Struggling to fight him off, Alfie squirmed under him as he pulled at his hands, feeling the blood from the gash in Chris's hand sticking to his skin.

Feeling the handle of the knife pushing against him, Alfie grabbed it, plunging it deeper inside of him. Jolting with a yell from the impact, Chris refused to let go of Alfie's neck, desperately holding on, knowing it was now or never. Alfie could feel his head lightening as the air in his lungs reduced. Feeling weak, he stopped clasping at Chris's grip. Reaching around for the gun, Alfie felt the cold, hard metal as he pulled it with his fingertips. Choking as he pulled the gun into the palm of his hands, he fought the urge to pass out. Taking hold of the gun, Alfie aimed it from his chest upwards, directed at Chris's chin. A loud, thunderous gunshot fired, exploding into the centre of Chris's jaw, blood splattering over Alfie.

Instantly releasing Alfie, he began to cough as he pushed Chris vigorously off him. Jumping up, he felt around his neck, gasping for breath as he moved cautiously toward the killer. Chris lay making noises, looking up at Alfie. Holding the gun over Chris's head, Alfie fired two rounds into his face, watching Chris still on the floor. Alfie kicked his legs, testing for movement. Regaining himself, he backed away from the body as he took the first step, firing another bullet just in case.

Walking up the stairs, it was silent; Alex and Ben were no longer kicking at the door. Standing at the door, Alfie removed the barricade and unlocked it. Pushing it open, he walked into the hallway, jumping backward, gun raised as Alex and Ben were about to attack him.

"What the fuck are you doing?" Alfie shouted as he shook the gun.

"Sorry, we heard gunshots and weren't sure if you or the killer were coming up," Ben replied sheepishly. Lowering their weapons, Alfie went and picked up the phones on the floor. He'd had another missed call from Lucy. Looking at Charley's phone, he was tempted to check the phone for any proof of what Chris had told him, but put the phone back into his pocket. Ben and Alex asked Alfie questions, which he ignored as he redialled Lucy, calling her back. Alex and Ben both went into the basement, seeing the dead killer. Lucy didn't answer the call.

"It was Chris, Charley's brother Chris!" Alex loudly said as Alfie turned to look at him. "Did you make him suffer?" He continued, vengeful for being held back and made to watch Jennifer die.

"It wasn't quick," Alfie replied, looking at Alex. He brushed past him, going into the kitchen. Making a glass of water, he took a gulp, then grabbed a tea towel hanging on a pole. Wetting the cloth, he wiped Chris's splattered blood off him. His phone rang urgently, and he answered it.

"Lucy, are you alright?" He spoke as if a weight had been lifted from him, knowing she was alive.

"You wish it was Lucy!" Stated the disguised voice, sending chills down Alfie's spine as he imagined the worst.

"Is she alive?" Alfie tried to maintain calmness, but his mixed emotions were getting the better of him.

"You'll have to come and find out for yourself," the intruder goaded, taunting Alfie with the unknown. Hanging up the call, Alfie stared through the hallway phone still at his ear.

Chapter 13

The gate closed with a thud. Lucy hurried barefoot along the concrete footpath at the back of Alfie's house. Tiny pebbles dug into her feet as she scampered along. The distance between the houses was greater than she had expected. The summer night's wind blew in her face, cooling her down as she overheated with adrenaline. Her blood-stained wet white T-shirt and damp navy lounge shorts blew against her as she got closer to her the house next door.

Standing before Emerson and Alice's garden gate, she looked around both sides, making sure no one was following her. The gun in her hand was ready to fire as soon as someone approached. Pushing the gate, but it was locked. Putting her hand through the gap, she hoped she could feel a switch or a key, to get through, but she could only feel the brick pillar.

Stepping backward, she looked up at the metal surroundings above the brick walls. Taking another step backward, she tripped and sat on the small wall dividing the footpath and the greenery behind. Pushing herself back up, she knocked a loose brick to the floor. After another look around to make sure no one was following, her knuckles whitened with her intense grip on the gun. Tucking the gun into her shorts, she jumped upwards, catching the gate above the wall, and pulled herself up.

Feet scraping against the brick wall, Lucy ignored the sanding of her feet as she ascended up the four-foot brick. Carefully placing her foot onto the flat surfaces of the beautifully woven gate that curved in places. Holding tightly to the cold metal, Lucy stopped to look at the height she would have to climb, which made her dubious of the fatality if she were to fall from the top. Clinging tightly to the metal in her hand, she tried to think of an easier way to tackle this obstacle, knowing if she was spotted by the black-masked killer, she'd be vulnerable to their gunfire.

Muted scraping and hard, wet footsteps seethed through the street, catching Lucy's attention. Turning her head to face the direction of Alfie's home, she noticed a distinct pink head with eyes shimmering in the fading moon's beam. Hand clenching onto the gate, Lucy reached for her gun but lost her footing. Holding herself up with one arm, she hurriedly pulled herself back up and began to climb up the gate.

Swishing their knife, the pink intruder viciously tried to slash Lucy, jumping in the air to catch her feet. Lucy quickly moved along the gate, going across to evade the pink killer as she ascended up the cold steel. Soaring up the gate, in a panic, Lucy stood on the tip of a curve. Jolting from the pain in her feet, she slipped, leaving her hanging. Air brushed against her foot as the killer swept the knife through the night air, a centimetre away from impact. Pulling herself back up cautiously, Lucy placed her feet back on the smooth part of the metal.

Frustrated as Lucy got further away, the pink killer jumped up, grabbing the gate, and scraping their wet boots against the wall, pulling themselves up. Bending the curves of the gate as they climbed carelessly, the killer ascended toward Lucy at a faster pace. Gaining closeness to their target, the killer held on tightly as they revealed their knife, gouging the air with a firm hold. Lucy squealed as she rushed to get away from the killer, stepping on another pointed curve. Firmly holding onto the gate, Lucy swung the bottom of her body toward the intruder as the killer swished their knife again, catching Lucy on the top of her thigh. Screaming as the knife cut her skin, she kicked the killer, causing them to lose their hold as they fell down, grappling the bottom of the gate, dangling against the wall. Dropping down to the ground, the pink intruder glared up in silent fury as they jumped back onto the gate and began climbing again.

Swinging her leg over the gate, Lucy straddled the top with one leg on each side. Peering down at the ground, the height stirred a wave of nausea in her stomach. Glancing back at the side she had just climbed; she spotted the killer rising up. Pulling out her gun, Lucy lost her balance, grabbing the top of the gate to steady herself. Dropping the gun into the garden, she murmured, "Shit," in a panic as she rapidly repositioned her leg and started descending the other side of the gate. The pink intruder stopped climbing, focusing on Lucy as she began scaling down. Lucy strategically moved in different directions so the killer wouldn't be able to catch her from the other side. Observing Lucy's movements intently, the killer shadowed her, aiming to seize any opportunity. Lucy stood on the edge of another curved point, attempting to descend quickly. Hanging again, Lucy looked below to see how far from the ground she was. Closing the gap between them, the pink killer grabbed one of Lucy's hands, but before they could get a full grip, Lucy let go.

Falling onto the grass and hitting her head hard, Lucy looked up to see the pink killer watching to see if she'd survived. Lucy lay with her eyes open, focusing on the killer and subtly tensing her body to assess her injuries. As the killer began to move, Lucy carefully got up, feeling pain shooting down her body. On her knees, Lucy felt around the grass searching for the gun.

Glancing back up, she noticed that the pink intruder had stopped moving. Feeling the gun under her palm, Lucy gripped the handle. Standing up, she pointed the gun at the intruder midway on the gate and fired. Her aim off, she missed, but as she fired again, the intruder fell from the gate.

Wobbling as she walked, Lucy staggered to the gate. She wanted to see the killer's body. Approaching, she leaned her face into the gate as the pink intruder's knife glided near her face. Jolting backwards, Lucy fell on the floor. Staring at the garden gate, the pink intruder stood glaring at her. Lucy stood up, catching her reflection in the mirrored eyes. "Who are you?" she asked as the intruder slashed her knife through the gate. Taking a step back, Lucy aimed the gun to fire again, but the intruder disappeared.

Hesitating, Lucy had the gun ready as she scanned the gate to check if the pink intruder was hiding. Checking from a distance, Lucy verified that the killer was gone. Turning around, she paced toward Alice and Emerson's house. Vigilant in her surroundings, but her mind was erratic, wondering how the pink killer had survived drowning when she herself barely caught her breath. She thought to call Alfie and give him a heads up that the pink killer was still alive, but she also didn't want to be caught off guard while she was out in the open.

Reaching the house, it bore an outside similar build to Alfie's home, but this house had a thick pipe sticking out, leading to one of the room's windows. As she stood opposite the kitchen door, she noticed a light beaming from the hallway. She put her hand to the kitchen door handle as a slight panic hit her, wondering what awaited inside the house. Taking an anxious breath, Lucy twisted the handle slowly, trying not to make a sound.

Pushing the unlocked door, Lucy crept inside, listening intently, ignoring the sound of her apprehensive heart pounding. She was careful with every breath, making sure not to make a noise. The kitchen was similar to Alfie's but brighter in colour, with bright blue walls and a white shinny floor. Creeping around, Lucy made her way to the door, peeping around sharply; it was empty. She snuck through the hallway, bumping into Alice who was exiting the living room.

"What are you doing in my house?" Alice demanded after a high-pitched scream, startled by Lucy's presence.

"I came to make sure you were safe," Lucy explained, grabbing Alice's arm. Seeing the gun in Lucy's other hand, Alice pulled her arm away from Lucy's hold. Looking at her up and down, the now pinkish bloodstain on her top and the cut that left blood dripping down her leg.

"Where's my husband?" Alice demanded with fright, backing away, her face went into panic as she imagined the worst, slightly turning her head toward the living room. "Where's Emerson?" Alice screamed backing away.

"He's fine! But we need to get to a safe place now!" Lucy shouted, frustration building inside of her as she walked closer to Alice, standing on the edge of the hallway. She looked at the corner of her eye, seeing the black masked intruder, she took a step backward, tensing her hold on the gun.

"You told me my Emerson was coming back!" Alice screamed, tears flooding from her face, looking at the black masked killer in the living room. The front door swung open; the pink masked intruder stared at Lucy before taking slow steps inside. Lucy fired her gun twice before sprinting up the stairs.

On the first floor, Lucy looked at the closed doors before her, the layout similar to Alfie's, so she could only assume what each room was. Rushing into the second room along, she stood in a homemade gym. A treadmill, a weight bench, and an exercise bike all spaced out to fill the room. Against the wall was a long rack of different-sized dumbbells. Lucy looked around; behind her was an ensuite, and in front of her were mirrored cupboards. She debated where to hide, not wanting to move around in the room too much to avoid being heard. Slowly walking backwards, she went into the ensuite, hiding inside the one-way glassed shower.

Back up against the wall so she could see anyone's entry. Holding the gun firmly in one hand, she pulled out her phone, putting it on silent just in case Alfie called her. Putting her phone back inside her pocket, she wrapped her free hand around the gun, arms balancing on her knees as both hands held the gun ready to pull the trigger. As she sat awaiting one of the killers pursuing her, she regretted her impulsive plan, worried that maybe now she would die, and the killers would be able to catch Alfie off guard.

The gym door creaked as it opened wider. Lucy stiffened her hold on the gun, more intense. Footsteps tapping heavily on the room's hardwood floor. Gritted teeth, Lucy readied herself as she tensed up. The ensuite door opened. Watching as the pink intruder stepped inside, without hesitation, Lucy fired the gun, shattering the one-way glass. The pink killer dropped to the floor, the bullet hitting them right in the chest. Standing up Lucy looked at the killer laying on the floor. Tip-toeing over the shattered glass, Lucy cautiously stepped over the killer's body, gun directly over them.

Sweeping her feet away, Lucy fell to the floor on her back, stamping her foot into the pink intruder's head. Swiftly jumping up, Lucy made a run for the door to escape. The pink intruder followed behind, grabbing Lucy's hair, pulling her back into the room. Firing the gun blindly, the bullet pierced into the wall. Turning around forcefully, the killer twisted Lucy's hair in their hand. Head down, Lucy wrenched herself free as the intruder pulled clumps of her hair out.

The pink-masked killer zoomed toward Lucy, tackling her to the floor. Lucy fired the gun twice into the intruder's chest, kicking her off. The pink killer, still standing, rushed toward Lucy. Dropping the gun, Lucy grabbed the intruder's wrist, wrestling for the blade. Spinning around, the intruder edged Lucy to the wall. Holding the killer back with all her weight, Lucy's eyes darted toward the weights near her. Kneeing the pink intruder in the groin, Lucy dodged as their knife penetrated into the wall. Lucy threw a punch then grabbed a six-kilogram dumbbell, smashing it into the intruder's face, shattering the mirrored goggles.

Holding their face, as one of the mirrored lenses impaled into the killer's eye, leaving it bloodshot, Lucy raced out of the room. Halting at the stairs, she realized that she'd left the gun. She doubled back toward the room; the pink killer rushed toward her as she sharply closed the door, trapping the pink intruder's arm. The knife in their hand cut Lucy's bicep, causing a narrow bleed, making her pull the door harder to hurt the intruder. Pushing the door inwards to open, Lucy knocked the killer backwards.

"Fuck!" Lucy muttered, realizing the gun was too far into the room. She bent down, grabbing the killer's knife. Getting away from the intruder, Lucy paced down the stairs, listening intensely for the black masked killer and the orange intruder. As she neared the bottom of the stairs, she could hear Alice's whimpering. She thought to wait for the right moment to run to the front door as the pink killer came charging down the stairs. Leaping off the stairs, Lucy sprinted to the front door, but it was locked. The pink intruder gave chase when a loud voice told them to "stop."

Lucy turned around, gradually pacing through the hallway. She stopped so that she faced the living room. The black-masked killer stood in front of a diamond-encrusted fireplace full of photos and ornaments, no weapon on display, staring blankly at Lucy. Before them, Alice sat on a long sofa, her shoulders shuffling as she whimpered in terror. Behind her, a table with a glass vase full of flowers, and two photo frames.

Lucy walked into the living room; it was as big as Alfie's house, the white carpet dirty from the intruders' boots.

Snatching the knife from Lucy's hand, the pink killer behind her pushed her into the living room. Catching the table to stop her from falling, Lucy looked up at the black-masked intruder. "Who are you?" Lucy asked, her eyes focusing on the mirrored lenses. A slight pause with a moment of silence just before the black-masked killer removed the balaclava revealing their face. Gasping, Lucy was shocked by the man in front of her. "How could you do this to Alfie?" She questioned with disgust, staring into the man's eyes. The pink killer walked around, standing next to the unmasked man.

"You'll find out when I kill him," The man replied, pulling the black balaclava over his face.

"You're gonna try and kill him!" Lucy confidently responded, picking up a photo frame, throwing it at the killer. Running back into the hallway, Lucy headed into the kitchen, closing the door behind her. She pulled open all the drawers until she found a knife. Bursting through the door, the pink killer ran at Lucy, who danced around the island, avoiding capture. Pretending to run one way, the pink intruder tried to intercept as Lucy made a run for the garden door. The pink intruder pushed the door shut, yanking Lucy away from the door.

Shoving the pink intruder into the door, the pink killer's head smashed through the window. Lucy made a run into the hallway. A gunshot fired. Lucy halted, turning to face the black-masked killer who held the gun toward her. The pink killer stomped through the hallway, pushing Lucy to the wall; they rammed their knife into Lucy's stomach. Lucy yelled as the killer pulled the knife out, causing Lucy to slide down the wall. Grappling at the shoulder of her top, the killer dragged her back into the living room. Lucy hunched over, holding her stomach. The pink intruder searched her pockets, finding her phone. Throwing the phone to the black-masked intruder, they pushed Lucy onto the sofa next to Alice. Lucy sat on the sofa, panting in pain, holding her stomach, swallowing the agony she was in.

"You shouldn't have done that," the black-mask intruder warned as he looked at the pink intruder and then back to Alice. No need for words, the pink intruder read the instruction well, a spiteful grip on Alice's hair, hurling her onto the floor face down. The pink killer sat on Alice's back, agonized screams and pleas screeching from her, begging for her life. The black-mask intruder called Alfie's phone from Lucy's.

Sitting on Alice's back like a horse, the pink intruder played with her, yanking her head backward, playing with the blade against her neck, teasing it down her back. Lucy begged them to stop as she helplessly watched. With palpable potency, the intruder jammed the knife into the centre of Alice's back. Alice cried in excruciating pain, scrapping the carpet to pull herself free. Feeling the struggle, the pink intruder revelled in the kill, repeatedly striking the knife into Alice's flesh. Blood splattered from her staining the white carpet with blood dying the fabrics a deadly pink.

Lucy closed her eyes, unable to watch the slaughter. Her stomach burned as she could feel the warm blood seeping onto her pressed palm, preventing too much blood from leaving her body. Tuning Alice's screams out of her head, Lucy worried about her own mortality as the wound was making her feel weaker. Opening her eyes for a second, she saw the pink killer turning Alice around, so they were face to face. Plunging the blade deep into Alice's chest, holding the knife inside. Leaning their head closer, the pink intruder listened as Alice gasped for every breath like it was music.

"If you had complied, this wouldn't have happened," the black-masked intruder said to Lucy as she closed her eyes again. Placing more pressure onto the injury in her gut, her heart raced as her mind was plagued by thoughts of death. She could feel her head lightening as she fought the urge to pass out. Hearing her phone ring, adrenaline surged through Lucy as she feared the killer had answered.

"Alfie, it's…" she shouted, hoping to warn Alfie of the danger he was about to face, but was cut off as the pink killer jumped up from Alice, the pink mask covered in blood splatters. Jumping on Lucy, their eyes met, and Lucy recognized who they belonged to. Covering Lucy's mouth, she squirmed. The black-masked killer called Alfie back. Struggling under the pink intruder, Lucy felt the side of her wound rip, causing her to scream into the killer's hand. As the killer ended the call, the pink killer got up from Lucy. Sitting on the sofa in agony, toppled by guilt, she felt responsible for Alfie's potential death.

Chapter 14

Frozen by the overwhelming concern and responsibility he placed on his shoulders, Alfie stood still, holding the disconnected phone to his ear. His mind flashed images of all the possibilities Lucy had endured, alive or dead. Alex and Ben called his name, standing behind him, trying to get his attention. His eyes glazed over blankly, staring out into the garden, all of Alfie's inner turmoil he'd forced out of his focus was scrapping to break free from the surface.

Placing his hand on Alfie's shoulder and giving it a soft squeeze, Alex felt a sharp sting from the cut on Alfie's shoulder, which broke Alfie out of his shock. Turning around, Alfie looked at Alex, who was gazing at the blood that seeped from the cut onto his fingers.

"What are we going to do now, Alfie?" Alex asked, wiping the blood from Alfie's cut onto his top. Silent with thought, Alfie's eyes darted over to Ben and then back to Alex. Chris's words about Charley echoed in the back of his head, distracting him.

Putting his phone inside his pocket, he felt Charley's phone. He pulled out the phone, looking at the blank screen. Feeling Alex and

Ben's eyes on him, he dropped his arm to face them. "I don't know, but we can't just charge into the house; they'll expect that," Alfie finally spoke.

"So how do we take them by surprise?" Alex asked, looking at Alfie who shrugged his shoulders as he tried to strategize a plan of attack. His eyes flicking between his friends as an idea came to him. Sizing up both of them, he deliberated the risk and if Lucy was dead, would it be worth putting them at risk.

"What are you thinking?" Alex asked, cautious of the look on Alfie's face. Barging past him, Alfie rushed out of the kitchen, heading into the basement. Grabbing the orange balaclava off the floor, he picked up the mask; it was heavier than expected. Turning it inside out, he found a small, rounded metal device, which was what they had been using to change their voices. "Testing," Alfie said into the device as it distorted his voice loudly. Moving near Chris's dead body, he checked the gloves on his hands, which were ruined. He then checked his attire, but his attack on him had destroyed the clothes, making them useless. Lastly, Alfie removed the boots. Running back upstairs, he went back into the kitchen, giving Alex the belongings.

"What's this for?" Alex asked as Alfie hurried back out of the kitchen. Sprinting up the stairs,

Alfie ran into every room, looking for something similar to the black clothing the intruders were wearing among his guests' clothes. Thomas had the same black top. Grabbing it, he went upstairs to his room to grab his own black jeans. Jolting back down the stairs, Alfie chucked the clothing at Alex.

"You want me to dress in Chris's disguise?" Alex stated with a questionable look at Alfie.

"Look, you are roughly the same height as Chris, and they don't know he's dead," Alfie explained as Alex shook his head, refusing to go along with the plan. He threw the items of clothing on the floor.

"Alex, they won't see this coming, and you can get to Lucy if she's alive and get her out while they are focused on me," Alfie explained assertively.

"He's right!" agreed Ben, "If Lucy is alive, then it's the best way to get close to her," he continued as both Alex and Alfie's eyes fell on him.

"Look, I want to kill these fuckers, but I don't want to single myself out," Alex said with a worried look on his face.

"None of us were meant to leave this house alive tonight. Look at how ruthless they were with the girls and Teddy, and the police officers. We were gonna get it worse than they did. If you want to go back upstairs into the panic room and wait for it to be safe, Alex, I understand, and I'll work something out. I don't want to force you into it," Alfie explained. Alex looked at Alfie and Ben, ridden with guilt. Reluctantly, he picked the clothing and mask off the floor.

"Fine, I'll do it," Alex said as he took himself into the corner of the kitchen and began changing. Alfie reached into his pocket, taking out Charley's phone. Unlocking the front screen, he began scrolling through the content. Messages were empty, her social media was blank, and there were no photos. Alfie double-checked everything, confused, as Charley was always taking photos, and he'd seen her texting the day they moved into the house. Where was the photo they'd taken outside their old home? Chris's words haunted him as he heard them repeating Charley's involvement. Frustrated, Alfie threw the phone into the wall, smashing it.

"What's wrong?" Ben asked nervously, looking at Alfie. Ignoring his question, Alfie was trying to get Chris's words out of his head and compose himself for the impending fight he was about to face. Rubbing his eyes, he turned back around, reassuring Ben that he was fine.

Dressed in the intruder's attire, holding the orange mask in his trembling hand, Alex displayed reluctance written all over his face as he took a deep breath, attempting to steady his nerves. "Do you really think this will work?" he asked Alfie, his voice shaking with nerves.

"I don't know, but even if it doesn't, it'll distract them long enough for me to make a move," Alfie replied honestly. "Use the voice box to disguise your voice," he pointed to the mask.

"What's the plan?" Ben asked, standing beside them. "What do I do?" he continued nervously. Alfie looked at Ben with a tensed smile as he started to explain their roles and instructions on how to play the part. Alex pulled the orange balaclava over his head, testing the voice box. Alfie noticed Alex's trembling worsening, so he reassured his friend that he wouldn't let anything happen to them, a promise he knew he couldn't guarantee.

Walking out of the house, Alex tensed his body to mask his nerves; his heart pounded so loudly he couldn't hear Ben's heavy breath beside him. Both of them paced slowly down the front of the house. His face burning hot as the orange mask made him feel suffocated, he couldn't help but assume he was walking into a doomed ending. Walking out of the front gate, Alex let Ben walk in front of him as he grabbed the scruff of his neck, revealing a knife that he rested the tip into his neck. Alex could feel Ben's legs giving way as he had to pull him up to stand, which made the tip of the knife cut his neck.

Standing at the wide-open gate of Alice and Emerson's home, Alex pushed Ben forward, marching him up the concrete path. Feeling the uneasiness and fear vibrating from his hold on the neck of Ben's clothing, Alex began to calm himself, reminding himself of the part he was going to play.

Knocking on the front door, they waited for what felt like minutes until the pink intruder opened the door wide. Every angst inside of him burned away as a fiery rage motivated him. Replaying the torture that Jennifer and his unborn baby had endured at their hands gave him an urge to repay the killer with the same treatment. Noticing the smashed mirrored eyes, Alex tried to guess who they were, but the bloodshot eye threw him off. "Where have you been?" asked the pink intruder with the disguised voice. Alex hesitated before replying, fighting the temptation to ram the knife into their face.

"I was in the house, I stabbed Alfie!" Alex replied with his now disguised voice concealing his identity and anger.

"Where did you find him?" the pink intruder interrogated, their eyes stripping Ben of his flesh.

"I found him hiding, No one lives remember!" Alex answered quickly with a monotone, trying to keep his cover.

The pink intruder moved to the side, gesturing for Alex and Ben to come inside. Walking confidently past the pink killer, Alex pushed and roughly handled Ben. The pink intruder closed the door, analysing Alex in the orange mask. Forcing Ben into the living room, Alex noticed the back of Lucy's head sitting up. Dragging Ben around, he pushed him onto the sofa, noticing Lucy holding her stomach and covered in blood.

"Lucy!" Ben impulsively shouted. Lucy looked at him just before Alex whacked him in the back of the head with the handle of the knife. Instantly, Alex noticed Alice's dead body bleeding out on the white carpet, disturbing him. His heart thumped harder as he looked at the pink intruder's artwork. The attacks were so similar to what the killer had done to Jennifer; for a second, he saw her lying on the floor and froze.

"Did I hear you say you stabbed Alfie?" asked the black-masked intruder, turning to Alex.

"Yeah, that's why I have this kitchen knife. He attacked me, so I stabbed him," Alex tried not to over-explain himself.

"Fucking idiot, Alfie can't die yet; that's not the plan. They'll kill you if you mess up the plan," the black-masked intruder explained in panic. Alex nodded his head as he wondered who the killer meant by "they."

Alex was quiet, thinking about what to say, concerned that he'd messed up. Calming himself, he responded as nonchalantly as he could. "Should I go and get him?" the voice box covering his nervous tone. The black-masked intruder shook their head.

"He's coming here anyway," the killer responded. Alex watched Lucy for a second as Ben looked at him, fearful that Ben would give away their cover. Alex turned around, looking out the side window in the house. He was hoping he'd see Alfie coming along any moment now, but the night was fading into quiet outside. Alex turned his head, looking at the black-masked intruder standing near the fireplace. His instinct was to attack and get the gun out of their hand, but he was held back by the plan and his own determination to survive.

"There's no point in him being alive!" The pink intruder said, standing behind the sofa as they began to brush his neck with their bloody-dipped hunting knife, painting the back of his head.

"No! We want Alfie to watch his friends die!" Alex quickly interrupted, preventing the pink intruder from their desire. Abruptly, the two killers looked at one another, which Alex noticed instantly, watching both of them trying to dissect their unspoken communications. The pink killer's naked eyes turned to Alex, full of suspicion, which worried him. "Fuck it, kill him, kill her, kill them all. I just thought we wanted Alfie to watch them die!" Alex spoke fast in defence, trying to recover his identity as the orange killer.

A vibration of grunts echoed from the pink intruder's voice box. Lunging at Alex, she grabbed his mask. With a firm grip around their wrist, Alex pulled them away. The black-masked intruder clicked the back of the gun, pointing it at him. Defeated and in fear of his life, Alex let go of the pink intruder's wrist, letting them take off his orange disguise.

Erupting through the house, a bullet tore through the air, penetrating Alex's shoulder with a sickening bang. The force sent him reeling, gritting his teeth against the searing pain, refusing to succumb. Before he could react, the pink intruder pounced, driving him to the ground with a heavy thud.

Alex fought back with every ounce of strength, his injured shoulder burning from the heat of the bullet. He grappled with the intruder; their bodies entangled in a fierce struggle for control.

Without thinking, Ben leaped onto the intruder's back, his hands wrapping around their throat in a vice-like grip. The pink killer choked, with an arm around their neck and a hand pulling the balaclava over the top of their mouth.

Knowing what the pink intruder was capable of, Alex clutched the intruder's foot in a desperate attempt to protect Ben from the intruder getting the upper hand. A brutal kick to the face caused his teeth to cut into his lip. Alex fell backwards to the floor as blood leaked down the side of his face.

Lying still on the floor as another explosion echoed within the house, the black-masked intruder fired a bullet straight into Ben's neck. Releasing the pink killer, Ben grabbed the side of his neck. Lucy let out a wailing cry as Ben collapsed to the floor.

The pink intruder instantly jumped over Alex, bending down knife raised ready to kill. Lucy begged for them to stop as she tried to move off the sofa to try and help Alex. The black-masked intruder pointed the gun at her, as the sound of shattering glass resonated in the room as the small shards rained down onto the white carpet. A brick flying through the room landed beside Ben's slowly dying body. The pink intruder stood up moving away from Alex and looking at the black-masked killer awaiting.

Chapter 15

Standing in the doorway, watching as Alex and Ben left his house, Alfie observed their slow walk out of his territory, wrenched in guilt. Knowing he had potentially sent the lambs to the slaughter, he filled with dread as he watched them vanish out of his sight. Turning around, Teddy's lifeless body caught his eye, and the sorrow he once felt was now mixed with animosity. Shaking his head to empty the images of Charley and Teddy from his mind, he rushed into the kitchen. Unloading the gun, he checked how many bullets were left—six. Reaching inside his pocket, he pulled out his phone and the butterfly knife, placing the three items on the kitchen island as he pulled out one of the drawers, rummaging through the junk. Finding a paperclip, he lodged it into the side of his phone's cover before putting the phone and knife back into his pocket and picking up the gun.

"Okay, let's do this," he encouraged himself. Placing the gun in his waistband, he walked over to the kitchen door. He looked at his reflection in the glass for a second before pulling the door open. Leaving the kitchen, he sprinted through the garden, the sky lightening as daylight approached. His feet stamped on the ground, propelling him forward. At the back of his garden, he opened the gate, swiftly racing up the footpath, the cobble pavement pressing against his feet.

Pulling the gate's handle, Alfie checked to see if it had been opened. Crouching down to eye level with the lock, he examined its vulnerability. Taking out his phone, he removed the paperclip, bending and twisting the wire metal until it was shaped properly. Carefully manoeuvring it into the keyhole, Alfie panicked and rushed, causing him to drop the unwound clip on the floor. Stumbling backwards, he threw his hand behind him, feeling the rough surface of a brick, which helped him regain his balance. Pushing himself forward, he felt for the paperclip on the pebbled floor, picked it back up, and took a deep breath, calming his worry as he concentrated on picking the gate lock. Fumbling with the metal in the keyhole, Alfie focused intently until he heard the clicking of the gate unlocking. Pushing the gate open, Alfie looked around, noticing the brick that he nearly fell on. Picking it up, he walked through the gate, scanning his surroundings.

Stopping halfway on the grass, Alfie surveyed the house from a distance, strategizing a way to get inside unnoticed. Following the length of the drainpipe up the wall, he hunched over, racing closer toward the house. Standing near the drainpipe, Alfie pulled at it with his free hand, testing its sturdiness.

Shifting around the kitchen, Alfie tried to peek inside the house, startled as a gunshot echoed through the house, vibrating against the windows. Dropping to the ground, his mind raced with intense fright. Staying low beneath the windows, Alfie shuffled around the house as quickly as he could. Approaching the side window of the living room, he eavesdropped in the hope of hearing his friends' voices. Peering through the bottom of the window, Alfie could see Lucy sitting injured, filled with relief as he had confirmation, she was alive. Ben jumped up from the sofa, diverting his attention as he watched Ben throttle the pink killer. Another bullet rattled through the house, leaving Alfie horrified to see the blood seeping out of Ben's neck. Stunned for a second, Alfie shuffled away from the window, crawling a couple of steps away. With tensed fingers on the brick, he hurled it with all his strength, shattering the window. Darting down the side of the house, Alfie heard the shattered shards falling to the ground.

Ducking down as he approached the kitchen, he took a quick look through the window, checking to see if any of the killers were coming for him. No one entered the kitchen, which made him cautious as he checked the side of the house.

Urgently, he ran to the pipe, firmly wrapping his hands around the cold steel. He pushed his feet off the ground as he ascended. With the window in his sight, he reached as near the window as he could. Feeling his hands slip down the pipe, he remained determined, readying himself before pulling himself back up. As he neared the window and reached his hand on the ledge, the sound of crunching grass made him freeze. Looking down, he saw the pink killer hunting for her prey. Fixed on the ledge, he toyed with the idea of getting inside unnoticed, but he knew he was risking more than just his life at this point. He remained in position, hoping the pink intruder wouldn't notice him as the sky was lightening, removing any shadowing.

Stomping through the garden, Alfie watched, deliberating when he could make an escape. Suddenly, his foot slipped, scraping against the pipe. Abruptly, the pink intruder turned around, catching the outline of Alfie holding onto the tube. Charging toward the house, the pink intruder flicked their knife through the air, trying to catch Alfie. Too high up to reach, the pink killer grunted as distortion resounded in the garden. Storming away from the drainpipe, the killer disappeared. Knowing he had only a short time, Alfie leaped upwards, taking the gun out of his waistband. He hammered the gun's base into the window before putting the gun back into his waistband. Throwing himself forward, Alfie

275

grabbed the window's ledge as he pulled himself through.

Inside the house, Alfie pulled himself into the home gym, dropping to the floor, where he landed on a metal object. He hissed in pain, quickly pushing himself up onto his knees. There, he saw Lucy's gun on the floor. Picking it up, he aimed it toward the open door as he gradually stood up.

Hearing the stampeding footsteps approaching, Alfie edged to the side of the room, standing near the dumbbells. The pink intruder, enraged, sprinted through the door, their knife ready. Alfie fired the gun, aiming at their leg. Instantly, the pink killer fell to the floor with a wail of pain emerging from the voice box. Alfie stayed in place as he watched the intruder struggle to stand up. The smashed mirrored eyes glanced at Alfie as they both intensely looked at each other.

"Who are you?" asked Alfie. The pink intruder ignored his question as they staggered with struggle to stand up. Alfie was still as he gave the killer a chance to stand, believing they would now reveal themselves, but they didn't. The killer limped toward Alfie, which made Alfie back up. They circled around until the killer was standing opposite the window. Alfie fired another bullet into the killer's arm, causing them to drop their knife. Firing another round from the gun, Alfie hit the killer in the chest, knocking them backwards out of the window. Rushing to the shattered window, the shards of glass cutting into his feet, Alfie looked below to see the pink killer lying still, their eyes staring up at him.

Backing away from the window, a shard of glass dug into Alfie's foot; sharply, he pulled it out, leaving drips of blood on the floor behind him. Sneaking down the stairs, he listened intently as he took each step. His back firmly against the wall as he gazed at the wall keeping him hidden from the killer in the living room. On the panel of the stairs, he climbed over the banister instead of walking down the final three steps that would put him in view of the living room. Blood from his foot dripped onto the laminated hallway floor. Dropping onto the floor, he skidded, grabbing the banister.

"Alfie, I know you're here," the disguised voice smoothly announced. Alfie let go of the banister as he moved silently towards the wall, his breathing becoming more intense as he swallowed the fear of death. Taking a chance, Alfie curved his arm around the wall's edge and blindly fired the gun.

"Missed!" the voice announced with arrogance.

"Who are you?" Alfie shouted through anxious, heavy breath.

"Throw away the gun and I'll show you," the voice offered, Alfie visualizing the killer's movements in his head as they spoke.

"No chance," Alfie replied sharply, his hands shaking with eagerness to end this with their death.

"Fine, throw the gun in here, or I'll put a bullet right through Lucy's head," the disguised voice threatened with the click of the gun. Lucy squealed, sending terror through Alfie.

Unclipping the gun, Alfie checked the bullets—three left. He threw the bullet cartridge into the room behind him and the gun into the living room. Heart pounding against his ribcage, he pressed his trembling body against the wall, listening intensely to what was going on in the living room.

"Come out, or she dies," the intruder demanded. Hesitant at first, Alfie stalled; he couldn't lose Lucy. Gradually, Alfie edged from the side of the wall, standing in the centre of the arch of the living room. The black-masked intruder fired the gun. Sharply, Alfie dived to the other side of the hallway, narrowly avoiding the shot that created a hole in the wall inches from his head. He knew his luck was running out as he gazed at the small, ragged tear.

Removing his gun from the back of his joggers, Alfie fired blindly again. Peering through the hole, Alfie got an idea of the black-masked intruder's position, firing another bullet that flew past the intruder's head, ripping through the mirror behind them.

Helpless, Alex pounced from the floor, grabbing the barrel of the gun despite his seething shoulder agony. Pushing the intruder against the wall, they fought for power over the gun. Bullets flew repeatedly through the air in the struggle, firing into the ceiling and causing small pieces of drywall to fall to the floor. Lucy screamed as the drywall hit her, and she dove to the other side of the sofa, still holding her stomach as the red blood stained the cushions.

Alex succumbed to the flaming pain in his arm as he lost strength against the black-masked killer, who pointed the gun downwards, firing again with a bullet penetrating into Alex's knee. Alex fell to the floor, as the killer pointed the gun in his face, pulling the trigger, but the cartridge was empty. They threw the gun out of the window as Alfie appeared back at the centre of the living room entrance, gun aimed and steady.

"Take the fucking mask off now," Alfie gritted.

"No!" the intruder plainly replied. Aggravated, Alfie emptied the last five remaining bullets into the black-masked killer. The gunfire reflected each spark from the gun before they dropped to the floor. Sidling into the living room, Alfie continued pointing the gun. Pulling the trigger and realizing there were no more bullets, Alfie dropped his aim.

"Are you both alright?" he asked as he turned to look at them both.

"No, I've been fucking shot," Alex wailed through gritted teeth, holding back the intense pain. Turning to Ben, Alfie tapped his face, then held his hand under his nose, checking if he was still breathing. No movement and no breath, Ben was dead. Alfie apologized to him, losing his grip on the situation for a second. His attention directed to Lucy as he helped her off the sofa. She told him the killer's identity, throwing him off guard.

"Do you think you two can make it back to mine on your own?" he said as he looked at the killer motionless behind him.

"Why aren't you coming with us?" Lucy replied as she stood hunched over, watching Alfie help Alex off the floor.

"The pink one's dead outside; I need to work out what the fuck is going on here," Alfie replied, checking Alex's knee. Rushed, Alfie swept the gun off the living room floor and the cartridge from the other room. He handed it to Lucy. Limping through the living room to the hallway, Lucy and Alex left the house heading back to Alfie's.

In the living room, Alfie uneasily kneeled beside the motionless killer as he reached over to remove their mask. Removing the masquerade, he looked at the killer's face, whose eyes were closed. Deep in concentration trying to piece the connection together, he leaned over the killer as dark blue eyes fluttered open, and a knife penetrated into Alfie's left side, leaving two slits between the flesh just above Alfie's hip.

Removing the knife aggressively, Alfie dropped backwards to the floor, holding his hand over the gash in his side and sliding backwards with his other arm. The killer stood up looking over Alfie.

"You were dead!" Alfie gasped, fighting the pain. The killer began mimicking sounds of their death, stopping with an eerie smile and tilted head.

"Was I... I seem to have a pulse. Silly Alfie!" Stewart replied sarcastically, revealing a bulletproof vest under his clothes.

"Why? Why did you do this?" Alfie asked, gritting through the pain, his hand still holding onto his side.

"Why not? You know what it's like to kill… It's fucking exhilarating… makes you feel like a god, slowly taking someone's life away, watching their eyes become empty… Fuck!" Stewart explained with enthusiasm, relishing in the enjoyment of power.

"I never enjoyed it," Alfie spoke defensively, with an angered look on his face.

"Oh, come on Alfie, don't kid a kidder. I saw the look in your eyes when you were firing that gun at me, you loved it. Pulling that trigger was too easy for you," Stewart replied insulted, his body stiffening.

"I didn't!" Alfie weakly defended, turning his face away from Stewart as he spoke before looking back at him showing his certainty.

"You did, and it's a shame because if we let this side of ourselves show, I think we'd have been even better friends, and maybe we'd be killing those who want to kill you" Stewart said with admiration.

"What do you mean those who want to kill me? You, Chris and the other one, why?" Alfie asked, confused by Stewart's words.

"The three of us, no Alfie, no. Someone has it out for you, Alfie Sayers. When you kill, you have to make sure your victims are not loved and there are no repercussions," Stewart playfully replied. "You see, like my first killing, no one even knew he was gone, and that first kill was better than losing my virginity," Stewart continued before Alfie cut him off.

"Who has it out for me, man, woman, who?" Alfie asked abruptly as he stood up face to face with Stewart.

"I'm not allowed to tell you just yet. You have to beg for your life first. I don't get to enjoy your final breath," Stewart said, wiping Alfie's blood off his knife.

"So why? Why are you involved in this? Why did you do this tonight?" Alfie asked as he shuffled towards the sofa.

"I'm a plant. Your death has been planned for a long time. I have no personal vendetta, which is why I wasn't as amateur as the other two were with the killings," Stewart boasted with a smile on his face.

"So, who has a personal vendetta against me?" Alfie asked as he leaned on the table behind the sofa, focusing on Stewart's face, trying to ignore the pain he was in.

"All I can tell you is that some people in that house, even dead ones… were or are involved. Here's the deal: I'm not going to kill you, but I am going to cut you up a little. I have to leave you alive for the others," Stewart continued as if he was speaking rationally.

"Charley?" Alfie asked, desperate for denial. Stewart nodded his head with a huge grin. Immediately, Stewart came charging across the room, jumping on the sofa, soaring toward Alfie. Quickly, Alfie grabbed the vase on the table, smashing it into Stewart's face as he grabbed his arm, yanking him over the chair. Backing away fast, his wound stinging as he moved away.

Amidst a loud eruption of psychotic laughter, Stewart arose from behind the sofa, revealing a bloody lip. Touching his lip, he began to praise Alfie, trying to distract him as he lunged forward, knife slicing the air. Alfie, in agony, avoided every slash and plunge aimed at him. Frustration became evident on Stewart's face as he failed to maim him as he desired. With every dodge, Alfie felt excruciating pain as his vest soaked up the blood seeping out. Stewart, relentless in his attack, tackled Alfie to the floor, falling next to Ben's dead body. Using both hands and putting all his body weight into his downward knife, Stewart tried to breach the blade into Alfie.

Holding Stewart's wrists with all his strength, Alfie held him at bay, fending off the impending stabbing. A quick glance at Ben, Alfie saw the drain cleaner tucked in his trousers. Stewart began moving closer to Alfie, as the pain Alfie felt was weakening his grip. Taking a deep breath and swallowing the burning in his side, Alfie knew it was do or die. Tucking his knees slowly upwards towards his stomach, the tightening in his core caused the two cuts in his side to throb and bleed out faster. His feet against Stewart's chest, Alfie power-kicked him backwards.

Rapidly, Alfie grabbed the chemical liquid as Stewart charged toward him. Uncapping the bottle, Alfie splashed it upwards, catching Stewart under his chin and on his nose. As Stewart continued to rage toward Alfie, he backed away, splashing more towards Stewart's face. Suddenly, Stewart dropped the knife on the floor, yelling as the drain cleaner began to eat his flesh. He attempted to touch his face, but the burning sensation travelled to his hands.

Backing away, Alfie watched as Stewart's skin began bubbling, a sizzling sound heard between his cries. Swaying as he ran through the living room, Alfie watched with enjoyment at the killer's suffering. Trying to stand up, Alfie fell back to the floor, noticing the brick on the floor. Placing his hand over it, he tensed his fingers in a wide grip. Slowly, Alfie stood back up, wincing at every movement. Wobbling into the hallway, Alfie looked toward the kitchen, watching Stewart splash water over his face. He paced through the hallway into the kitchen.

In the kitchen, he silently snuck toward Stewart. Standing behind him, Alfie whacked the brick into the back of Stewart's head. With force, Stewart's chemically burned face collided into the edge of the tap, ripping open the top of his nose. Grabbing the back of his black jumper, Alfie vigorously pulled him backwards. Disoriented, Stewart tripped, smashing the back of his head into the edge of the island in the middle of the kitchen. Standing over him, Alfie looked at him with a smile, pushing his arm with his bare foot. Stewart now lay flat, looking up at the ceiling. Alfie kneeled over him, brick still in hand, as he repeatedly struck the brick into Stewart's face. Teeth broke out of his mouth, and blood splattered everywhere, continuously striking the brick violently until his face was dented in and his skull bones were shattered.

Standing up, Alfie looked down at the art he'd created, losing control. "That was exhilarating," Alfie breathed, dropping the brick on top of him. Clutching at his side, Alfie fell into the island, feeling his head getting light from the shock of being stabbed. Pushing away from the corner of the countertop, he balanced himself. Taking a slow walk towards the kitchen door, he opened it, stepping outside. Ready to unmask the pink killer, he felt flustered as he walked outside; the body of the pink killer had vanished. Uneasily, he reached into his pocket, unlocking the butterfly knife. He looked around, fighting the pain surging through his body.

Looking around the house, blood-stained grass caught his attention. He followed the trail leading out of the neighbour's house. Diligent of his surroundings, he took his time, listening intently to the sounds around him, vigilant in his surroundings. The blood trail ended at the front of his gate. Glancing at his house from the distance, Alfie forgot about the pink killer for a moment as he prepared himself for confronting Charley and ending this once and for all.

Chapter 16

Overwhelmed as he staggered towards his home, Alfie collapsed outside the front door, the knife still firm in his grasp. Pushing himself up with his elbows, pain seared through his body. He looked at the dead officer near him, filled with guilt, all the victims of the night piercing his sight and weighing heavily on him. "Sorry," he muttered under his breath. Staring at the ground, he gradually pushed himself up, grabbing the sides of the door to support himself as he stood. Teddy's body was cantered in his view. He replayed his death, and then the words of Chris echoed through his ears. Alfie didn't know how to feel; anger was equal to loss.

Pulling himself into the house, Alfie stepped slowly into the hallway. Giving her a wide smile, which she returned, he ignored the pain and moved slightly faster, wrapping his arms around her tightly. He couldn't contain his relief at her survival, which allowed the anger from Chris's reveal, the betrayal of Charley, and the loss of friends to flood to the surface, letting the tears flow freely from his eyes. Alex appeared in the kitchen doorway, looking at them both.

"Who was the pink one?" Lucy muffled into Alfie's shoulder.

"They disappeared," sniffled Alfie, pressing his eyes on Lucy's shoulder before pulling away to look at her.

"We need to kill them; they can't get away," Lucy stated with concern as she winced from the pain in her stomach.

"Whoever it is, they're injured; I shot them in the leg," Alfie assured, looking at both her and Alex. "Where's the gun?" he asked, looking at both of them. Lucy pulled the gun from the side of her shorts, handing it to Alfie. Pulling up his vest, Lucy and Alex's eyes spotted the wound seeping down Alfie's bloody skin.

"Oh my God, Alfie," Lucy gasped, soaking her hands in blood as she pulled his vest up to check the severity.

"It's fine, looks worse than it is," Alfie lied, pulling his wet vest down to cover his injury. "I need to get you out of here," Alfie stated, looking at Lucy and Alex.

"Don't you mean we need to get out of here?" Alex replied, looking at Alfie unsure. Alfie fell silent for a moment before revealing his intentions, confessing all that had been revealed to him. Lucy tried to sway his plan, but Alfie was adamant. Standing in the doorway, Alex initially hesitated before subtly nodding, agreeing to Alfie's plan.

"Let's get everyone out of the panic room," Alfie said, cutting Lucy off as she tried to rationalize what he had told her. Alfie ascended the stairs followed by Lucy and Alex; the injured trio took slow steps, fighting the anguish of their wounds. Alfie's mind was heavy as the dangers of the chaos seemed to have calmed. He replayed every death and words spoken internally; he was fighting an army of anxious soldiers ready to win their war.

"Are you sure you can do this?" Lucy said, midway on the stairs, stopping everyone. Alfie turned to face her, looking at Alex behind her; he felt so grateful for them. He knew what Alex had lost and what Lucy had risked, but they walked through the fire to save him. Nodding his head, Alfie turned away; he couldn't allow himself to get into the emotional side of what he had to do.

On the second floor, the three of them walked into Alfie's bedroom. Catching his reflection in the window opposite, he assumed the fight Oscar would put up upon seeing him like this.

Grabbing a black T-shirt and black joggers from the corner of the walk-in wardrobe, Alfie spoke, "Give me a minute; I can't let Oscar see me in this state," before disappearing into the ensuite and closing the door.

Removing the gun from his joggers, Alfie placed it on the side of the sink. Twisting the taps, he let the water run before splashing it over his face. Dirt and blood filled the sink as he washed the torment of the night away.

Taking off his vest, he grabbed some cotton wool from the cabinet and dampened it. He dabbed it on his shoulder, removing the dry blood from his cut. In the mirror, Alfie examined the bruise on his side, a deep purple of pain.

Stretching his arm up, the two cuts sent a sharp sensation down his body, causing him to stumble to the side; quickly, he grabbed the side of the sink, knocking the gun to the floor. "For fuck's sake," he muttered through gritted teeth, grimacing in pain.

Sucking the agony through his clenched teeth, he grabbed his black T-shirt, pulling it over his head. Looking into the mirror, Teddy's reflection stared back at him. Freezing as he watched Teddy's slit throat filling the mirror, Alfie clenched his hands tightly on the sink, his body beginning to shake.

"Look what's happened to me because of you!" Teddy's bloodshot eyes glared at Alfie, appearing demonic.

"Sorry," Alfie cried with blame, trying to avert his gaze away from the haunting reflection.

"You keep secrets from me, pretend that we are friends, and you left me to die!" Teddy shouted venomously.

"I'm sorry," Alfie said a little louder, clenching his jaw to steady his nerves, avoiding looking at the mirror but the image etched inside his head.

"You're not sorry, you're the cause. All this death because of you and what you hide," Teddy's haunting voice echoed. "I lost everything because of you," Teddy continued.

"And you took Charley from me," Alfie retorted, his own anger fighting his guilty conscience. Teddy began to laugh.

"I did, and she loved every moment of it. I pleased her in ways you could never," Teddy mocked with a sinister grin, blood leaking from his bottom lip. Enraged, Alfie punched his hand through the mirror. The voices in his head stopped blaming him as he stared at the shattered cabinet. A shard of glass etched into his knuckle; he pulled it out, looking at his reflection. Dropping the shard into the sink, he closed his eyes, hearing panicked breaths coming from the shower. Carefully bending down, he reached for the gun, aiming it.

"Get out now!" Alfie demanded. The heavy breathing stopped, and suddenly the one-way glass slid open. Ivy stood in front of him, shaking. Alfie sized her up, his suspecting mind darting to her legs, checking for any blood. "Where the hell have you been?" He asked, the gun still raised.

"I... I, Lucy, she... Lucy said everyone needed... that they needed to, uh, come up... up here, and I... I... I hid in here," Ivy stuttered, explaining to Alfie. Alfie lowered the gun. "What's going on?" Ivy asked as she began to cry. Alfie looked at her still suspecting.

"Let's just get you out of here," Alfie softened, realizing she was going to be in turmoil when she found out about Ella. Taking Ella out into his room, Lucy, sitting on the bed, stood up defensively.

"Where have you been all night?" She interrogated. Ivy stuttered, trying to speak, but Lucy pressured her as she kept urging her to answer.

"She's been hiding in the bathroom," Alfie answered, feeling sympathy for her.

"You haven't changed your trousers, you don't want Oscar to see you with them on go and change," Lucy instructed, taking a short glance at Alfie before focusing on Ivy again. Alfie looked down at his trousers, then at Lucy and Ivy, then at Alex with a look asking him to settle the tension. Alex limped between the two girls.

Back inside the ensuite, Alfie closed the door, inhaling a deep breath, his eyes closed before changing into the black joggers. Turning around to leave the bathroom, a man appeared before him, wailing in his face.

"KILLER!"

Alfie staggered backward, falling to the floor. The man from his past bent down, putting his face in Alfie's. Heart racing, hands shaking, Alfie could feel his breath trapped in his throat. Tightly, he squeezed his eyes shut. Reopening his eyes, the man he murdered was gone.

A tentative knock on the ensuite door startled Alfie, prompting him to swallow his fear as Lucy peered inside to check on him. Assuring her he was fine, he maintained a composed facade, calming his nerves before returning to his bedroom. Casting a quick glance at Ivy, who still wore a fearful expression, Alfie realized that Lucy and Alex hadn't informed her yet. With a purposeful stride, he made his way to the walk-in wardrobe. Expecting his mother to have already opened it, he was surprised to find it still closed. With a firm knock, he signalled for the hidden door open. The door slowly creaked open as his mother opened the door armed.

Seeing her son, Alfie's mother threw herself at him, wrapping her arms tightly around his neck. He winced in pain as he fell backwards, tensing his body and causing a sharp infliction of pain.

"Are you okay?" She asked with a mother's panic, scanning him all over to find the cause.

"Yeah, I'll be okay. Why didn't you open the door when we came into the bedroom?" Alfie asked, trying to ignore the pain.

"The rest of the cameras went off after you and the boys went downstairs, so I couldn't see who was coming in and out," Alfie's mother explained, instantly triggering Alfie's overthinking about how that could be possible. Lifting up his T-shirt, his mother looked at the wound in his side. "We need to get that covered up or that won't stop bleeding," she stated calmly.

"Do it out here," Alfie insisted. His mother gave him a look of confusion before going back into the panic room to get the first aid box. Lucy, Alex, and Ivy went inside the room. Alfie watched them as Ivy rushed over to Charley, embracing each other firmly. Lucy and Alex went over to Thomas sitting on the chair, Emerson standing alone against the wall. Bulldozer stared at Alfie from the bed across the room, his tail wagging, as Oscar remained peacefully asleep.

Coming out of the room with the first aid box, Alfie removed his T-shirt as his mother pushed his side puncture together, taping it shut before wrapping a bandage firmly around his waist.

"Who were they?" Asked Alfie's mother as he sat on the bed.

"One was her brother Chris, and another was Stewart, who we thought was dead. I don't know who the third one was; they got away," Alfie explained. His mother knew the look on his face; she'd seen it before, but this time there was a reluctance blended in. Briefly he told his mother about what the killers had told him before revealing his final act.

"Can you do it?" asked his mother with concern, "Are you sure?" she continued as Alfie silently nodded, unsure. "I can do it if you can't," she affirmed before their conversation was disturbed by a loud cry from the panic room.

Jumping up, Alfie grabbed the gun, both he and his mother running into the panic room. Ivy roared howls of torment, collapsing into Charley. The tears awoke Oscar as Bulldozer barked at the emotion in the room. Putting the gun back in his joggers, his mother handed him his T-shirt. Putting the T-shirt back on, he walked over to the bed, patting Bulldozer on the head before sitting next to Oscar, giving him a loving hug and kissing the side of his head.

"Why's Ivy crying?" innocently whispered Oscar in his ear.

"She had some sad news," Alfie replied, squeezing Oscar tighter.

"What's going on?" Oscar asked innocently as he looked around the room. Alfie's mother walked over to the bed, standing in front of the two Sayers.

"Nothing's going on, but you need to stay with Nanny till we leave this house," Alfie said, looking at his mother. Standing up, Alfie let his mother sit as she scooped Oscar onto her lap. Watching everyone around the room, Alfie walked into the centre. "Right, we all need to get out of this house," Alfie declared, speaking to the room.

"Where's Alice?" Emerson interrupted. Alfie looked at him with an apologetic look, then dashed his eyes toward Oscar, pleading with Emerson to not make a scene. "Where is she?" Emerson continued louder. Ivy stopped crying as an awkward silence filled the room. Alfie's mother covered Oscar's ears as Bulldozer jumped off the bed.

"Not now, mate," Alex interrupted, knowing Alfie's concern.

"Where the fuck is my wife?" Emerson shouted with a broken voice, desperately hoping for an answer. Lucy stood up, holding her stomach, Thomas standing to help her balance.

"She's dead! And I'll tell you what happened when we get out of here. There's a child in here!" Lucy abruptly spoke, annoyance on her face. Irritated, Emerson charged toward Lucy. Quickly, Alfie grabbed him, pushing him to the wall, removing the gun and putting it under Emerson's chin.

"You chose to stay in here. You have no idea what we have dealt with, so I suggest you calm yourself down before I add another body to my kill count," Alfie spat venomously with his fury, wetting Emerson's face. A sudden burst of tears instantly calmed him down as he heard Oscar crying. Charley walked over to her son, taking him from Alfie's mother, reassuring him as she gave Alfie the same death stare she'd given him earlier that night. Putting the gun back in his waistband, he backed away from Emerson with a calmer tone. "We're going to go downstairs, and whoever's got a car big enough to fit everyone drive to the hospital. My mother, Charley, Oscar, the dog, and I will follow behind."

Alfie led the way out of the panic room, with everyone trailing behind. Emerson, Ivy, Thomas, and Charley exited the bedroom, heading downstairs. In the hallway, Alfie turned to his mother. "Go into Oscar's room with him and

298

Bulldozer," he instructed, handing her the butterfly knife. Lucy and Alex followed as Alfie began descending the stairs. Halfway down, Alfie halted them, leaning in to instruct Lucy quietly. "Wait thirty to forty minutes, then call the police," he whispered, ensuring only they could hear. Lucy opened her mouth to respond, but Alfie turned away, continuing his descent down the stairs.

Downstairs, Alfie heard Charley and Ivy's fright at seeing the dead bodies and blood in the hallway. Emerson was waiting at the front door, the breaking of daylight glimmering light into the slaughtered abode. "We'll be right behind you, once we work out how to get Oscar out of here without seeing this," Alfie said, ushering everyone out of the house. Walking down the front path, Lucy and Alex kept looking back at Alfie with anxious looks until he saw them near the front gate and closed the door.

"Oh my god, Alfie, what happened here?" Charley asked as she looked at the victims on the floor, her eyes catching the splatters of blood around the hallway. Edging into the living room, Charley gasped as she looked at Jennifer, Ella, and Grace's bodies sat upright under the window. Bursting into tears, she rushed over to Ella, kneeling opposite her as she touched her face.

Alfie took slow steps into the living room, staring at the back of Charley's head. "Can you believe your brother did that to Ella?" Alfie informed Charley, his tone of voice sarcastically playing along with her emotions.

Charley spun her head, confused. "What... What do you mean Chris did this?" Charley said, disbelief evident in her voice.

"Yep, Chris... He was one of the assailants that broke in here tonight. Want to see him now?" Alfie smiled, with the same sardonic tone and folded arms. Charley looked at him with scepticism, but he wasn't buying her act.

She was silent as she looked at Alfie standing up, trying to figure out his coldness. "Where is he?" Charley stuttered.

"He's in the basement. Come on, let's go and see," Alfie gestured toward the kitchen, urging Charley to lead the way.

"I don't want to. This is too much," Charley replied wearily, sensing the defensiveness in Alfie's body language. She took a step backwards. Unfolding his arms, Alfie walked toward Charley with intensity, grabbing her wrist forcefully and pulling her out of the living room and into the hallway. Begging and pleading, she cried for him to let her go, which only caused him to squeeze her wrist tighter as he dragged her towards the basement door. She tried to turn into the kitchen, but he slammed his palm against the wall, blocking her escape. Opening the basement door, he shoved her forward.

"Alfie, stop! What is going on with you?" Charley halted, turning to look at Alfie, her vulnerability written on her face. Barging past her, he yanked her down the stairs. In the basement, he pulled her to Chris's body. She turned her head, avoiding looking at him. Alfie grabbed her head, forcing her to face him.

"That is what I am capable of when someone threatens me. This is what I am capable of to protect the people I love. This is what I am capable of when someone betrays me," Alfie vilified himself as he pressed Charley for a true reaction. Charley pushed Alfie off her, running back up the stairs. Watching her storming footsteps run away from him, he looked at Chris on the floor before following Charley up the stairs.

In the kitchen, Charley grabbed a knife from the kitchen, tears flooding from her eyes as she hid behind the island. Standing in the kitchen doorway, Alfie gave Charley a sadistic smile "So, you want to dive right into trying to kill me," Alfie said offhand taking a step into the kitchen.

"I don't want to kill you," Charley pleaded, her footing ready to run either way. Alfie pulled out the gun from his joggers' waistband, showing his hands, before placing it on the countertop.

"So, where do we start?" Alfie mocked, placing his hands on the opposite side of the island, his intense gaze fixed on Charley. She looked at him puzzled. "Shall we start with you and Teddy?" Alfie said, his tone calming but loaded with the hurt he buried. Charley tensed her hold on the knife, her palms sweaty as her eyes narrowed. She questioned what Alfie had meant, feeling insulted by his attempt to influence her to tell him the truth.

Charley looked at him guiltily before begrudgingly telling him the truth. "You weren't ever meant to find out. It happened once, that time when you disappeared, leaving me in the dark about where you were and what was going on with us. It was an accident," Charley confessed, her face flushed with remorse as she trembled under the pressure Alfie put on her.

"So, you did sleep with him? How did it happen?" Alfie calmly asked.

"I was distraught when you left and… and he took me for a drink… he… he was reassuring me that we would be okay, and… I… I… I kissed him. He pulled away, I left, and he walked me home… then it just happened. We

302

swore you'd never find out," Charley stuttered in her explanation as she trembled, putting the knife down. Shifting around the island Charley moved closer to Alfie as he lowered his defences.

"Why did you hate Eva if it was a one-time thing?" Alfie said softly, causing Charley to freeze at the end of the island. Their eyes met, and Charley screwed up her face, unsure what Alfie had meant. "You weren't jealous Teddy had moved on?" Alfie scrutinized her face as he said the words, trying to catch her off guard.

"No, God no, our thing happened long before she came on the scene… I didn't like her because Teddy became distant and she rarely joined in on things we did as a group," Charley explained, edging closer toward Alfie. Placing his palms on the countertop of the island, one over the gun, he clenched the gun in his hand. Frustration filled him as Chris's words echoed in his head; he couldn't bear to see her vulnerability; he wasn't going to be duped by her.

"Explain to me why Chris told me this was all your idea? Why Stewart said you were a part of this?" Alfie's voice trembled with unwavering conviction as he released the bottled-up information, his disturbance boiling over.

"What? Alfie, no... that's a lie!" Charley exclaimed desperately, placing her hand on Alfie's arm. Feeling himself soften at her touch, Alfie grabbed her by the shoulders, pushing her against the wall she gasped as her back knocked against the surface.

"Why would he lie, Charley? Why would your own brother put the blame on you? How would he have known the code to get into the house? It's the only thing that makes sense; is that you planned all of this," Alfie shouted in her face, his eyes intensely staring into hers.

"Alfie, you're hurting me," she cried, trying to get out of his clutches. Firmly holding her shoulders, he slammed her against the wall, demanding the truth. Tears began to fall from her eyes as she begged for him to let her go. He ignored her pleas as he wrapped his hands around her neck. Slapping at his hands, she tried to free herself from him. "Alfie, stop," she gasped in a low whisper as his hands closed her airways. Panicked, Charley bent her knee into his groin, forcing Alfie to let go. Coughing as she caught her breath, Charley looked at Alfie like he was a monster. He tried to grab her again, but she pushed him backwards, running out of the kitchen.

Grabbing the gun off the countertop, Alfie, fuelled with adrenaline, rushed to the kitchen door. Aiming the gun, he commanded Charley to halt before he readied the gun to fire. Turning around to see Alfie pointing the gun, fear setting in, Charley began to cry, her whimpers echoing through the hallway. "Why have you been so distant with me all night? The photos on the table, the questions, the arguments, the slap... We're meant to be by each other's side whatever happens, and you turned against me," Alfie bombarded Charley with his suspicions.

"I was scared, and I was angry… you kept me in the dark and look at everything that's happened tonight, I know you were trying to protect us, but that loyalty you wanted from me, is the same as the trust you didn't put in me," Charley cried her voice cracking.

"I want you to be telling the truth, I love you, and It has destroyed me inside when they said you were behind this, you, Oscar and my mum are everything to me… but I don't know if you're lying right now and that scares me… and I hate that all this has made me so uncertain of you, of us!" Alfie broke, his voice trembling with emotion as his own tears streamed down his face, unable to contain the overwhelming flood of feelings any longer. His gun-wielding hand shook violently as he struggled to steady himself, the weight of uncertainty crushing him like a vice.

"Alfie, please!" Charley begged through tears, her terrified eyes pleading for help. Suddenly, a menacing silhouette with a pink head lunged from the living room, tackling Charley to the floor. Taken aback, Alfie stopped for a second. In a whirlwind of chaos, the injured pink killer held their knife over Charley as both engaged in a desperate struggle. The knife edged closer to Charley's throat. Her anguished scream tore through the air, reaching Alfie's ears like a gut-wrenching plea for help.

Reacting swiftly to Charley's helplessness, Alfie moved like lightning. Kicking the pink intruder off Charley, who lay on their side, Alfie rapidly emptied the final three bullets of the gun into the side of the pink killer's head. The room fell into momentary silence. Charley stood up, watching Alfie's face as he analysed the pink intruder's dead corpse. The pink-masked assailant slumped to the floor; the threat now extinguished.

"Believe me now," Charley stated sternly. Alfie turned to her for a moment before pulling the gun's trigger a final time, but with no result. Dropping the gun to the floor, he bent down, pushing the body so it was facing the ceiling. "Who is it?" Charley asked. Alfie ignored her question, carefully removing the mask from the intruder's head.

"What the hell is going on?" Alfie asked himself as he examined the body. His mind reeled in confusion as he stared at Eva's lifeless form, a cold sweat breaking out across his brow. He couldn't fathom what was happening—people faking their deaths to catch him off guard—the mystery haunting his thoughts like a lingering shadow.

On his knees, Alfie leaned in closer, hoping to figure out the mystery of why these three had banded together, when a sudden impact jolted the back of his head, sending a shockwave of pain radiating through his body. Disoriented and off-balance, he stumbled forward, slanting over Eva's body. He could feel his adrenaline trying to fight the urge to close his eyes, but the impact of the blow overcame him, forcing his eyes to close.

Chapter 17

Waves of agony radiated through Alfie's temples, accompanied by a pounding at the back of his head. His skull tightened from the impact of the blow, and a tingling sensation ran down his body, leaving his legs numb. Breathing slowly and steadily, he felt the firmness of the sofa pressed against the front of his face. Opening his eyes, he was greeted by the brightness of the sun shining through the window, but his vision was blurred as he tried to make out his surroundings.

Closing his eyes as footsteps approached, he tried to listen carefully, but the pounding migraine blocked his concentration. Taking slow-paced breaths into the sofa's cotton fibres, he attempted to relax his body to ease his suffering.

Images of Oscar and his mother slithered into his aching head as it dawned on him that they were out of the panic room. The urgency of protecting them overcame the pounding in his head. Opening his eyes again, they were still blurry. He could make out an outline of someone sitting against the wall opposite him on the sofa. Vibrations from stomping footsteps shook through the house, accompanied by a heavy breath of frustration.

Shutting his eyes, Alfie knew there was more than one person in the room. Charley, obviously, but who was her accomplice? He began suspecting people in his head, praying his mother and Oscar wouldn't make an appearance.

Suddenly, thoughts of Eva and the other assailants raced through Alfie's mind—a chaotic swirl of confusion and dread. The enigma of Chris, the madness of Stewart, and the mysterious Eva—each one a piece of a puzzle he struggled to assemble. Stewart's insanity, Chris's inexplicable hatred, and Eva, a once-stranger who entered his life through Teddy just two years ago—all were woven into a tapestry of uncertainty. As he mentally tallied the victims— Teddy's mother, Ronnie, Teddy himself, Grace, Ella, Jennifer, Alice, and Ben—the randomness of their deaths struck him profoundly. The only common thread among them was Alfie.

Shifting uncomfortably on the sofa, he felt an inexplicable restraint, his arms bound by handcuffs, amplifying the gravity of the situation. Footsteps receded as they left the living room, turning the room into a still silence. Alfie opened his eyes, slightly blurred; he squinted to take a peek at who was opposite him. It took a moment until he regained his sight. A woman sat, her arms arched out, revealing that she too shared the same cuffed bracelets as Alfie. Her long blonde hair spiralled around her sides. His eyes slowly came into focus, and he realized Charley was also bound and helpless. He wondered if it was a trick—a cheap tactic to make him feel guilty for believing it was her behind all this—or was it genuine?

Lifting his head, Alfie scanned the room, taking note that the lifeless bodies were now cleared from the living room, although the grim remnants of blood splatters still stained the floor. When Charley shifted her head, Alfie quickly dropped back onto the sofa, feigning unconsciousness. Footsteps echoed through the house, growing steadily closer. Alfie remained perfectly still, his body tense. Hands gripped the top of the sofa, and a heavy breath grazed the back of Alfie's neck, causing him to stiffen even further.

"Wakey, wakey, Alfie," a male voice taunted. Alfie's heart raced as a wet hand placed two fingers on his neck, checking his pulse. The touch heightened Alfie's panic, accelerating his heartbeat. "Don't pretend you're asleep, Alfie, or I'll have to go upstairs and kill your bitch of a mother to kill time," the voice threatened, sending a shiver down Alfie's spine. He gritted his teeth, contemplating how to escape this perilous situation.

Opening his eye, he glanced at Charley, who met his gaze with terrified tears streaming down her face. Sensing the sofa slightly tilt, a hand firmly gripped the centre of Alfie's back, clutching his T-shirt and the top of his joggers. With force, the unknown assailant thrust Alfie downward, lifting him off the sofa and propelling him onto the glass table. As Alfie fell through the shattered glass, shards crunched underneath him. Groaning, he attempted to turn and push himself up, only to feel a sharp slice on the side of his cheek.

Pressing his hand hard against the shards, Alfie could feel and hear them cracking underneath him as the assailant lifted him from the centre of the glass table and hurled him across the room.

"Stop, please stop," Charley begged through tears. Alfie attempted to stand up, but his legs felt like jelly, causing him to wobble and fall to the floor. A kick to his gut caught the side of a large bruise around his side, eliciting a sigh of discomfort from Alfie. He tried to get back up, but his feet were swept away, flooring him once again. With his face down, touching the cold wooden floorboards, Alfie rolled to the side just as the assailant attempted to stamp his foot into Alfie's head.

Making a run for it, Alfie tried to escape the living room, but his legs felt weak. The man grabbed the scruff of Alfie's top, heaving him toward the wall. With a loud thud, Alfie's back hit the wall as he slipped down, the savage attack preventing him from seeing the attacker's face. Charley continued to beg for the attacker to stop, her painful screeches shooting through Alfie's heart and making him feel guilty.

The attackers halted their assault on him, leaving Alfie lying on the floor helpless, watching as his attacker's feet moved toward Charley. Digging his fingertips into the floor, Alfie pulled himself forward towards Charley, but his body was too exhausted to move quickly enough. He could feel blood soaking onto his bandage from the cuts on his side. He watched as Charley was lifted from her feet, her legs kicking in the air.

"Stop," Alfie coughed, still pulling himself forward. Charley dropped to the ground as the feet stormed back to Alfie. Grabbing the chain between Alfie's bracelets, the assailant dragged him over to Charley, throwing him at her side. Charley rapidly threw herself on top of Alfie, her hair covering his face and soaking in blood from the gash on his cheek.

"I'm sorry," she whispered into his ear as her tears dropped onto his earlobe. Alfie closed his eyes, tormented by his failure to protect his family. His eyes were blank as he stared up at the ceiling through Charley's blood-dampened hair, a flash of all his kills replaying in his memory. He wondered if karma was finally catching up to him and if this was his ending.

"Why are you doing this?" Charley screamed as she looked up at the attacker, her body covering Alfie to protect him.

"Alfie needs to confess his sins," the voice replied from the sofa where they now sat.

"He won't be confessing anything, the way you're hitting him," Charley shouted abruptly, her voice cracking from the tears she'd been crying. The attacker stood up from the sofa, disappearing into the hallway. He was gone for a short time before reappearing.

"Move," the attacker demanded. Hesitant at first, Charley slowly moved away as the attacker threw a glass of water over Alfie's face. The blood seeping from the cut on his face washed away, then started to bleed again. Alfie coughed as the water went down his throat and up his nose. Lifting Alfie's head, Charley cradled his face, trying to help him catch his breath. Alfie looked up at her, apologizing to her.

Alfie's eyes moved to see his attacker standing over him and Charley, his breath trapped in his throat as he stared at the assailant's face. Shock and disbelief overtook all his guilt. His mind raced, struggling to comprehend the sight before him. The familiar features twisted into a mask of aggression sent a shiver down Alfie's spine, a deep-seated disturbance gripping his soul.

His heart hammered against his ribs, each beat echoing in his ears like a thunderous drum. The realization crashed over him like a tidal wave, leaving him gasping for air as he grappled with the enormity of the betrayal. The weight of disbelief pressed down on him, threatening to suffocate him with its crushing force. He felt as though he had been plunged into a dark abyss, his world upended by the revelation.

As he struggled to come to terms with the chilling reality before him, Alfie's mind reeled with unanswered questions. Disturbance etched into Alfie's expression mirrored the turmoil raging within him, a restless storm of emotions threatening to consume him whole. Grappling with the devastating truth, his brain flashed to Teddy holding his throat falling onto the hallway floor. He couldn't fathom how his so-called friend could have done this to him, how this so-called friend could fake his death and silently enjoy the torment of the night.

"Teddy!" Alfie staggered as it slowly hit him. "How are you alive?" he asked with confusion as he slowly sat up. Putting his hands behind his head, he pulled a band from around his neck, revealing an empty plastic bag from under his blood-smothered T-shirt.

"A bag of pig's blood. Cut it just right and it'll look like your throat's been slit, if you hide it well enough," Teddy amused as he watched the confusion on Alfie's face. A psychotic laugh emerged from Teddy's mouth, enjoying the chaos over Alfie's face. "Come on, Alfie. Who else would be able to make you believe it was Charley? How was the front door open without any damage? Who else could've put a dummy outside your house undetected? I saw the look on your face that night," Teddy continued, mocking Alfie.

"Why?" Alfie asked as he straightened himself on the floor. Charley held onto Alfie's wrist as they both stared at Teddy.

"Why? Why?" Teddy said calmly, then shouted, ending with his sinister laugh. A hundred questions raced through Alfie's head.

"Yes, why? What have I done to you?" asked Alfie, his heart pounding like a hard kickdrum.

"You know what you've done to me, and I'm going to hear it from your mouth today!" Teddy declared with an eerie coldness.

"What about your mother? Is she even dead?" asked Alfie, slowly sliding himself in front of

Charley. He was starting to feel his adrenaline kicking in, taking his pains away.

"Yes, she's dead... but first, I want you to tell me the truth," Teddy said, his tone turning normal. Alfie looked at Teddy, then glanced behind him, noticing an iron bar on the floor near Eva's body. It was the weapon he hit Alfie over the head with. Slyly tugging the handcuff chain, testing how restrained he was, Alfie deliberated how he was going to get out of this trap.

"Fine, I've wanted to tell you for years, so let's get it out in the air, but... before I die, will you answer my questions?" Alfie tried to bargain, knowing Teddy would be impulsive once he heard the truth. Alfie knew that whatever the outcome of this, Teddy was going to have to die, with or without him.

" I already know what happened... so don't lie to me!" Teddy instructed, glaring at Alfie in the eyes.

Chapter 18

19 years ago

Alfie's eyes glossed over with darkness, a hatred burning inside of him, unleashing its flames on its ignitor. The knife clenched tightly in his hand as he repeatedly plunged it into his father. Lost in his fury, unable to recognize that his father was dead, every piercing of the blade only added to the mutilation.

"Alfie!" the blonde-haired man, Eddy, shouted with distress. Alfie was too far gone to hear the man's calling. He blankly continued his attack on his father's corpse. "Alfie, stop!" Eddy pleaded once again, the realization that the young boy had lost control startled him. Taking slow steps toward Alfie, he continued trying to break his murderous trance. Realizing that no matter what he said, Alfie wasn't responding or snapping out of it, he bent down, placing his hand on Alfie's shoulder. Lost within his own rage, Alfie turned sharply, screaming in rage as he plunged the knife deep into Eddy's chest.

Looking into his victim's eyes, Alfie froze, staring into Eddy's eyes. Gazing down at the knife in Eddy's chest, Alfie snapped back into reality, consumed with regret. Immobilised on the spot, watching as Eddy slowly fell backwards, lying on the floor.

A heavy pounding in Alfie's chest, a drumbeat of dread, as he watched in horror the unintended consequences of his wrath unfold before him. His hands trembled uncontrollably, a wave of fear hitting him like icy vines creeping up his spine. His breath grew heavy with a tight pressure as the realization sank in, a knot of worry tightening in Alfie's stomach as he struggled to comprehend the extent of the harm he had caused.

Watching the pain and worry etched on Eddy's face, Alfie flushed with anguish, dropped to his knees beside his unintended victim. Constricted with a suffocating sense of remorse, his throat tight with unshed tears as he struggled with the depths of his shame.

"I'm sorry," Alfie stuttered, debating whether to pull out the knife or not. Loud, stampeding footsteps echoed from the passage. In panic, Alfie glanced at the door, believing the police were coming to arrest him. An older man stopped in the door frame, his mouth slightly open, hiding his shock. His hazel eyes darted onto Alfie, who shot up to stand desperately looking at his grandfather showing his guilt. His grandfather's eyes shifted to Alfie's father's mutilated body on the floor.

"What happened?" he asked, stunned, walking into the room. Alfie's mother sat in the corner, cradling Alfie's younger brother.

"It's going to be okay; it's going to be okay!" she muttered as she kept kissing his head.

"I didn't mean to," Alfie confessed, looking at the grey-haired man with guilty sadness.

"Alfie, Alfie," Eddy breathed, spaced, calling out to Alfie, his voice a desperate plea. Reactively, Alfie bent down, grabbing Eddy's wrist, his heart racing with a mix of fear and guilt, his breaths shallow and uneven as he professed his apologies.

"Teddy... he is... he's your... brother... Please..." Eddy's voice trailed off, his strength waning as he struggled to convey his final message. Closing his eyes, Eddy succumbed to his fate, his words hanging in the air, heavy with urgency and unspoken sorrow. He lay there, with staggered breathing, each exhale a reminder of the fleeting moments left.

Alfie's mind raced, trying to process the flood of information bombarding his senses. The words echoed in his mind, each syllable a sharp jolt to his senses, leaving him reeling in confusion. Teddy was his best friend; they had grown up together. He always saw him as a brother. Questions swirled in his mind, each vying for attention as he grappled with the enormity of the revelation. His thoughts collided in a tangled mess of emotions.

"What do you mean?" Alfie's voice trembled with disbelief as he searched the eyes of the messenger, hoping for clarity amidst the chaos. Rubbing the man's face, Alfie tried to wake him up, tapping Eddy's cheek, but it was too late.

"Alfie?" his grandad called to him as he took a step closer. Alfie felt a sense of security as he ran, crying his fear and sorrows to his grandfather. Pulling Alfie away, his clothes cloaked in spatters of wet blood, he held onto Alfie. A howling screech from his mother made Alfie and his grandfather look in unison.

"He's dead… My boy's dead!" Alfie's mother shrieked. Her face contorted in agony; every line etched with the pain of a mother's shattered heart. Her cries grew louder, more desperate, as though pleading with the universe to bring Oscar back to life. Tears flowed freely, tracing silent rivers down her cheeks as she cradled her son's lifeless form in her arms.

Overloaded with so many emotions, Alfie's legs gave way as he collapsed to the floor. His body was limp and trembling, consumed by a whirlwind of emotions that engulfed him. The events of the night replayed in his mind on a loop, hauntingly, each memory crippling him with intense regret, fear, loss, and anger.

Shock held him in its spiteful grip, numbing his senses and leaving him disoriented. He struggled to make sense of the chaos that had unfolded before him, the weight of his actions pressing down on him, suffocating him. His chest tightened, a crushing sensation that constricted his breath and sent waves of panic coursing through his veins. A cold sweat broke out across his forehead, his body trembling uncontrollably as he struggled to regain control of his fractured reality. His vision blurred, the world around him fading into a hazy blur of shapes and shadows.

Alfie clutched at his chest, his fingers clawing desperately at the fabric of his shirt as he fought to stave off the rising tide of panic. He was consumed by a darkness so profound, it threatened to swallow him whole. His first-ever panic attack took hold, wrapping around his chest tightly. He gasped for air, his body convulsing with each ragged breath as he struggled to hold onto the fragile thread.

Curled up on the floor, Alfie stared blankly across the room. His grandfather knelt beside him, a hand gently resting on Alfie's shoulder. He felt a pang of helplessness as he witnessed the overwhelming distress his grandson was experiencing. Amidst the chaos, Alfie's mother's cries pierced through the air, diverting his attention from Alfie's anguish.

"It's going to be okay, Alfie," his grandfather spoke sympathetically, his voice a soothing balm amidst the turmoil. Alfie's panic momentarily broke as he looked up at his grandfather, tears streaming down his cheeks.

"I didn't mean to," Alfie muttered through his tears.

"I know you didn't. But right now, Alfie, I need you to focus. This is important," his grandfather said, extending a hand to help Alfie up from the floor. With tears still cascading down his face, Alfie swallowed hard and pushed himself upright, grasping his grandfather's hand for support.

Bending down so that he was at eye level with his grandson, he began to give Alfie instructions. "You haven't done anything wrong tonight. I did. Your father killed that man, not you," he instructed Alfie, who nodded silently. Standing up, Alfie watched as his grandfather meticulously tampered with the crime scene, ensuring it appeared as though Alfie was responsible.

While calming Alfie's mother, his grandfather began explaining his plan to her. It was then that she broke away from her grief over losing a child and realized the chaos within her home. Carefully laying her son on the floor, she rushed over to Alfie and embraced him tightly.

"I'm sorry, I'm so, so sorry," regret weighed heavily in her voice as she acknowledged that her son had saved them at a heavy cost. Alfie's grandfather approached them, detailing his plan for the next steps. He instructed his daughter to call the police once they had their story stable.

Taking in all the information, Alfie walked to the living room door and slid down its frame, silently watching his mother and grandfather until flashing blue lights flooded the house.

Chapter 19

"After everything that happened that night, a few days later I asked my mum why your dad was in our house. She told me they found out your mother and my father were having an affair. We'd had a few times when him and my mother had gotten into fights, but that night your father came round because he'd got the results of a DNA test, and he wasn't your father. My dad was your father," Alfie finished, revealing his long-hidden secret to Teddy.

Teddy sat frozen, the weight of the truth he thought he'd known tipped upside down. A confused look on his face was accompanied by fury in his eyes. Alfie watched as Teddy was unsettled by the revelation that had just rocked his memory of his father. Teddy couldn't bring himself to look at Alfie as a tear fell from his eyes, the hurt inside of him battling internally to get to the surface.

Carefully, Alfie stood up, taking slow steps toward Teddy. He could see the vulnerability emanating from Teddy. Getting closer, Teddy looked at Alfie, both still as they gazed at each other.

"I'm sorry," Alfie apologized, his bound hands reaching out to comfort Teddy. Grabbing Alfie's hand, Teddy bent his fingers backwards as he kicked him back down on the floor.

"This doesn't change anything, Alfie. This is bigger than you think," Teddy said with a calmness, all his turmoil disappearing at Alfie's moment of kindness.

"What do you mean it's bigger than I think it is?" Alfie asked, puzzled as he eyed the room, trying to figure out how he would survive this.

"It doesn't matter now. I'm going to do you a Favor and kill you and Charley, your mother, and Oscar so none of you have to find out," Teddy replied authentically.

Alfie moved back next to Charley, who had muffled sobs of fear fighting her restraints. Silence cloaked the room with a heavy atmosphere. Alfie's mind deliberated his next move, Teddy was still taking in the information he'd been told, forgetting what he'd believed to be the truth. Charley's gaze was fixed on Teddy, trying to understand the man she thought she knew; someone she'd trusted was now someone she feared.

The sunlight beamed through the living room, birds tweeting in the sky as the day had risen. The living room brightened by the sun shining through the window, the air in the room thick with tension. The weight of captivity was suffocating Charley, who resisted giving into her own anxiety.

"Teddy, please don't do this," Charley broke, begging. Alfie stiffened, angered by his own guilt of Charley's helplessness. Teddy stood, taking a step toward them, the wooden floorboards creaking under his heavy foot. Both Charley and Alfie's breaths became shallow, anticipating what was about to occur.

Teddy loomed over Alfie and Charley, his menacing presence devouring the essence of their fear. Alfie backed himself so he could feel her legs on his back, making sure he took all of Teddy's stare. Teddy was confusing him; one moment he was showing vulnerability, the next he was revealing the true villain inside. Alfie couldn't decipher what his next move was going to be.

Pushing Alfie out of the way, Teddy grabbed the chain on Charley's handcuffs, pulling her towards the hallway. Terrified screams ruptured through the house. Quickly, Alfie jumped up, punching Teddy in the back of the head. Letting go of the chain on Charley's handcuffs, Teddy dropped her to the floor. She fearfully crawled away from them both getting out of the way.

Teddy swung a punch toward Alfie, who ducked, avoiding his touch. Diving into the hallway, Alfie grabbed the iron bar, batting it into Teddy's face. Teddy placed his hand to his face as Alfie swung again. This time, Teddy fell backwards, avoiding the collision.

"I don't want to kill you. I've been wrecked with guilt all night thinking you were dead. So here's what's going to happen: I'll answer anything you want to know, and you're going to do the same. Thirty-two years we've been in each other's lives, and I know you don't want to do this. I know you," Alfie stated, holding the iron bar ready to swing if Teddy moved.

"Fine, let's do this," Teddy smirked, humouring Alfie.

"Alright, first question, Eva, why?" Alfie stood ready to attack if Teddy moved. Touching the side of his face Teddy laughed with a sinister smirking knowing the revelation would throw Alfie.

"Richard Gein… He was her father!" Teddy gleamed with satisfaction. Alfie's eyes widened in sheer disbelief, the weight of the revelation settling heavily on his shoulders, sending a shiver down his spine. Questions surfaced on his face as he looked upon Teddy, who smirked at him.

"Who's Richard Gein?" Charley asked, noticing the puzzled look on Alfie's face. Still stunned, Alfie wouldn't take his eyes off Teddy.

"He's one of the men Alfie murdered that time he disappeared, remember? It was that time we slept together," Teddy revelled in Alfie's confusion, trying to provoke an attack. Charley turned back to Alfie, her own questions racing through her mind. Tempted, she stopped herself from asking anything for now.

"How did she find out?" Ignoring Charley, Alfie asked coldly, with an intensity that was unlike the Alfie both Charley and Teddy had known for so long. His hazel eyes deepened as he began to estimate what Teddy had meant by "This is bigger than me." Clenching his teeth, he held back the toxic indulgence he'd once released in revenge.

"You made an error, Alfie boy, you and your stupid mother," Teddy continued to gloat, enjoying watching Alfie edging on the verge of the killer he discovered him to be.

"If I made an error that caught me out, why now eleven years later? What changed?" Alfie's brows furrowed in concentration; each word was measured, deliberate, carefully constructing the web together. A hunger burned in his gaze, a thirst for understanding as he delved deeper into the depth of what was happening.

"I changed it?" Nonchalantly speaking with a boosted ego, Teddy dug the hurt deeper into his betrayal.

"How?" Alfie asked directly as he edged slightly forward. Teddy gleamed a teeth-showing smile as his and Alfie entered an intense stare-off. "How!" Alfie shouted impatiently.

"By killing my mother!" Teddy exclaimed with a cocky tone, proud of himself.

"Tell me what happened?!" Alfie demanded.

Chapter 20

Strolling leisurely beneath the scorching summer sun, Teddy made his way home along his usual route, engrossed in conversation with Eva over the phone. He vented his frustrations about Alfie's upcoming TV appearance.

"Why does everything work out for him? He has the perfect life, and I'm stuck working a shit job doing heavy labour every day," he moaned, as Eva reassured him that Alfie's luck was running out. Continuing to walk, his pace mirrored the passion of his resentment. Each word spoken into the phone dripped with venomous contempt as he unleashed a tornado of complaints about Alfie. Every syllable uttered was soaked in his own bitterness and hidden jealousy.

Pulling the phone away from his ear, he noticed Alfie was calling. Sighing, he ended his call with Eva and answered Alfie, changing his tone to chirpy and friendly.

"Sorry Alfie, I drew the short straw at work, and I have to work late tonight. I am so sorry, I wish I could make it," Teddy lied convincingly, rolling his eyes and mocking Alfie's sincere disappointment.

"I know Alfie, I tried to get out of it, but you know what it's like there. No one wants to do the night work, and when it's someone's turn, there's no changing it," Teddy continued his lie convincingly as his face showed how unbothered he really felt. Teddy hurriedly ended the call with his fake regret.

"Fucking arsehole," he muttered to himself, putting his phone into his pocket.

Continuing his walk home, Teddy ranted to himself until he reached his front door. Hearing the front door open, Teddy's mother called him into the kitchen. She'd made him a sandwich sitting on the table waiting for him, holding a newspaper she was reading the article written about Alfie. Teddy rolled his eyes, annoyed that she could support him after what Eva had told him about his father. Sitting down, he noticed that she had another newspaper beneath her on the table.

Sitting down, Teddy thanked his mother for the food, but she dismissed his politeness, beaming with pride as she eagerly thrust the newspaper into Teddy's face as soon as she noticed him sitting. Pushing her hand away, he nearly choked on his food.

"I'm eating!" Teddy moaned with his mouth full and annoyed, dismissing her son, she sparkled with admiration as she pointed to Alfie's photo prominently displayed on the front page.

"Look at Alfie! Isn't he just remarkable?" she exclaimed; her voice filled with genuine pride. Reading the article out loud, she burdened Teddy's ears with noise he was tired of hearing. Every praise in the paper excited her, making her voice high-pitched. Resentment built inside Teddy like a fire burning brighter.

"Oh, I am so proud of him. He's been through so much, that poor kid. It's so nice to see it all going well for him," Teddy's mother said with a lovingly tone as she gazed at his photo. "He deserves all of this; he has worked so hard!" she exclaimed, intensifying Teddy's deep-rooted hatred and envy.

"Mum, give it a rest. All I hear anywhere I go, is Alfie this and Alfie that, it's getting on my nerves," Teddy barked, unable to contain his infuriation any longer.

"That's not very nice. You better cut that attitude when you go to his show today," his mother replied sternly, with a look of disappointment.

"I'm not going, I've got somewhere to be," Teddy replied, putting his sandwich back on the plate.

"What do you mean you're not going?" Teddy's mother asked in shock. Teddy stormed out, his shadow reflecting off the white walls as he dragged his feet behind him, circling the table in the centre of the room. "Teddy! Where's your moral support for your friend?" she continued in a rage, sliding the wooden chair out from the table as she stood up to watch Teddy leave the room. She followed Teddy, who was walking up the stairs right next to the kitchen door. "Don't ignore me, Teddy!" she shouted angrily.

Teddy slowly ascended the stairs, still ignoring his mother's pestering. She shouted his name one final time, and Teddy stopped in the middle of the staircase. "Alfie, Alfie, fucking Alfie, just shut up about fucking Alfie!" Teddy vented his frustration to his mother. Annoyed by his tone and hostility towards his oldest friend, she looked at him in shock. Silently, she watched as Teddy walked up the stairs and slammed his bedroom door facing the staircase.

Teddy huffed as he sat on the bed, which was cantered in the room. His phone began to ring again, and it was Alfie calling. Annoyed by the caller's name, Teddy threw the phone on the pillow of the bed. Standing up, he walked over to the white wall he faced. He looked at the photograph in the middle of the wall, a photo of him as a child standing with his father. Taking the photo frame off the wall, revealing a brown square, Teddy pushed his hand onto it, causing the brown square to pop out from the wall, revealing a secret hole holding a load of documents and photos. He placed a photo of Charley and Oscar inside, then replaced the covering with his precious photo.

A knock on his bedroom door interrupted his thoughts, and his mother let herself in before Teddy could invite her. "I'm sorry, Teddy. I know I have been going on about Alfie, and I shouldn't. I know how you are feeling," his mother said caringly. Standing in the doorframe, she awaited his reply, but he didn't respond. "You need to talk about it, Teddy. It's not healthy to let feelings like that linger," she continued sympathizing with Teddy.

"What feelings?" Teddy turned to look at his mother, initially worried he'd been caught.

"Jealousy. It's not healthy to feel that angry and resentful about a friend, especially one who's been there for you," his mother replied, trying to console her son and be there for him.

"It's not jealousy. Alfie killed dad! He killed your husband!" Teddy fumed, taking a step towards his mother.

"What? No! Alfie's father, Freddy, killed Daddy," Teddy's mother reassured him as

Teddy's face began to lose emotion at her response.

"No, Alfie killed him. His grandad took the blame. Freddy was innocent!" Teddy said coldly.

"No, Teddy. Now, this is enough! Alfie, like you, has been through hell and back, and maybe that poor boy suffered more than you did that night. You lost Daddy, and it hurt both of us. He was traumatized by that night. You know what he was like after, you know what he lost. You deserve the same success he has gotten; you both suffered a lot, but you don't push yourself. He pushed himself, and look where he is," Teddy's mother went into a lecture, defending Alfie and asserting the events of his father's death.

As they continued their conversation, they were interrupted by the doorbell. "Come in!" Teddy shouted from behind his mother. The front door opened, and Eva walked in, closing the door behind her. Her dark grey eyes looked up the stairs at Teddy and his mother, her rounded face and heavy pink lips smiling at them.

"Oh no, you, this is all because of you. Get out of my house, you tart!" Teddy's mother shouted at Eva, whose smile quickly dropped.

Consumed by rage, Teddy tightly wrapped his hands around his mother's neck, strangling her with great force. The pressure of his fingers pressed down on her larynx, making it impossible for her to talk. Teddy's grasp tightened, a sinister satisfaction creeping through him as he revelled in the pulse of his mother's fading life beneath his merciless fingertips—an eerie acknowledgment of the humanity he callously extinguished. The air grew thick with the putrid scent of fear.

"Kill her, that's it, do it, baby, kill her!" Eva dropped her bag, encouraging Teddy with a sinister smile. His mother slapped at his hand, silently pleading for him to let her go. In a fleeting moment of morality, Teddy released his grip on his mother's neck. She stumbled, plummeting down the stairs. Teddy, a statue of malevolence frozen at the apex of the staircase, grappled with the abyss of emotions devouring him—a tempest of unrelenting guilt, festering anger, and a newfound feeling of power and lust he'd never known.

His mother dropped onto her back, right by Eva's feet. Her eyes widened in shock and pain as she slowly tried to pull herself up from the floor. Reacting quickly, Eva grabbed her arms, attempting to push her back down to prevent her from escaping. Teddy remained statue like at the top of the stairs, his emotions a tumultuous whirlwind inside him.

"Get away from me," croaked Teddy's mother, trying to get out of the house. Eva pushed her out of the way, locking the door. Eyes fixed on Teddy's mother, Eva bent down, grabbing a hunting knife out of her bag. Teddy's mother tried to scream for help, even looking to Teddy, who began to walk down the stairs at the call of his name. Eva, hungry for the kill, began to taunt her, swishing the knife in her direction.

"Please!" Teddy's mother begged. Teddy, downstairs, took the knife from Eva's hands. His mother apologized as Teddy stood opposite her. She could see the battle in Teddy's eyes; he hesitated, while Eva watched his moment of weakness, unsatisfied.

"Your father wouldn't want this," begged Teddy's mother, her voice croaky and desperate, pleading with him to reconsider. Blind hatred surged through Teddy at the mention of his father; his eyes scorned his mother as he viciously plunged the blade into her chest. A dry, cackling screech erupted from her; a failed scream muffled by Teddy's hand. Leaving the knife buried deep, he forced her on to the living room floor, her fingernails clawing desperately at the old wooden surface. Releasing her mouth briefly, Teddy ripped the knife free, casting it aside. Kneeling on her arms to restrain her, he covered her mouth again, pinching her nose to suffocate her. She struggled for air, her body jolting in a primal fight for breath as Teddy held her down tightly, sealing her fate.

Eva picked up the knife, her thumb rubbing the bloodied blade as she licked it, savouring the taste of fear-tainted plasma. Dark grey eyes glittered with excitement as she watched Teddy commit matricide, a bloodlust bubbling inside her, hungering to join in.

With a shudder, Teddy released his grip on his mother's lifeless body, sitting atop her. Every detail of her motionless form heightened his senses; he noticed every cell and hair follicle on her face and head, the scent of death filling his nostrils. A deep sadness washed over him as he surveyed what he had done, his hands trembling as he realized the blood staining his clothes. His fragile mother was gone.

"How are you feeling?" Eva gloated, adopting a sympathetic tone as Teddy turned to her, overwhelmed by the weight of his actions. Silent and broken, Teddy offered no reply as Eva embraced him, a smirk concealed from his view.

"This is Alfie's fault! If Alfie hadn't done what he did to your father, if he didn't vilify innocent people, you wouldn't have done this," Eva explained, planting a kiss on Teddy's head.

338

"The plan's over. I'm going to prison," Teddy replied, shattered.

Pulling away, Eva grabbed her bag and headed into the kitchen. Teddy remained seated over his mother's body, consumed by guilt and emptiness, unable to tear his gaze away. Frozen in time by the magnitude of his actions, he was lost in the chasm of his remorse.

Returning to the living room, Eva held out a newspaper article featuring Alfie, pushing it into Teddy's face. "Remember, this is all his fault!" she asserted, igniting a surge of anger within Teddy. Jaw clenched tightly, he hurled the paper across the room, Eva sensing she had provoked him enough to follow her instructions.

Heading upstairs, Teddy changed his clothes, stowing the bloody ones in a bag. Rifling through the contents of his hidden wall compartment, he tossed them into the bag. Descending the stairs, he approached Eva, embracing her one final time, kissing her intensely before leaving the house.

Chapter 21

Revolted as Teddy recounted the gruesome details of his mother's death with unsettling happiness, Alfie could tell that the friend he'd once known was gone. The vivid imagery painted by Teddy's words left a sickening curl in Alfie's stomach. "Tonight was because of you, Alfie," the words on the note echoed in his head; her joy for his success had been what made her son kill her. Hiding his guilt as he stood over Teddy, he could see the darkness inside Teddy's soul.

"Who came to your house when you left? Why fake Eva's death? How did you get a police officer to confirm Eva's death?" Alfie asked, every question lingering in his mind, standing hesitantly to finish what Teddy had started.

"You've destroyed lives, Alfie. Your actions have consequences, and they are catching up to you. If, by a miracle, you manage to get away from this alive tonight, more are coming."

"So, who sent the notes and photos?" Alfie quizzed, trying to gather all the information he could before the inevitable happened.

"I don't know, but I gave the photos to them," Teddy replied honestly. Alfie intensely took in every word, dwelling on "them." He had many questions for who was behind all this; he knew Teddy wouldn't reveal.

"Who killed Ronnie? It wasn't you; you were here. Was it Chris?" Alfie questioned as Teddy stood up from the sofa. Alfie took a step backward, fixed on Teddy's movement. He knew eventually how this was going to end, but the years of friendship burdened him to make a move.

"That idiot... No, I don't know who killed Ronnie. I wasn't involved in that! But like I said, Alfie, the consequences of the past are catching up," Teddy said, eyes looking over to Charley. Charley sat on the floor, her posture tense and uneasy, her fingers fidgeting nervously as she cast anxious glances between Alfie and Teddy, unable to shake off the feeling of impending dread. "I have a question, all this time, we've been related, and you never said anything... so tell me, what was it like killing the man who I knew as my father?" Teddy started, genuine as he glided into a sadistic tone. "Did that knife impaling him feel good? Did you enjoy it?" Teddy continued, raising his voice, taunting Alfie. "And that poor baby brother, Oscar, is that why you named your son Oscar, guilt over killing him too?" Teddy's words hit Alfie hard, feeling as though a dagger was piercing his heart. "For years, it was, don't mention Oscar in front of Alfie; he's traumatized!" Teddy cruelly spoke. "That little boy would still be alive if it wasn't for you… And then you name your son Oscar. Was that the guilt, hoping for a second chance to protect the uncle that child will never know?" Teddy's words were venomous.

Internally, every word hit Alfie hard adding to years of his historic conscience. Externally, Alfie seemed composed, years of practice at faking his stability. The iron bar in his hand, Alfie awaited Teddy's movement.

Taking a step toward Alfie, he clenched the base of the bar with all his strength, awaiting Teddy's quick attack. Lunging to the side, Teddy dove to the floor to grab Charley. Swiftly, Charley dodged Teddy's attack, rolling to the side of the room. Reacting swiftly, Alfie turned and kicked Teddy in the side of the face, the same spot he'd previously hit with the iron bar. Teddy dropped to the floor, but as Alfie swung his leg again, Teddy grabbed his ankle, pulling him down. Striking the iron bar in Teddy's direction, Teddy took a thrash to his arm as he grabbed hold of the other end of the iron bar. A tug-of-war battle between both men, neither willing to release the weapon. Alfie stamped the bottom of his foot into Teddy's shoulder.

Suffering the blows, Teddy crawled up Alfie's legs, still holding the bar. Lying on Alfie's legs, Teddy shuffled up until he was on top of Alfie, both still holding the bar. Alfie's bracelet-chained hands near his face refused to release the iron bar. Teddy poured all his weight into his hold, putting full pressure on top of Alfie, angling the iron bar straight as he forced it down on Alfie's neck. Charley, on the other side of the living room, just before the three women's dead bodies, watched in panic.

"Stop, please stop!" She yelled as she watched Alfie struggling to maintain his strength under Teddy's body weight. Flinching forward, she stopped herself, anxious to get involved. She pleaded with Teddy again, but her words fell on deaf ears amidst the chaos. Coercing herself through the fear, she rushed over, grabbing a clump of Teddy's hair. As hair ripped out, she grabbed another clump.

Teddy took one hand off the iron bar, punching Charley in the stomach. Winding her, she let go of his hair, falling to the floor. Seizing the opportunity of Teddy's distraction, Alfie bit Teddy's remaining hand. Abruptly, Alfie smashed the iron bar into the top of Teddy's forehead. Jolting back, Teddy grabbed the iron bar, yanking it from Alfie's hands, throwing it across the room. Locking eyes as they stood opposite each other, Teddy breathed heavily with rage.

"All this tonight, so you could kill me. You had to get three other people to do your dirty work to get here. Now, you're weak, Teddy, you're a coward!" Alfie taunted Teddy. Consumed in his anger, Teddy charged toward Alfie. Eyeing Teddy's movement carefully, Alfie dodged out of the way, diving for the iron bar Teddy had thrown. Teddy quickly ran, kicking the weapon further away. Lifting Alfie from the floor by the handcuffs chain, he punched Alfie repeatedly.

Charley ran behind Teddy, throwing the chain between her handcuffs over his head. Jumping on his back, she dropped her body weight, tightening the chain around Teddy's neck. Teddy's fingers desperately tugged at the chain, but Charley tightened her hold, preventing his escape. He thrashed wildly in the living room, struggling against Charley's relentless hold. Watching Charley struggle to hold him, Alfie swept Teddy's feet out from under him, causing him to smash into the ground face-first. Teddy, powerless, Alfie pinned him down while Charley applied pressure, choking the life out of him.

Struggling underneath Alfie and Charley's hold, Alfie kneeled on Teddy's hands, placing his hands firmly on the back of his head. Charley kneeled on Teddy's back, pulling her arms up until Teddy stopped moving.

"He's dead!" Charley declared. Alfie took his hands off his head, checking Teddy's neck, searching for a pulse.

"I can't feel anything," Alfie said, looking at Charley. Moving his knees off Teddy's arms, Alfie lifted Teddy's head so Charley could remove the chain and get up. Standing up, he quickly embraced Charley, placing the handcuff chain over her. "I am so sorry," Alfie apologized for his reaction earlier.

"It's fine," Charley reassured, kissing Alfie's cheek. Pulling his arms over her head again, Alfie bent down, checking Teddy's pockets for the keys to release him and her. He didn't have it. Rushing, Alfie jumped up, going to the police officer in the hallway; the dead police officer didn't have it either.

"Look, go upstairs, let my mum know I'm fine, we need to get Oscar out of this house without seeing all this. I'm gonna find the key to get these off," Alfie instructed, feeling the frustration bubbling inside him. He watched as Charley made her way up the stairs. A rising heat began to fill Alfie's body, anxiety triggered by his bindings and the threats he'd faced. Gritting his teeth, he took a deep breath through his nose and stood up. As Charley vanished up the stairs, Alfie went outside, scavenging for the key to undo his binds. He went directly to the body of the police officer, checking through every pocket he had.

"For fuck's sake!" Alfie fumed. "Where is it!" His panic and frustration built from the chaos he'd fought through the night. The air was thick with tension, each second feeling like an eternity. Surveying the scene, he suddenly remembered the officer handing him the key earlier in the night to release the handcuff he'd put on him and dropping it on the floor.

Patting the ground beneath the dining room window, he felt the cold metal of the key. Relieved, he picked it up, releasing his wrists from the clenching bracelet. He looked around at the blood on the ground, walking onto the grass; he began to feel faint. Sitting down on the green grass, he took in a deep breath, slowly exhaling, his head spinning from everything that'd happened. Looking up at the sun, he squinted with a eased smile, grateful for seeing another beautiful day.

Quickly kneeling over his hands on the ground, Alfie was violently sick; coughing, he wiped his mouth. Closing his eyes, he could feel every emotion he'd restrained through the night. Emotions overwhelmed him, tears falling from his eyes as thoughts of the lost friends and the betrayal by one of his oldest friends rushed through his mind. Scraping his fingertips on the ground, his nails filled with dirt; he let out a frustrated, painful screech.

Angry, sad, and hurt, Alfie felt the pain from his wounds burning. Consumed by the trauma he had relived and the new trauma that burdened his future. Attempting to calm himself with deep breaths, he realized he was in too deep. Palms firmly on the ground, he let out a tormented shriek again, staring at the bloodstain on the ground as he yelled louder, his larynx erupting with pain. Curling his hands, he banged his clenched fist on the grass, fighting to regain control.

Trying to catch his breath, Alfie's mind replayed the night's events. "You had to do it!" he breathed to himself repeatedly. Suddenly, flashes of his father pierced into his thoughts, rekindling the old childhood fear. The demons in his life intoxicated his mind; Teddy's mother appeared standing opposite him.

"He did this because of you," Motionless, she spoke as she stood gormless and bloodied, staring hauntingly at him. Alfie apologized to her. She glared at him with accusations that Alfie could feel.

"You weren't there; you don't understand," Alfie pleaded with her; she stared at him soullessly. Feeling a grip on his shoulder, Alfie jumped up, terrified by Ronnie, who also stared at him silently. Flashes of his altercations with Chris and Stewart replayed in his mind. He squeezed his eyes shut, trying to regain a clear mind, but as he opened his eyes, Ella, Grace, Ben, Jennifer, and Alice appeared, reminding him that their deaths were his fault.

Pushing past them, Alfie was met by Eva, Stewart, Chris, and Teddy. Throwing punches at the hallucinations, Alfie swung wildly at the phantom enemies he believed were back to get him. His fists sliced through empty air with desperate fury. Each punch carried the weight of his fear and confusion as he grappled with his imaginary opponents, his movements a chaotic defence.

Falling backward, Alfie closed his eyes; all his ghosts disappeared. Confused, Alfie looked around for them, wondering where they had gone.

"I'm going crazy!" Alfie muttered to himself, wiping his hands over his face. A chilling realization swept over Alfie as his body calmed itself from the hysteria. Waves of horror washed over him as he reflected, acknowledging his emotions. He brushed his face with his hands, looking upon the little boy from his past.

"It was never your fault, Alfie," said the young boy. Alfie knew it was all in his head; his psyche was finally healing after all the revelations, he forgave himself, knowing he was never the cause of any of the innocent's deaths.

Alfie looked at his young brother, welling up with grief as a sudden chill enveloped him, sending shivers down his spine. Childhood memories flooded back, tears streaming down his face as his heart clenched.

"I wish you were here with us now," Alfie whispered as the hallucination of his young brother faded away. The air tasted different as Alfie inhaled and exhaled again, looking around at the front of the house. The heaviness he'd once carried on his shoulders was now lighter. He felt different, he felt free.

Walking back inside the house, stepping through the hallway, Alfie paused as he looked into the living room. Teddy's body was gone.

"DADDY!" Alfie heard Oscar's cries from a distance. Ignoring the burning from his wound, Alfie sprinted up the stairs, jumping up steps to get there faster. On the second floor, Alfie saw Bulldozer scratching at his bedroom door, hissing as he pinned at his closed door. Alfie was silent, carefully approaching. He knew he couldn't act on instinct and had to be shrewd.

Opening Oscar's bedroom door, he saw Charley out cold on the floor. Preparing himself for the worst, Alfie left Oscar's room, standing outside his bedroom, he cautiously pushed the door open. Bulldozer lunged, but Alfie grabbed his collar before he could attack. Commanding the dog to stay, his heart sank watching Teddy holding Oscar in the air with a knife to his throat a cut on his arm.

Alfie edged inside the bedroom, Bulldozer by his side. Alfie's mother stood near the bed, pleading with Teddy to not do this to a child.

"Go and check on Charley!" Alfie instructed his mother. Hesitating to leave her son and grandson, Alfie's mother took slow steps toward Alfie. She couldn't bear leaving without her innocent grandson.

"Now Mum!" Alfie said sternly; she could hear the worry in his voice as she left the room.

"Let him go Teddy!" Alfie continued, his sternness masking his internal worry about what could happen to his only child. Alfie took a step further into the room, his foot knocking the baseball bat Lucy had dropped. Teddy took a step backwards, an inch away from the window. A hatred like no other consumed Alfie as he watched Teddy parade Oscar around helplessly.

"Look at what you're doing to him, Ted. He's terrified. Are you really going to kill the child who calls you Uncle Ted, the child you held as a baby?" Alfie desperately tried to appeal to Teddy's better nature.

Watching Teddy's hold get tighter, a surge of paralyzing fear coursed through Alfie's veins as he stood helplessly. Scanning every inch of his son's vulnerable face, his paternal instinct rattled with his self-control to stay calm. Realizing that Teddy had no better nature, that man was long gone.

"Let's just keep this between me and you!" Alfie shouted, losing his composure, Bulldozer stepping forward before Alfie commanded him to stay.

"Why would I let him go? I have nothing to lose. I have nothing because of you!" Shouted Teddy frantically. Oscar slipped from Teddy's hold. Lifting Oscar up in the air, repositioning him so he had a grip around his waist.

Oscar frantically began to kick his feet, his cries piercing the air as he fought against Teddy's hold, his tiny frame trembling with fear. Desperation flickered in Teddy's eyes as he struggled to maintain his grip on both the squirming child and the deadly weapon. With a chilling determination, Teddy tightened his hold on the knife, pressing it menacingly against

Oscar's quivering chest. His gaze locked onto Alfie's, a sinister glint reflecting his intent as he slowly raised the blade, inching it closer to the innocent child's delicate face. Positioning the knife, Teddy's arm hovering near Oscar's mouth. Innocently reacting, Oscar sank his tiny child teeth into the flesh of Teddy's wrist. A roar erupted from Teddy's lips as he dropped the knife. Oscar's teeth ripping into Teddy's flesh opening the cut on his arm. Releasing his hold on Oscar, the child fell to the floor.

"Get him!" Alfie shouted, instructing Bulldozer, who soared at Teddy. Rapidly, Alfie picked Oscar up from the floor, rushing him into his bedroom with his mother and Charley. "Go and hide somewhere!" Alfie urgently instructed as he raced back into his bedroom, closing the door behind him.

Bulldozer clung to Teddy's arm, while Teddy struggled to get the dog off him. Alfie lifted the baseball bat from the floor, swinging with great force. The first strike caught Teddy in the face, followed by a second blow to his shoulder. Teddy punched Bulldozer in the nose, forcing the dog to release its grip, his arm dripping blood from the dog's pierced teeth holes.

Alfie swung the bat a third time, but Teddy grabbed it, pulling it off Alfie and throwing it at Bulldozer. Recalling Bulldozer, the dog backed away growling at Teddy. Alfie didn't want the dog to get hurt. "Is that how low you've sunk? You'd kill a child?" Alfie asked disappointedly. Teddy didn't reply, running at Alfie, swinging a punch. Alfie countered the punch, connecting and taking a hit as Teddy grabbed Alfie by the throat, backing him toward his bed.

Falling backwards, Teddy began to choke Alfie, while Bulldozer jumped on the bed, gnawing on Teddy's arm to free Alfie. Alfie hit Teddy in the nose with the palm of his hand, reaching down the side of the bed frame for his grandfather's Bowie knife. Teddy pushed Bulldozer off the bed as he strangled Alfie aggressively. Bulldozer jumping back on to the bed, snapping at Teddy's leg. Ignoring the attack of the dog Teddy shook Alfie's head, determined to feel his life fade in his hands.

Alfie felt the handle of the Bowie knife, pulling it from the side of the bed and thrusting the blade into Teddy's shoulder. Teddy was relentless, consumed in his wrath, still choking Alfie. Alfie plunged the blade into Teddy's back, finally releasing his grip. Leaning over Alfie, he punched Teddy in the throat, Bulldozer released Teddy's leg as Alfie pushed Teddy backwards with his feet. Falling off the bed, the knife embedded in his back deepened as he hit the floor.

Rapidly, Alfie jumped off the bed, watching as Teddy turned over crawling for the knife he'd dropped with Oscar. Wrenching the knife out of Teddy's back, Alfie kicked him in the side, shouting, "You threaten my child!" then kicked him again. "You've killed my friends!" Alfie continued, stamping on the back of Teddy's head, forcing his face to rebound off the floor.

Picking up the knife Teddy had dropped; Alfie threw it into the walk-in wardrobe. Rolling Teddy on his back again, Alfie sat on top of him, punching him with his free hand. "You were my best friend, the one person I thought I could trust," Alfie vented, punching Teddy again. Putting his hand up over his face, Teddy tried to defend himself as Alfie plunged the Bowie knife into the palm of Teddy's hand.

Standing up, Alfie dragged Teddy into the centre of the room as Teddy weakly grabbed at his ankle. "You set all this up tonight so you could kill me, and now I get to choose if you live or die," Alfie said calmly as he and Teddy stared at each other.

Teddy coughed as he tried to speak. "I'll see you soon in hell, Sayers," he said, defeated. Stamping on Teddy's head, then ramming the Bowie knife into his thigh, Alfie stood, indulging in Teddy's helplessness. He debated how he would kill him, fixed on the numerous ways he could. Bulldozer sat on the floor, watching his master's victory.

Pulling out the knife, Alfie walked to the bedroom door, his back to Teddy. "Go for the throat!" he maliciously instructed Bulldozer as he walked out of the room, closing the door, eager to hear Teddy's torture. Bulldozer prowled slowly over to Teddy; a predator ready to strike. Lying still as his body turned cold, the blood seeped out, staining the floor. From the corner of his eye, he watched Bulldozer approach, his paws dirty with Teddy's leaking blood. A menacing growl emerged as Bulldozer pounced, his wide-open jaw biting into Teddy's neck with ferocious hunger. He shook and pulled at the flesh on his neck, ripping it wide open, the sound sickeningly audible. Sinking his teeth in deeper and deeper, repeating his shake and pull, until his teeth touched his hyoid bone, feeling the satisfying crunch as he ripped it out, a gruesome trophy of his victory.

Alfie stood outside, listening to every squeal from Teddy and grunt and growl from Bulldozer as he attacked. Opening Oscar's bedroom door, he looked inside. Routing through some of Oscar's stuff, Alfie found an old clown mask and blanket. He picked it up, leaving the bedroom. Opening his bedroom door, he called Bulldozer out of the room as he saw Teddy lying in a pool of blood, his body twitching. As

Bulldozer left the bedroom, Alfie closed the door, leaving Teddy to die slowly and painfully.

Checking each room on the second floor, Alfie found where his mother, Charley, and Oscar hid. He wondered if they'd gone down to the first floor as he peered at the attic stairs at the end of the second-floor hallway. He wiped Bulldozer's face with the blanket, removing Teddy's blood from his snout, before they both ascended the stairs, opening the attic door. Brightened by the sunlight glowing through the window, he looked at his mother, his eyes confirming to her that it was over.

"All safe?" Charley asked, Alfie nodded as he walked over to Oscar picking him up, he embraced him tightly.

"I told you he'd be fine," Alfie's mother said to Charley smugly. The pain from the gash in his side began to burn through him as he held Oscar in his arms, it was a pain he suffered as he looked at the innocent sadness and fear written over his face.

"Alrighty, brave man, can you put this mask on? We need to go and see Aunt Lucy, and you know how she's scared of clowns," Alfie playfully encouraged Oscar, trying to erase his fear. Oscar gave a false smile, taking the mask silently and putting it on. Slowly, they all walked down the attic stairs. Standing on the second floor, Alfie looked at his mother, subtly warning her of the carnage downstairs and instructing both her and Charley to avert Oscar's view. In an unnerving silence they descended the stairs. On the ground floor, his mother took in the bloodshed around numb to such scenes.

"Mum, get my car keys. They are in the kitchen," Alfie instructed softly as he took Oscar out of the house. Charley followed behind him, pointing to the key on the floor outside as she finally uncuffed herself. Police and ambulance sirens pierced through the street. Charley took Oscar from Alfie. Standing in the garden, they watched as the emergency services arrived at Alfie's home. Several police cars and three ambulances piled up inside and outside of Alfie's house. Limping over to them, Charley stayed in place with Oscar as his mother came running out of the house with his car keys.

Two police officers got out of their car, the first one introducing himself. "Hi, my name's Officer Henby. We had a call from a Lucy Caden. She reported a break-in and several murders," said the officer. Alfie fell to the ground, overcome with the pain that had been inflicted on him, the stab wound bleeding through. Two paramedics rushed over, helping him off the floor as they took him into the back of an ambulance. Alfie's mother handed Charley the car keys as she rushed over to her son and the paramedics.

"Is he okay?" she panicked asking the paramedics helping him into the back of one of the ambulances.

"He'll be fine, ma'am," replied Officer Henby behind her, "But we need to go over what has happened here?" The police officer stated.

"Officer, we'll tell you everything, as will the others, but can we get my son to the hospital and my grandson far, far away from this crime scene," Alfie's mother replied as the officer gestured for Alfie's mother to get in the ambulance with Alfie, then gestured for Charley and Oscar to get in the back of the police car.

Chapter 22

In a dimly lit warehouse, a group of individuals congregated around a large table, their faces illuminated by the soft glow of a single light hanging overhead. A newspaper lay spread out in the centre, its headline declaring Alfie's survival. Rising from their seat with a swift motion, one of the members drove a blade into the photo of Alfie's face with an intense rage. The room erupted into heated arguments, some lamenting their premature actions while others seethed at Alfie's unexpected survival. The atmosphere was tense, punctuated by the slamming of a door and the echoing footsteps of an enraged individual approaching the table. With a furious gesture, they threw another newspaper onto the table, displaying the faces of all the victims. "She wasn't supposed to die!" they roared, their voice filled with a mix of frustration and rage. The room in awkward silence as the rage from their arrival fumed. "We need a new plan, and I'm killing Alfie Sayers!" they declared.

Chapter 23

Dream:

Alfie walked barefoot along the front of his former home, enveloped in an eerie silence. Suddenly, a small boy darted past him and rushed into the house. Alfie called out for him to stop, but the door slammed shut behind the child. Racing up the path, Alfie forcefully barged into the door, only to find it locked. He attempted to open it by slamming his body against it repeatedly, but to no avail. Frustrated and desperate, Alfie dashed to the window. Peering inside, he saw his son Oscar standing frozen in the hallway. Alfie's heart raced with fear as he elbowed the window in a frantic attempt to shatter it and reach his son, but the glass remained intact. Meanwhile, a masked assailant approached Oscar, sending Alfie into a panicked frenzy, relentlessly pounding on the unyielding glass.

"Get away from him!" Alfie shouted repeatedly, his desperation mounting. Suddenly, a hissing sound caught his attention, and he noticed his little brother motioning towards an entrance at the back.

360

Without hesitation, Alfie followed his brother to the rear of the house. As he burst through the door, he halted abruptly in the hallway, face-to-face with the masked assailant, while Oscar was nowhere to be seen.

"Take off your mask!" Alfie demanded; his eyes locked intensely on the figure before him. With bated breath, he watched as the assailant slowly removed the mask, revealing a faceless void beneath.

Abruptly opening his eyes, Alfie lay in his bed, staring at the ceiling. Sitting up, he yawned, wiping his forehead. Leisurely, Alfie got out of bed, preparing for the day. Incapable of living in his dream house, Alfie bought another, slightly smaller than the last, but still spacious. Heading downstairs, he entered the kitchen where Charley, Oscar, and his mother sat around the table, eating breakfast. Oscar slyly fed Bulldozer and their new brindle bullmastiff, Gufi. On the TV mounted on the wall, Lucy sat doing an interview about the events she and Alfie had endured.

"Are they really still going on about that night?" Alfie's mother asked, looking at Alfie.

"Yep, they keep harassing me for more details. For what she did for me, for us, she deserves to milk this for all she can," Alfie replied. Catching Oscar feeding the dogs under the table, Alfie gave him a smile as he broke up a piece of toast, giving pieces to both Bulldozer and Gufi.

"So, what are your plans for today, Alfie?" asked Charley, quickly changing the subject from the events of the night. She placed a mug of coffee on the table for Alfie and sat down next to him. Glancing at his watch and realizing the time, Alfie jumped up, kissed his mother, Charley, and Oscar goodbye, grabbed his car keys from the hallway, and left the house.

Stepping outside his home, cameras flashed in Alfie's face, their lenses uncomfortably close. He pushed them away as they bombarded him with questions, their persistence irritating him. Ignoring their attempts to corner him, Alfie made his way toward his car, shrugging off their attempts to provoke a reaction. Inside his car, he drove slowly, navigating through the nuisance in his path. Roaring the car's horn, he resisted the urge to knock them over.

"Get out of his way!" shrieked his mother, emerging from the house with a bucket of water that she threw over the paparazzi. Distracted, Alfie quickly drove off, heading to his therapy appointment. Hurriedly parking his car, he rushed inside his therapist's office, running late.

"I'm so sorry I'm late; I had a bit of a crowded situation this morning," Alfie said, calming himself from the rush.

"No worries, I expect it now, what with all the stories that have been coming out. How do you feel about the attention?" the therapist asked, observing Alfie's restless movements.

"I have a mixed relationship with it. I'm grateful for all that it has brought me, but there is always something invasive about it. I let my friend Lucy take the front of what we went through because I don't want to keep reliving it, but it's never good enough. They want me to speak and give greater details," Alfie explained, fidgeting with his hands.

"What about that night do you not want to relive?" the therapist asked, analysing Alfie's uncomfortable body language. Alfie took a deep breath.

"That night was full of betrayal, and while it helped me overcome a lot of my anxiety, it traumatised me in another way. That's why we have never spoken about it and focus on keeping the anxiety at bay," Alfie admitted, feeling the therapist probing for details. The hour-long session delved deeper into Alfie's mental state, revealing that while he had overcome his anxiety, his nights were still troubled by unsettling dreams. However, these dreams were no longer haunting recollections of past events but rather ominous glimpses into unknown futures he'd been threatened by. Alfie described them as vivid visions of scenarios he couldn't comprehend, leaving him with a sense of foreboding upon waking.

Expressing gratitude to the therapist for the discussion, Alfie left the building. Lucy called him on his mobile phone.

"I'm running late today for everything; could you meet me at the office?" Alfie asked as he jumped inside his car, driving as fast as allowed to get to his office. Navigating his way through the congested streets, he weaved between cars and pedestrians. Spotting Lucy walking on the pavement, he pulled over beside her. Lucy got into the car as Alfie drove further up the road, turning to enter the carpark at the front of his office.

He and Lucy got out of the car, walking into the glass building. Stopping at the reception area, he collected his mail, smiling at the new receptionist as thoughts of Ronnie flicked into his mind. Thanking the receptionist, he and Lucy went to the elevator, getting inside. Alone in the lift, Alfie made a confession.

"Every time I go to that reception desk, I feel bad over what happened Ronnie," Lucy touched his arm, reassuring him that it wasn't his fault. The lift doors opened. Alfie and Lucy walked into the office.

"So, what do you have to get from here?" Lucy asked, watching Alfie drop the letters on the centre table.

"I left my other laptop in the office; it has CVs for me and Thomas to go through for our new hire," Alfie said, walking into his private office. Lucy walked toward the office window, now repaired from the crime scene. She watched the people passing by.

Unlocking a drawer in his desk, Alfie pulled the drawer out, removing his laptop. Beneath the laptop, a photo faced down lay flat with writing on it. Alfie placed his laptop on the tabletop, picking up the photo. Ignoring the writing, he flipped it over, revealing a photo of Teddy, Eva, Stewart, and Chris, each with a red cross over their bodies. Flipping the photo around, he read the writing he previously dismissed.

"Behind every false smile, lies a darker truth." Alfie called out to Lucy, handing her the photo. She looked at it confusedly. Alfie's mobile phone rang. Lucy put the photo down on the table. Looking at his phone, Alfie read the private number notification.

"What do you want?" Alfie answered sharply, a familiar heavy breathing down the phone remained silent, awaiting Alfie to break. Lucy looked at him confused, mouthing questions. Alfie dismissed her. The heavy breathing irritated Alfie as he turned the phone on speaker, placing it on the table. Lucy moved closer to the table, listening to the breathing. She went to say something, but Alfie threw his hand up, stopping her. Frustrated, Alfie ended the call. The phone rang again. Alfie picked up the phone, answering.

"Who the fuck is this!" Alfie shouted down the phone, causing Lucy to move closer to listen. The caller began to laugh down the phone.

"You can't escape your fate… It's only just begun," the voice said eerily as they ended the call. Lucy hearing the warning vaguely asked Alfie to repeat it. Both had a worrying look on their face. Alfie picked up the photo avoiding Lucy's gaze as he declared.

"It's starting again!"

The End… For Now!

Thank You For Reading!

Thank you for picking up a copy of Disquiet. I hope you enjoyed the story as much as I enjoyed writing it. I'd like to start by thanking my best friend, Casey Laurence. Throughout this journey, she has read through drafts of chapters, been a cheerleader, and a great critic. Next, I would like to thank Liam Walton. Though I know he didn't think I was going to get around to publishing this book, he was a great supporter and encouraged everyone to get involved and support. Next, I would like to thank Andrew Garce, not only my boss but also a good friend. He listened to me when I would go on and was always supportive. Next, I would like to thank Lisa Bryan. She read the first chapter and offered to read through it for me, which I really wanted to let her, but I also wanted to keep the whole plot and surprises secret from everyone. I have a list of people whom I give thanks to, but I have three I've saved for last because they have had a huge impact on my life…

Sian Waters, as a child, Sian always gave me books and encouraged my creative side. She was a prominent person in my life that has played a huge part in my love of stories.

My Grandad George, losing my grandad impacted my life a lot, and while this story has been with me a long time, it was wanting to create a story he would love that made this as violent and as brutal as it became. I know the comments he'd make if he were still here and had read this book, and he'd probably tell me to make it more aggressive.

Most importantly, Sarah Reed, my mother, a strong woman who has always given me the freedom to fly in whatever direction I want (not without critique) and always supports and believes in me no matter how ambitious my ideas become. I'm grateful to have such an amazing mum.

Printed in Great Britain
by Amazon

44835247R00205